MORE THAN THIS

CHRISTMAS KEY BOOK FOUR

STEPHANIE TAYLOR

STEPHANIE TAYLOR

For O—
Red Croc to my blue one.
One half of the unlikeliest friendship on this pale blue dot.
It's an honor and a privilege to know you.
~S.

"Your heart knows the way. Run in that direction."

— —Rumi

1

"We're fine," the woman next to Holly chants. "Everything is going to be fine. We've got wings and engine power and prayer," she whispers to herself, rocking forward and back in her small airplane seat.

"Hey," Holly says, reaching over and putting a hand on the woman's forearm. "Nervous flier?"

The woman breaks her chant long enough to turn her glassy gaze on Holly. "Yeah," she croaks. "Just a little."

"Why are you going to London? Business? Pleasure?"

"My father lives there—well, not in London, but outside the city —and I need to see him," the woman says, pieces of her blonde hair falling out of her ponytail. She puts a shaky hand to her forehead and sweeps them back. "He's turning seventy, and he has Parkinson's."

"So are you British?" Holly probes, watching as the woman clutches the armrests with both hands.

"No, and neither is my dad. But my stepmom is." She looks at Holly and smiles.

"Sounds like a good trip," Holly says calmly. "What are you guys going to do?" It's not that she's overly interested in a stranger's trip, but the idea of spending the next eight hours sitting beside a basket case who looks like she's on the verge of hyperventilating is a little daunting.

The woman takes a deep breath, not letting go of the armrests. "Probably take it easy. I just want to spend time with my dad." She puts her head back against the seat and closes her eyes briefly before opening them and looking straight at Holly. "Will you tell me about your trip?"

The seatbelt sign dings and the captain's voice comes on. Holly points in the general direction of the cockpit to indicate that she wants to listen.

"Welcome aboard Flight 513 with nonstop service from Miami to London Heathrow," the female voice says. "I'm Captain Walters, and I'm flying today with Captain Allender and a full flight crew to serve you in all of our cabins. It's not often that we have a totally female crew on our trans-Atlantic flights, but we're thrilled to have you on board with us, and we hope you enjoy the eight hour trip. Skies look clear ahead, but just stay buckled up when you're seated anyway, and let us know what we can do to make your journey more comfortable."

"What do you think of that?" the woman asks Holly. "All women. I'm nervous no matter who's in the cockpit. Sometimes I want to know their names, and sometimes I—"

"How about if I tell you a story?" Holly offers impulsively, cutting the woman off before she spirals into gibberish and starts to foam at the mouth. "I'm from this beautiful island about fifty miles beyond Key West. It's called Christmas Key, and it's decorated all year long with tinsel and lights. We have a bar that looks out onto the beach and live music there on Friday nights, and there are no cars on the entire island—just golf carts."

"Oooh," the lady says. She loosens her grip on the armrests. "I'd drive a pink golf cart."

Holly turns to her and smiles. "You know, it's funny you should say that..."

2

"It's going to be strange around here without her, isn't it?" Bonnie Lane is standing on Main Street just outside the Christmas Key B&B, making small-talk with Jake Zavaroni as his police cruiser/golf cart hybrid idles at the curb.

Jake's jaw clenches almost imperceptibly and he eyes the thick trees at the end of Main Street where it intercepts with Cinnamon Lane. "Yeah, it'll be strange. But we'll get used to it. We have to." Bonnie's left eyebrow hitches towards her hairline, but she says nothing. "And it's only for two weeks, right?"

"She'll be back on June first, so technically it's three weeks," Bonnie says gently. "It's a long trip for our girl, and a long time for us to get by without her."

Jake swats at the key ring that dangles from the ignition of his electric cart. "We'll survive," he grumbles, but Bonnie isn't convinced.

"How's Pucci doing?" Bonnie fishes around in her handbag for her sunglasses.

"He's fine, but I think he's still moping around, waiting for Holly to walk through the door. He wouldn't even eat for the first two days."

"Ah," Bonnie says, sliding her black cat-eye sunglasses up the bridge of her nose.

"Don't say 'ah' to me, Bonnie Lane," Jake insists. "I'm not the one dragging around here with my tail between my legs because she's gone. We needed a break from each other, and if she hadn't left, then I was going to."

"I can't say I'm glad it was her," Bonnie says, putting her purse back over her shoulder, "but I sure would've missed you if you'd gone, doll."

Jake glances to his left and waves as one of the triplets drives by in her own golf cart. "Thanks, Bon," he says in a low voice. "But we both know that if it came down to a vote over who gets to stay and who has to go, I'd be on the next boat to Key West." It will never come to that, of course, but Jake isn't entirely wrong: as the mayor and owner of the majority of the island, Holly Baxter's popularity with the locals is firmly entrenched. She'd grown up on Christmas Key right under the noses of most of the island's residents, and is truly the backbone of pretty much everything that happens on the island.

"Oh, come on now," Bonnie scoffs. "We love you, too. In a perfect world the two of you would get your heads and your hearts straight and be back together, but..."

"But it's not a perfect world," Jake finishes, putting both hands on the steering wheel like he's ready to move on. "Listen, I'd better get back to policing these mean streets."

"Of course you should," Bonnie says, taking a step away from the curb. "And if that dog of Holly's wants to come hang out in the B&B office with me, well, you just run him on over here. He's used to sitting there while she works, and it might make him feel less lonely for her if he sticks with his usual routine."

"Got it," Jake says. He gives Bonnie a wink and a two-fingered salute as he pulls away from the curb. Main Street is paved, but the sand and shells that cover ninety percent of the island always manage to migrate to the road somehow, and Jake's tires crunch over the gritty surface as he drives west and hangs a left onto Holly Lane.

Holly Lane, he thinks, leaning back in his seat and driving with one hand. Of course it's named after her. Everything on the island reminds Jake of her. He drives by the chapel and slows for a moment, staring at the small, rustic church at the bend in the road. Just a month or so earlier, Jake and Holly had shared a moment behind the chapel that raises goosebumps on his arms now just to think of it. Sure, they'd been back there under weird circumstances, searching for the misplaced cremains of Sadie Pillory that her husband had buried after a storm, but Holly's gentle, caring nature had touched him then, and he can't stop himself from picturing her there now, bent over the headstone her grandfather had placed there years before.

Jake punches the accelerator of his golf cart and moves on. Thinking back on all of Holly's good qualities isn't going to help him move on. And imagining her in Europe with a former pro-baseball player holding her hand as they stroll the romantic streets of Paris isn't helping either. In just a year, Jake's been through a lot: he'd proposed to Holly, but instead of getting married, they broke up; River O'Leary—the baseball player—showed up on the island for a vacation and swept Holly away almost instantly; and a reality show blew into town over the holidays and turned the island upside down. But the real significance of the reality show had been Bridget, the actress/contestant who had wooed Jake for the cameras, but then burrowed her way into his heart for real. He'd asked her to stay. They'd been living together. They'd almost had a baby...

Jake steers his cart into the sandy lot of the Jingle Bell Bistro and pushes the image of Bridget and all thoughts of the painful miscarriage and their eventual break-up out of his mind. It was for the best —he knows this now—but being the one who always gets left behind is getting old.

With a firm jab of his foot, Jake sets the park brake and jumps out, taking the steps up to the beachside bistro two at a time. It's lunch time and he's hungry. And when all else fails, he can always count on Iris and Jimmy Cafferkey's clam chowder to put him in a good mood.

3

By the time they land at London's Heathrow airport, Megan, the woman next to Holly, has long been breathing normally, and she's completely convinced that Christmas Key should be her new home.

"It sounds *so amazing*," the woman says for the umpteenth time as they make their way towards the baggage claim area. "I can picture everyone: Cap, Bonnie, Pucci, *Jake.*" She jabs Holly with an elbow. "I can't wait to see it all."

"Well, we'd love to have you," Holly says. "And you have all of our contact info on that card I gave you, right?"

"Got it," the woman says, patting her purse to indicate that she's got the card with Christmas Key's social media links and email address tucked safely inside. "Okay, I guess this is good-bye—I need to freshen up and then find my dad and stepmom."

"Have a great time!" Holly calls after her, watching Megan as she ducks into the first ladies' room they see. Megan throws her an excited wave back and disappears into the restroom with a crowd of short women in dark *hijabs.* The exotic mix of travelers at Heathrow is already dazzling Holly, and as she looks around at the variety of humans surrounding her, she feels a thrill of excitement at being off the island.

Holly didn't sleep much on the flight, and the unfamiliar sights and smells around her make her stomach twist and turn with anticipation. She's somewhere totally new, in a city and a country that are so much more metropolitan than Christmas Key that it's almost like the two places don't even share the same planet. Two men speaking French close in on her from behind and Holly pulls her shoulder bag to her body more tightly, remembering the lectures she'd gotten from her neighbors about being aware of her surroundings no matter where she is.

At the baggage claim she waits patiently for the carousel to start spitting out suitcases and boxes. A woman next to Holly in chic knee-high suede boots takes her in from head-to-toe, no doubt pegging her as a country bumpkin on a backpacking trip through Europe. Holly stares at the laces of her own Converse sneakers and wonders if she should have chosen something more attractive for her travels than her olive green cargo pants, a gray t-shirt, and her blue Yankees baseball hat. But it doesn't matter now; she's on her way to the rental apartment that River's picked out, and she'll have time to shower and change before he gets there.

The baggage carousel beeps loudly and grinds into action. Men and women of various sizes, shapes, and colors step forward and pull dinged and well-worn suitcases from the conveyor belt as Holly stares at the mouth of the machine, waiting to spot the hardshell suitcase Bonnie has loaned her. It's hot pink with white polkadots, and as it makes its slow trek around the belt, Holly flushes at the sight of it. The suitcase is fun and cheerful, but it's also loud and American. She suddenly wishes she'd borrowed something in black.

"Darling," the woman in the suede boots says, touching Holly's elbow as she heaves the oversized suitcase off the conveyor, "what agency are you with?" The wheels of the pink suitcase land on the floor loudly.

"Huh?" Holly squints at the woman, whose face is clean and

unlined. Her black hair is long and straight, and everything about her smells like money.

"Agency, love. Which agency are you with?" The woman is watching Holly intently, making mental calculations and tabulations of the width of Holly's eyes, the length of her nose, the smoothness of her skin, and the broadness of her shoulders.

"I'm sorry..." The lack of sleep on the flight is catching up to Holly while she stands there, sweating in her gray t-shirt as a multitude of languages flow around her. A voice comes over the loudspeaker and says something unintelligible in a British accent. All Holly wants to do is blink her eyes and magically be in the apartment, ready to take a hot shower.

"You are a model, yes?" the woman asks, sweeping one manicured hand through the air in front of Holly.

"A model?" Holly parrots. "Oh, good lord, no!"

A tiny frown creases the woman's forehead. "But why not?" she asks, as if this is the most obvious next question in the world.

"Why not? Because I'm thirty. And I'm the mayor of an island. And, and...I don't know—I'm just not."

"Huh," the woman says, still appraising Holly. "But your structure is fabulous. I bet you look amazing in a bikini." She reaches out and touches Holly's upper arm as she tilts her head back and laughs. "Don't take that the wrong way—that isn't a pick-up line!"

Holly looks around at the people still waiting for baggage; none of them are listening to this odd exchange.

"I basically live in a bikini at home," Holly says, relaxing a little when she realizes that this woman isn't joking.

"That sounds like paradise. I should visit in August."

"August is pretty humid. Lots of bugs," Holly adds.

"Well, August is our slow month in Europe. Most places close down almost entirely, and we all vacation."

"*That* sounds like paradise." Holly folds her arms over her chest and bumps the pink and white suitcase with one knee. "Listen, I need to get to the Heathrow Express and then to Paddington Station. Any idea where I catch the train?"

"I'm headed that way, darling. Let's walk and talk." The woman pulls up the handle of a clean, unmarked suitcase and drags it behind her like it weighs five pounds. Holly grabs the handle of her own case and it nearly knocks her over as she buckles under seventy pounds of shoes, summer dresses, jeans, t-shirts, and bathing suits. She has no choice but to follow the woman through a tangle of people all fighting to squeeze onto one escalator.

"Follow, please," the woman says crisply over her shoulder.

Holly falls into a single-file line as the crowd merges and people step onto the escalator with their baggage. She panics as she sees the narrow space and the small step that she'll have to fit her suitcase onto.

"I don't think I'll—" She's about to step out of line and find an elevator when the man behind her touches her lower back, shoving her forward.

"Coming?" the woman asks casually, not glancing back at Holly. The people who've wedged her in place on the escalator spread out at the bottom as they go in different directions, and Holly trips over the grate, dragging the suitcase with her as she's freed from the tightly packed group of travelers.

"Coming," Holly says breathlessly. The woman's flat heels click on the hard floor as she leads the way, shoulders back, head straight. Holly double-steps to keep up.

"We can catch the express train here," the woman says, wheeling her suitcase through an archway and onto a platform, "and I can have a better look at your bone structure while we wait." She comes to a stop and turns to Holly.

"Oh." Holly takes an involuntary step back as the woman leans in and puts one hand on Holly's chin, turning her face from side to side.

"Thirty is definitely at the upper end of the range I'd be looking for," she says. "But I do think there's an earthy, natural quality to you that could really translate in photos. How long are you in London?"

It takes everything in Holly not to pull her head away and out of the woman's hand. Being assessed this way is a totally foreign feeling to her. Even in college she'd never been one to feel comfortable under the scrutiny of others, and her life on Christmas Key has never been about glamour and beauty. Being described as "earthy and natural" by this woman who sees extreme beauty on a daily basis doesn't bother her at all, whereas some women might prefer to be considered chic and polished.

"I'm here for a few days with my...boyfriend," Holly says, getting hung up only briefly on how to describe her relationship with River. Is he her boyfriend? They'd parted uncomfortably on Christmas Eve, and the road back from there has been cobbled together with long phone conversations, the rebuilding of trust, and lots of mutual understandings.

"Is he as gorgeous as you? Because that would really be something," the woman says as she digs through her leather purse. "Here's my card. We'll probably get separated on the train here, as it's going to be full. Call me. My office is near Buckingham Palace."

The express train sweeps through the tunnel with a rush of air, blowing the stray pieces of hair from under Holly's Yankees cap. She holds the business card tightly. "It was lovely to meet you—what was your name, darling?"

"Holly."

"Yes. Just lovely, Holly."

The doors whoosh open and people spill from the train as others fight their way through the crowd with baggage in hand, trying to get on. Holly steps onto the train and turns around, gripping her heavy suitcase with both hands as she yanks it over the ledge.

"Mind the gap," warns a recorded female voice with a British accent. "Mind the gap."

"I'm minding it," Holly mutters, giving one final tug on the handle. The suitcase bumps over the lip of the train and she reels backward, nearly bumping into a woman with a baby in her arms. "Sorry," Holly says, straightening her baseball hat. As promised, the woman she'd followed to the train platform is already gone and Holly is left in the standing room only section of the car, her huge pink suitcase leaning against her thigh as she stares at the business card of a woman who—completely improbably—has mistaken her tired, travel-weary self for a model. As the train pulls away from the plat-form, she almost laughs out loud.

THE TAXI STAND at Paddington Station is through a series of long hall-ways. Holly moves as quickly as she can, following the flow of humans as they make their way to other trains. The air that hits her as she walks out of the station is cooler than she's used to in May, and the skin on her arms prickles uncomfortably.

"Join the queue, miss!" a man in a coat and hat says, blowing a whistle and pointing at a line that's roped off by a guardrail. Holly falls in behind an elderly couple, her big suitcase banging against the metal rails awkwardly.

"Where to?" A man dressed identically to the man with the whistle looks at Holly with disinterest when she reaches the front of the line.

"Portobello Road, Notting Hill," Holly says, consulting an address that she's saved on her phone.

A taxi wheels into place at the curb next to her. "Put this in the boot for you, love?" the driver asks, coming around to help Holly. He's got large, stained front teeth and the friendliest smile Holly's seen since she got off the plane.

"Please," she says, stepping into the back of the black, domed-roof cab as the taxi stand attendant opens the door grandly.

"Oooh, it opens backwards," Holly says, nodding at the way the car opens up like it's got French doors.

"Suicide doors," the attendant says with a smirk. He slams the door and moves on to the next person in line.

"So we're off to Portobello Road, are we?" The driver slides into the front seat and punches a few buttons on his dash. A thick piece of clear plexiglass divides the front and back of the cab.

"Yes, please."

Holly sinks back against the seat and exhales deeply. She's made it. London. Three weeks of vacation. No village council meetings, no ringing office phones, no island drama. She spends the fifteen minute ride through the busy city taking in buildings and people, and watching all of the other black taxis speed down the wrong side of the road. A new city, a big adventure, and—best of all—in a few hours, she'll be with River again.

4

"Christmas Key B&B, this is Bonnie."

"Hi, Bonnie. Is Holly in?" She doesn't identify herself, but the demanding, entitled tone of the woman's voice crackles over the phone line and sends ice shooting through Bonnie's veins. It's Holly's mother.

"No, I'm afraid she's out. May I take a message?" Bonnie reaches for a pen and a notepad, trying to keep her voice even. What did Holly say about calls from her mother? Put her through to voicemail? Tell her Holly's out of the office sick? Hang up on her and unplug the phones for the next three weeks?

"You know damn well I don't want to leave a message for her, Bonnie Lane," Coco says. "When will she be back?"

Bonnie arches a penciled eyebrow and purses her lips. Everything about this woman sets her on edge, and the ongoing, unspoken drama between her and Holly's mother is only exaggerated by the well-known fact that Bonnie is the mother Holly *wishes* she had.

"She's out of the office, Coco. She said she wasn't feeling well." Pucci, Holly's golden retriever, ambles past the desk that Bonnie normally shares with Holly, his thick tail swatting Bonnie's bare calf.

Jake had taken Bonnie up on her offer to drop the dog off at the office, and, to be perfectly honest, Bonnie is enjoying the company.

"Fine. I'll call her cell phone. I know she won't answer when she sees that it's me, but I need to talk to her immediately."

"Is there something I can help you with?" Bonnie offers mildly. Her heart is racing at the prospect of whatever Coco might need to discuss with Holly urgently, but she keeps her cool.

"That'll be between me, my daughter, and Leo," Coco sniffs. Leo would be Leo Buckhunter, Coco's half-brother and the third owner of the island and all its assets. Coco's parents had divided the island three ways between her, the illegitimate half-brother who has always been a thorn in her side, and Holly, and this fact is the only thing standing between Coco and a profitable sale of Christmas Key. She's made no secret of her desire to have the island off the books and the profits *in* her bank account, and her willingness to do away with the only home her daughter has ever known is a major point of contention.

"Well, you can try Buckhunter if you want. I suppose you have his number."

"I suppose I probably do. If you hear from Holly, have her call me." Coco clicks off without saying good-bye and Bonnie ends the call on the office's cordless phone, setting the handset facedown on the white wicker desk.

The afternoon is brilliant and blue outside the B&B's huge picture window, and Bonnie rests her elbows on the desk, folding her plump hands and resting her chin on her fingers. A call from Coco always stirs things up like a violent summer storm, and she doesn't like the frosty, commanding way that Coco sounded on the phone just now.

Life is just getting back to normal for Bonnie after an ill-fated romance that pulled her away from the island and into the arms of a swashbuckling weekend pirate, but once she'd realized that life on the mainland with a loud, overbearing beau wasn't for her, she'd fled back to the safety of Christmas Key and to her happy life with the other islanders. She watches them through the window now, smiling as Maria Agnelli totters down the sidewalk in oversized black sunglasses that make her look like an ancient, Italian Jackie O.

Cap Duncan steps out of his cigar shop across the street with Marco, his parrot, on one shoulder, a rakish smile on his face as he clamps an unlit Cuban between his lips. Dr. Fiona Potts, Holly's best friend and the island's only doctor, opens the door of Poinsettia Plaza on the other side of Main Street, guiding Hal Pillory out by the elbow and settling him into the passenger seat of the golf cart that's being driven by his middle aged son. It's a good life—one she won't make the mistake of trying to change ever again.

"Hey." A male voice in the doorway breaks into Bonnie's thoughts and she pulls her eyes away from the view of Main Street. Buckhunter himself is standing in the doorway, his white t-shirt covered by a stained apron. His bar, Jack Frosty's, is just a few steps away from the B&B.

"Oh, hey, sugar. Is the lunch rush over?" Bonnie asks, pulling her laced fingers apart and trying to refocus.

"Yeah," Buckhunter says wryly. "All eight of my customers have been served and rung up."

"Slow day?"

"Nah, it's fine. Usually a small lunch crowd means a bigger turnout for dinner. It all works out in the wash." Buckhunter shrugs and runs a hand over his recently shorn scalp. He normally wears his sun-bleached hair in loose waves, but he'd lost a friendly bet with Holly and the outcome was that he'd agreed to shave his head. Millie had done the honors across the street at Scissors & Ribbons, the island's only salon, and Buckhunter's girlfriend, Dr. Fiona Potts, has grown to love the clean cut look and the short, graying-blonde hair that feels like suede.

"So what's up?" Bonnie asks, pushing back her chair. She stands and tugs at the legs of her pink capri pants to loosen them around her pillowy thighs.

"Coco. That's what's up." Buckhunter makes a slow-blinking, deep-inhaling-for-patience face that reveals his true feelings about his half-sister. "She just called."

"Yeah, she called here, too. I told her Holly was out—I'm not supposed to tell her that the boss is off the island for three weeks."

"And see, I didn't get those same instructions," Buckhunter says, putting his hands on his hips over the apron. Underneath the cooking attire, he's wearing cut-off Levi's and a pair of Birkenstocks. "I guess Holly figured that Coco almost never calls, and she might get away with a little vacation with her mother being none the wiser."

"Oh, no." Bonnie puts both hands over her face and shakes her head.

"Yeah," Buckhunter says, making a smacking sound with his lips and pulling a guilty face. "I kind of told her Holly was in Europe."

"Oh, *no*," Bonnie wails. "What did she say?" Her hands fall from her face and she looks at Buckhunter, who is staring at the floor in front of him.

"That she's on her way down."

They stand in silence for a moment, pondering the implications of a visit from Coco.

"When?" Bonnie asks. Her brow is furrowed as she tries to figure out the best way to break this to Holly.

"Tomorrow."

"So much for giving fair warning." Bonnie shakes her head. "Can we stop her?"

"Have we ever been able to stop her?" Buckhunter tips his chin down and looks at Bonnie from under his brow.

"That woman," Bonnie says, her chest huffing as she starts to get worked up. "She's meaner'n a wet panther, in't she?" Her Georgia accent is always thick and entertaining, but when Bonnie gets herself worked up in a lather, the colloquialisms and overall Southernness get cranked up several notches.

"Mmhmm, she is," Buckhunter agrees. "But there's more."

"More what?" Bonnie slaps the back of her wicker desk chair with one hand. "I'm not sure I can take any more, doll." She picks up a file on her desk and uses it to fan her face dramatically. "I'm about to overheat like a '57 Ford on a dusty country road in Joo-lahh," Bonnie adds, making 'July' sound like a distant relative of a mint julep.

Buckhunter exhales and rips off the band-aid. "She's bringing a group of investors. And they're staying at the B&B."

"Soooo..." Bonnie runs through the scenario in her head, her eyes focused on the ceiling as she takes it in. "Starting tomorrow, we've got to provide maid service, meals, and general boot-lickin' to a group of people who want to come in and buy us up like we're property for sale?"

"So it seems." Buckhunter moves his apron aside and jams his weathered hands into the pockets of his shorts. "Do you want to call Holly, or should I?"

"Now there's a fine question," Bonnie says, walking over to the white board on the wall where she's written out Holly's planned whereabouts. "She's in London for a couple of days, and then they're moving on to Amsterdam and Paris. That's the most romantic city in the world!" She turns to Buckhunter. "Right?"

"So they say," Buckhunter agrees.

"We don't want to ruin her good time, do we?"

"I don't," he says.

"But we have to tell her, right?" Bonnie asks, clearly hoping that the answer is no.

"Seems like the right thing to do."

Bonnie sighs and turns her head to the window and the bright blue sky beyond. "Okay," she says with deep resignation, "I'll tell her."

5

The cab ride to Notting Hill is quick and Holly is utterly charmed by the area. Busy streets are filled with people sitting at outdoor cafés; florists have sidewalk displays of rainbow-hued bunches of hydrangea, tulips, sweet peas, and peonies; and the buildings are a wash of bright colors and cheerful front doors. There's a huge mural on Ledbury Road of a man reading a book on a park bench, and Holly cranes her neck as they pass, taking in the details of his painted on shoelaces, pink socks, and bowler hat.

"Here we are, miss," the cab driver says, coming to a stop in front of a tall, narrow building the color of butter. It's sandwiched between pink and baby blue buildings. The whole street reminds Holly of Easter.

With the instructions that River has sent her, Holly punches in a code next to a shiny, navy blue front door with a brass knocker. The lock clicks, letting her in. The foyer is all hard wood and white walls covered in matted and framed artwork. A tall bookshelf stuffed with hardcover books sits next to a curving staircase and an opulent crystal chandelier. Holly looks down at the floor: she's standing on a rug that's a reproduction of Andy Warhol's self-portraits in a rainbow of neon colors. It's so bright and artsy, so inviting that she actually laughs out loud. She kicks off her Converse and drops everything right there in the entryway.

The stairs lead to a landing with three doors and Holly peers into one with wide eyes; it's a master bedroom with a painted white brick fireplace and an enormous bed. There's a second bedroom with a desk and a view of the busy street below, and a huge bathroom with a clawfoot tub and white subway tiles on the walls. Several potted orchids line the windowsill, each flower craning its neck to eagerly pull in the indirect sunlight from the southern exposure.

Without thinking, Holly puts the stopper in the tub and turns on the hot water. Her clothes land in a pile on the black and white tiled floor, and she sinks into the bathtub gratefully, ready to soak away the long trip before River arrives.

"HONEY, I'M HOME!" comes a voice from downstairs.

Holly wraps herself in the plush white robe that's hanging from a hook in the bathroom. "Oh my God—you're here!" she shouts back. Her feet are still damp from the bath, and she takes the stairs gingerly, holding onto the banister as she rushes down to greet River.

He's standing in the doorway, two small suitcases at his feet, watching her with a lopsided grin. "You look clean," he says. His eyes crinkle at the corners as he looks down at her. Holly pauses at the bottom of the stairs and touches her wet hair self-consciously.

"I guess I could have run a brush through my hair or put on some clothes," she says. There's a weird moment where she feels shy and awkward, and she isn't sure whether to run to him or hurry back upstairs and change.

"Get over here," River says, letting the backpack he's still wearing on one shoulder slip to the floor with a thud. A grin spreads across Holly's face and she takes the five steps that separate them, throwing her arms around his neck happily.

River picks her up off the ground and holds her tight. "I was just going to mess up your hair and take off your clothes anyway," he says in her ear. Holly's laugh catches in her throat.

"You look good," River says, setting Holly's feet on the floor again. He gazes into her eyes as they both process the past four months and the way they'd parted on Christmas Eve. There was a lot said that day and a lot left unsaid, and the time that's passed between then and now has been filled with texts and calls. There are words on the tip of Holly's tongue as she thinks about how to apologize in person for pushing River away over the holidays. Looking into his eyes now, she remembers his sadness as he'd stared at her Christmas tree mournfully, the realization that she wasn't really over Jake yet hanging between them both like a heavy curtain that morning in her bungalow.

"River," she says, putting her hands on the sides of his stomach.

"Hey. No." River sets his big hands on both of her cheeks, his fingertips touching her earlobes. "Let's just start from here," he whispers, moving his head down so that his lips meet hers. It's the first time Holly's been kissed since Christmas, and a tingling sensation starts on her scalp, prickling its way down her neck and spine.

"Or we could start upstairs," she suggests, pulling her lips from his reluctantly.

River bends and lifts Holly in his arms easily, scooping her up like a damsel he's about to carry across a puddle. "I like the way you think, Mayor," he says, carrying her up the stairs and leaving his bags in the entryway. "I really like the way you think."

HOLLY WAKES up and reaches for her phone in the unfamiliar room. It's three in the morning. They'd fallen asleep tangled in the sheets of the master bedroom, the early summer sun still hanging over the buildings of Notting Hill, and River is still snoring softly in the dark.

By the light of her cell phone, Holly tiptoes through the bedroom and into the bathroom where she'd discarded her clothes so many hours earlier. She digs her toothbrush and toothpaste out of her toiletries case and holds the brush under the faucet.

"You're awake, too?" River materializes in the doorway to the bathroom.

Holly spits toothpaste into the sink. "Well, we fell asleep at about five, so it felt like a good time to get up."

"You hungry?" River folds his arms across his bare chest and tucks his hands into his armpits, squinting at her through sleepy eyes.

"We forgot to eat." The water rushes over Holly's toothbrush as she rinses it and drops it into her toiletries bag again. "And I think I skipped the last meal on the plane." She re-ties the robe around her waist. "But," Holly adds, remembering the woman she'd met at the baggage carousel, "I should probably skip a few more meals—I mean, if I'm going to be an international supermodel."

River gives a confused laugh and reaches for his own shaving kit and toothbrush. "Come again?"

"I met this lady at Heathrow who wanted to know if you were as hot as me," Holly says, leaning a hip against the edge of her sink as River gets his own toothbrush wet in the other sink.

"I hope you told her I was hotter," he says, squeezing paste onto the brush. "Way, way hotter."

"It would have blown her mind too much," Holly says, tossing a hand towel at him and hitting him on the cheek. "She already thought I was the most perfect specimen she'd ever seen—she even said something about how good I must look in a bikini."

River stops laughing. "Wait, you aren't kidding? This really happened?"

"I know it's hard to believe," Holly says defensively, "but yes, it really happened."

"It's not hard to believe, it's just...random. Did she offer to turn you into a star?"

"She gave me her card and asked me how long I'd be in London." Holly brushes past River and kneels before the suitcase he'd carried up the stairs and into the bedroom for her.

"Wow. I could be dating the next Cindy Crawford," River says as he falls onto the edge of the bed, facing Holly.

"You could be." Holly looks up at him from the floor as she sifts through the stacks of clothes she's brought with her. "But right now you're just dating a very hungry woman."

"Then let's go see what we can find." River unzips his own bag and pulls out a pair of jeans and a sweatshirt.

"At three in the morning?"

"Why not? If all else fails we can always find a McDonald's."

Holly pulls on a pair of jeans and a lightweight gray sweater with a flowered scarf, then ties her Converse and grabs her cross-body purse.

They're at the door, double-checking for keys and wallets when River pauses and frowns at Holly. "You're missing something," he says.

Holly looks herself up and down. "I think I have it all."

"Hold on." River puts one finger in the air and dashes back up the stairs, taking them two at a time. Holly has no idea what he's talking about, so she takes the minutes he's gone to pull a tube of pink lipgloss from her purse and lean into the mirror in the foyer to apply it. "Here," River says, jumping down the last two steps. "This is what's missing."

Holly twists the top of her lipgloss back on and drops it into her purse. When she looks up at River, he's standing in front of her with a crumpled, faded blue item in his hands. It's his Mets baseball hat. Holly holds her breath.

"Are you sure?" She glances up with just her eyes as he unfolds it and sets it on top of her long, loose hair.

River smiles as he tugs the hat into place. "I'm sure."

Everything that's passed between them since they laid eyes on each other in this foyer just over twelve hours ago has felt momentous, but this move is the biggest. Holly had worn his hat for months after his initial visit to the island the previous August, and she'd given it back to him on Christmas Eve before he'd hopped a boat to Key West. Having it back on her head now feels good—it feels right—and she grins at him happily, knowing that there are no words needed at this moment.

"Let's get some grub," River says, pulling open the front door and holding it for her. "I'm hungry for some bangers and mash."

"That just sounds gross." Holly steps down onto the deserted sidewalk. River closes and locks the door behind them.

"It's delicious, trust me. And if we can't find an open pub, then I promise to feed you Big Macs and fries, deal?"

"Deal." Holly slips her arm through his and moves in close so that their sides are touching as they walk.

The shops and bistros are all closed, the flowers and tables and chairs pulled inside for the night. Lights are off in all the businesses and most of the residences on the street, and a single black cab putters near the curb ahead, its driver focused on the dim glow of his cell phone screen.

"Should we catch a ride?" River asks, nodding at the taxi.

"Let's walk. It feels good after sitting on a plane for so many hours."

They stroll through Notting Hill in the middle of the dark night, stepping to the side so that two rowdy guys with thick accents and the drunken strides of pub-hoppers can pass them. Holly doesn't make eye contact with them, nor does she pay them any mind as they carry on, looking for an open pub of any sort.

"Hey!" shouts a voice from behind them. Holly stops, but River keeps moving, grabbing her hand and yanking her along. "Are you two Americans?"

"They're drunk, Holly," River says, still not breaking stride.

"Come back, we just want to talk about American baseball," says the other voice. "I love the Mets."

The trusting, caring part of Holly—the part that's been sheltered for most of her thirty years by small-town island life—wants to chat with the tipsy younger men, but River isn't having it.

"Keep moving," he says through gritted teeth.

"Hey, beautiful," says the first guy. "You're boyfriend is a real wanker. I see you want to talk to us, but he won't let you."

"Why don't you ditch him and come with us?" the other guy offers, yelling now to bridge the growing distance between them.

Holly picks up her pace to match River's stride and they hit a crosswalk as the sign turns to walk, rushing across to the other side of the street.

She resists the urge to glance over her shoulder, hoping that the silence behind them means that the men have given up and decided to go on to find their next pint—or a bed in which to sleep off their current buzz. But later on she'll kick herself for not looking back; later on she'll wonder what could have been different if she'd just paused and taken stock of their whereabouts, because from out of nowhere a strong force yanks her back, causing her to trip and fall.

As she sprawls on the sidewalk and River spins to catch her, she sees one of the men standing at the end of the street, hands in the pockets of his jacket as he dances back and forth from one foot to the other. The other man is standing over her brandishing a knife, the sliced strap of her purse gripped in one hand as he assesses her with glinting eyes. River springs into action and the man sidesteps him, deftly reaching out and plucking the Mets hat from Holly's head before he turns and bolts. He meets his friend at the end of the street and they take off running, their pounding footsteps echoing on the quiet street as they round the corner and disappear into the night.

6

"Hoooo, boy," says Millie Bradford as she rolls a strand of Fiona's strawberry-blonde hair around her curling iron wand. "Holly is going to be steaming mad over this one."

Fiona meets Millie's eye in the mirror she's facing at Scissors & Ribbons. "It's almost like Coco knew she was leaving, and she planned to swoop in with these investors the minute Holly was off the island."

"But how could she have known Holly was leaving?" Millie asks, setting the curling iron on the counter of her hair station.

"Could be she's got a bit of the witch in her," offers Calista Guy, the new island masseuse who doubles as Millie's salon assistant.

Millie and Fiona laugh.

"She's definitely a bit of a witch," Millie says, shaking her head. "But there's no magic in that woman."

"What does that even mean?" Fiona asks, twisting in her seat to look at Calista. "Are you talking about real witches and potions and stuff?"

"You know, that she's into sorcery and spells and witchcraft. Like my mother-in-law." Calista shrugs nonchalantly.

"Oh, now you're pulling our legs! Your mother-in-law can't be that bad," Millie says, waving a dismissive hand in the general direction of the front desk.

"You just wait," Calista says with big eyes. "You all talk about this Coco woman like she's made of lizard tongues and vinegar, but none of you have met Idora Blaine-Guy. That woman will turn you to stone if you stare at her too long. Make no mistake."

"When does she get here?" Fiona asks, turning back to the mirror so that Millie can finish curling her hair. It isn't like she needs a weekly hair appointment to get by on a tropical island where the dress code allows everyone—even the resident M.D.—to wear bikinis as underclothes and to pad around unpaved roads in flip-flops, but Fiona is a firm believer in supporting the local economy, so she stops by every week like clockwork for a wash and style and a manicure.

"Idora-ble the Horrible?" Calista asks, eyebrows raised so high that they nearly meet up with the hairline of her perfect afro. "Last I heard she was closing on the sale of her condo in Toronto and was planning on being here sometime in the next week. I actually don't want to know when—it would be kind of like knowing too much about the details of your own death." Calista shudders.

"Does Vance know that you refer to his mother as 'Idora-ble the Horrible'?" Millie asks with genuine amusement.

"Lord, no!" One hand flies to Calista's heart. "I mean, he knows we aren't the best of friends, but I don't think he'd be a fan of the nickname."

"But she's really coming down to help with the boys, right? So maybe she'll stay out of your hair," Fiona says.

"She'll be living at our house, Dr. Potts," Calista says, dropping her chin to her chest and throwing Fiona a serious look. "So she'll be 'in my hair' already based entirely on her proximity. But yes, her main job is to help with Mexi and Mori." Calista's six-year-old twin boys are currently the only children living on the island—the only ones ever to live there, in fact, aside from Holly and her friend Emily Cafferkey—and Calista and Vance had quickly realized they were in over their heads when they'd discovered just how much mischief two little boys could get into on Christmas Key.

Fiona shrugs. "Sorry—I've never had a mother-in-law. I'm not sure what kind of advice to give here."

"Has Buckhunter's mom been down to visit?" Calista asks, punching a few keys on the computer at the front desk.

"His mom passed away a long time ago," Fiona says. Millie turns her chair so that she can work on the back of Fiona's hair.

"I'm sorry. I didn't know." Calista slides a pair of square-framed reading glasses on so that she can see the screen in front of her. "And though it'll sound crass, frankly, I'm a little jealous."

Fiona smiles. "Yeah, she died of cancer about twenty years ago, I think. He doesn't talk about her much."

"So, wait," Calista says, taking the glasses off again. "Buckhunter's mother would be..."

"Holly's grandpa's mistress." Fiona fills in the blanks of the Baxter family tree for the island's newest resident.

"Wow. Weird. And he and Holly really didn't know they were related until last summer?"

"Nope," Fiona says, staring out the window at Main Street. She can see Calista out of the corner of her eye. "He and Coco agreed to keep it quiet for as long as possible, and Holly's grandpa moved Buckhunter onto the family property to watch over Holly just before he died. She had no idea until Buckhunter told her everything."

"Family secrets, man..." Calista shakes her head, one fisted hand on her hip. All three women are facing Main Street, watching as golf carts drift by on the island's only paved street.

"Family secrets are a doozy," Millie agrees, spinning Fiona's chair so that she's looking in the mirror again. "And this hair looks pretty magnificent, if I do say so myself."

"Looks fab, Millie. Thanks." Fiona pats the beachy waves on either side of her head. "Now I need to get Buckhunter to take me to the Ho Ho tonight to show it off."

"Is Joe playing tonight?" Millie walks over to the front counter while Fiona grabs her purse from the hook near the styling chair and follows her.

"Wouldn't be a Friday night without Mr. Sacamano and his guitar, would it?" Fiona asks, pulling her wallet out of her bag.

"I'll have to see if Ray is up to it," Millie says, ringing up the services on her cash register. Fiona slides a credit card across the counter. "He's been feeling a little under the weather lately."

Fiona frowns. As the only doctor to a population of just over a hundred, she has the medical records of her neighbors neatly filed away inside her brain, for the most part.

"Has he been taking the vitamins I recommended?" she asks.

"Sure has," Millie confirms. "I even bought him one of those boxes with little dividers for the days of the week and I fill it every Sunday night. He's just been sort of low on energy."

"I could see him again this afternoon if you can get him over here," Fiona says, looking at the watch on her wrist. "Maybe just do a quick check and see if I can figure out what's up." She'd been hoping to close up shop after lunch and just take emergency calls on her cell phone, but the thought of boisterous, fun-loving Ray Bradford not feeling well enough to join them at the Ho Ho Hideaway on a Friday night has her concerned.

Millie closes the drawer under the computer and tears off a credit card receipt for Fiona. "Could you really? I'll go get him now," she says with obvious relief. "Calista—can you watch things here for twenty or thirty minutes while I go and pick up Ray?"

"Sure, sure. Go on. I don't have a massage client until four o'clock." Calista slides a stool up to the counter and sits down, resting her weight on her elbows. "I've got all the action I could ever want right under my nose," she says, making a sweeping gesture at Main Street. "So you all go on, and I'll be right here when you get back."

FIONA DRAWS SOME BLOOD, takes Ray's vitals, and hits him with a shot of Vitamin B12 before sending him on his way. She'll need to run a quick test to see if he's low on iron, but other than some complaints about feeling listless, he seems fine to her.

"I'm walking out of the building right now," Fiona says into her phone as she locks up the front doors of Poinsettia Plaza.

"I can see you. Do you want me to drive?" Bonnie asks, getting up from her desk in the B&B's office and tidying papers hastily. She sticks the pens and pencils back in the jar next to her computer and pushes in her chair. "I should've gone home to change, but it doesn't much matter now."

"Change into what, Bon?" Fiona looks both ways and crosses Main, her phone cradled between her ear and shoulder as she searches her purse for gum and lipstick.

"I don't know. Maybe a summer dress. Or a bustier and hot pants."

Fiona rolls her eyes and shoves a stick of gum in her mouth. "For Wyatt?" she asks, smiling as she takes a step up onto the curb.

"Oh, you bite your tongue, girl! Wyatt Bender, my patootie..." Bonnie says with disdain as she takes her purse off the hook by the door. "I'll meet you in the lobby." She ends the call and fluffs up her red hair as she turns off lights and heads for the front of the building.

There isn't a single visitor on the island this weekend, so Bonnie stops and takes a careful listen. The B&B is silent.

"Hey," Fiona pops her head in. "We've got no one, right?"

"Not a soul. A rare weekend without anyone to cater to."

"So lock this joint up and let's go meet up with everyone." Fiona walks all the way in and pokes her head through the doorway so that she can see the hallway. "Leave the lights on, or turn them off?"

"Might as well turn everything off. Feels kind of spooky, doesn't it?"

"A little," Fiona admits. "I keep thinking I'm going to see Jack Nicholson pop his head around the corner and say, 'Heeeerreee's Johnny!'" she says with a menacing grin.

"Oh my stars in heaven," Bonnie says, coming up behind Fiona and grabbing the fabric of her tank top. "Let's get out of here. I've got the willies now."

The women share a ride in Bonnie's golf cart, chattering the whole way about who might turn up at the Ho Ho Hideaway, and what Holly and River might be up to on their European adventure.

"They probably haven't left the hotel yet," Fiona says, consulting her watch. "It's about six o'clock here, which means it's eleven p.m. in London, right?"

"Sounds about right to me."

"I hope they have an amazing time—Holly deserves it," Fiona says loyally. "I hate watching her go back-and-forth with Jake, and that whole mess with Bridget..."

"We all dodged a bullet when Bridget left the island." Bonnie turns the cart into the sandy lot of the bar. The sun still has a few hours until it sinks into the water for the night, and the golden haze of evening wraps around them as they look out at the beach. "She wasn't one of us."

"And neither is Coco," Fiona says. She steps out of the cart and follows Bonnie to the steps of the open-air bar. "Bon," she pauses, "I really think we need to call Holly."

Bonnie stops on the bottom stair and turns to face Fiona. There's a steel in her eyes that's borne of protectiveness and love for their young mayor, and she takes a deep breath before answering.

"You're probably right," she says, "but let's have a drink first, huh? We'll call her—I promise."

Fiona ponders this as the waves crash nearby. "Okay, one drink. I could do that. It might give us time to figure out how to break it to her."

"That a girl." Bonnie's smile is wide as she reaches out a hand to take Fiona's. "Let's get you something with rum in it, and take a spin on the dance floor, doll."

Within a half hour, the bar is full of nearly everyone Bonnie and Fiona know, and they're laughing and talking their way through the crowd as Joe Sacamano pours shots, mixes drinks, and fields song requests for when he takes the stand at dusk. When Chubby Checker comes on the sound system, Jake grabs Mrs. Agnelli's wrinkled hand and carefully dances The Twist with the sharp-tongued octogenarian. Wyatt Bender flirts mercilessly with Bonnie all night long, and Cap Duncan nurses a Diet Coke and chomps on an unlit cigar. He's been off the sauce for months, and the only way that Heddie Lang-Mueller will stay by his side is if he stays away from the hard stuff. He puts one hand on Heddie's lower back and leans in close, laughing at something she says in German, their shared language. The only thing missing from the happy scene is Holly.

At ten-thirty, Fiona finds her phone in her purse and punches in Holly's number, motioning for Bonnie to walk down the stairs with her and onto the beach. They sink to the sand together, holding the phone between their ears as the sound of faraway ringing competes with the rolling of the waves and the merriment of their neighbors in the bar.

"It's three-thirty in the morning there now, isn't it?" Bonnie hisses. She pulls her knees up and hugs them close to her ample chest.

Fiona nods. They listen to the lonely sound of the phone ringing on the other side of the Atlantic until Holly's voicemail finally picks up.

"Hi, this is Holly Baxter, mayor of Christmas Key and proprietor of the Christmas Key B&B. Please leave me a message and I'll get back to you..."

7

"This is a real start to your trip, innit?" a uniformed police officer says kindly, offering Holly and River paper cups full of black coffee inside a small room at the Notting Hill station. "Fresh off the plane and you get knocked over by two blokes on the street who're as bent as a nine-bob note."

Holly and River exchange a look. A female officer enters the room, her dark hair swept into a neat bun at the nape of her neck. "You must be gutted, lass," she says in a distinctly Irish accent. "So sorry about your purse and phone and all your stuff. Was your passport in the bag?"

The room they're in has a wall of windows that looks out onto a hallway that's surprisingly busy at four in the morning.

"No, my passport is back at the flat we're renting."

"Thank Job for that," the first officer says. "Okay," he pats the table and stands, "let's get this report filed and see if we can't turn up your stuff, shall we?"

Holly answers as many questions as she can about what was in her purse and about the two men who took it. She doesn't remember their faces well, but the rough-looking rose tattoo on the neck of the guy who'd knocked her to the ground stands out distinctly, as does the black Adidas track suit worn by the guy who'd waited down the street. It isn't much, but it's all she's got.

Once the report is filed, Holly and River leave the station and are greeted by the first signs of daylight. The late spring sky is turning from ink to pink above them, and River takes Holly's hand in his.

"Sorry about your purse and your phone," he says, leaning over and kissing her on top of the head.

"Sorry about your hat." Holly puts one hand on her bare head, giving River a glum look.

"Eh," he shrugs, "it's just stuff. We'll live. And hey—you know what the good news is?"

"What?" Holly asks hopefully.

"It's breakfast time. We can probably find some beans on toast to soak up that disgusting coffee we just drank."

Holly makes a face. "I'm not sure about the beans on toast bit, but I'd say amen to the disgusting coffee part."

They walk along the sidewalk, watching as the early morning vendors open shop for delivery trucks. The tired-looking proprietors trade signatures for stacks of newspapers, boxes of freshly-made bread, and bundles of clean linens for bistro tables.

"Hey, I have an idea," River says, stopping at a red light and turning to her as they wait on the street corner.

"I'm all ears."

"Let's make this a 'yes' trip," he says, his eyes dancing. "Starting now."

"A what?"

"A 'yes' trip—we have to say yes to anything that comes along." He looks up and down the street eagerly. "If a guy walks up to us right now and asks if we want to buy a cheap Rolex from inside his trench coat, we say yes. If we go to a restaurant and the waitress asks us if we want a squid omelet for breakfast, we say yes."

"Ew," Holly says, wrinkling her nose. "Cheap watches and squid omelets?"

"Okay, bad examples," River says, letting go of her hand and holding both of his hands up in defense. "More like this: a lady asks you to be a model and you say yes. Why not? Or, wait—was her card in your purse?"

"No, it's on the dresser back at the apartment."

"Perfect. And some douchebag steals your purse and leaves you without a phone—"

"*And* without my cash, my lipgloss, and my favorite sunglasses." Holly pouts.

"We'll buy lipgloss and sunglasses," River reassures her. "But he took away your tether to the island and to work. Say *yes* to that, Holly. Say yes to three weeks of rambling around a whole new continent without having to think about whether Mr. and Mrs. Weinershnitzel-heimer from Tulsa are happy in the Seashell Suite."

Holly snorts at the name of the imaginary guests. "Yeah, the Weinershnitzelheimers were a real pain in the butt," she says, getting in on the joke.

"Exactly! And don't worry about the next village council meeting while we're here. Heddie and Bonnie will get everything lined up and set the agenda, won't they?"

"Yeah, I'm sure they will..." she says, looking at the sidewalk as she contemplates what three weeks with no contact really means.

"Listen," River says, taking both of her hands in his as the light changes and gives them permission to walk. They ignore it. "We took this trip to find out whether there was really something here for us to work with. We left the island behind to see if this, this *thing* between us really has wings, right? So let's dedicate three whole weeks to finding out. What do you say?"

Holly thinks for a minute. She lifts her eyes from the sidewalk and meets his gaze. "I say what about you?"

"What about me?"

"You've still got your phone, so you aren't cut off from your life."

"It's off," River says immediately, pulling his iPhone from the back pocket of his jeans. He holds down the button and powers it down. "As soon as we get back to the flat, I'll bury it in the bottom of my suit-case and I won't look at it for three weeks—I promise."

"Hmmm," Holly ponders this. "I trust you, but I feel like it would be safer in the bottom of *my* suitcase," she says. "That way you won't be tempted to check your email or look at Facebook or anything."

River laughs. "Oh, I think I can live without social media for three weeks. No problem there." He looks into her eyes. "Okay," he acquiesces. "You've got a deal."

They grin at one another on the street corner as black cabs and early morning commuters whiz by. The light to cross the street changes again, but still they stand there, smiling like loons.

"So, what do you say to that squid omelet?" River asks.

Holly sighs, letting the idea of this 'yes' trip permeate her whole body. "I guess the only thing I can say to that is *yes*."

8

The chartered boat slides into shore late in the afternoon on Saturday. Bonnie and Fiona have agreed to meet up at Mistletoe Morning Brew right near the dock to assess the situation.

"What do you think?" Bonnie asks eagerly, standing beside Fiona and peering out the window.

"I can't tell yet, Bon. They haven't even gotten off the boat." Fiona watches intently as the captain ties the boat up and starts removing luggage. The vessel bobs in the choppy water and the palm trees nearby dip and blow in the wind.

"I see Louis Vuitton luggage," Bonnie points out. "And a *really* cute boat captain. Hey, how old do you think he is?"

Fiona rolls her eyes. "Focus, focus, focus," she chants jokingly. "It's Coco we're worried about, not the fresh man meat that's just landed on the island."

"Right, okay. He's probably just dropping off his cargo and heading out anyway." Bonnie shrugs, looking the captain up and down appreciatively as he bends over in his white shorts and striped shirt. "Unless I can convince him to stick around and join us at Jack Frosty's for a few minutes." She narrows her eyes, wondering how much convincing that would take. "I bet he'd let me wear his captain's hat."

"*Bonnie*," Fiona says in a firm voice. She turns and puts both hands on the shoulders of the older woman. "We cannot pounce on every man who sets foot on this island. Remember Sinker McBludgeon?"

Bonnie's face contorts in pain in response to the reminder of her short-lived romance with the man who'd come to Christmas Key for a pirates' weekend.

"And," Fiona continues, "we need to get as much info as possible on Coco and the investors so that we can tell Holly what's up when she calls us back."

"You're right," Bonnie says with defeat. "You're right as rain, doll. I have a problem, and I'll be the first to admit it." She spins around to face the small crowd that's sitting around drinking afternoon coffees in the bistro. "My name is Bonnie," she says loudly, "and I'm a manaholic."

A smattering of bored applause fills the shop. Cap Duncan doesn't even look up from his newspaper.

"The first step is admitting it, hon," Carrie-Anne Martinez says as she passes by with a tray of dirty cups in her hands. "But for the record, none of us are blown away by the revelation."

Bonnie shrugs and turns back to the window. "It's a curse."

"It's an obsession," Fiona corrects. "Oh—here they come!" She snaps her fingers to get Bonnie's attention. Coco is the first off the boat, extending one thin hand to the boat's captain so that he can help her traverse the tricky steps from the rocking boat to the dock. She puts one foot on the weathered wood and steadies herself as the captain sets his hand on the small of her back. The next person off the boat is a tall man with long, dark hair that shines in the sunlight. He's wearing simple khaki pants and a shirt in the same color that's buttoned to the chin.

"That guy looks like a prisoner," Bonnie says frankly.

"Oh, Bon." Fiona wants to disagree, but his outfit *does* look like a prison-issue ensemble. "Maybe he's just not into fashion?"

Bonnie purses her lips and looks at Fiona from the corner of her eye. "Right. Maybe."

The next two people off the boat are an older couple. The man is wearing a navy blazer with a hot pink pocket square and a gold chain at his neck. The woman is wrapped in a floaty floral shift that stops at the knee, revealing wrinkled, tanned knees and still shapely calves. She's dripping in diamonds.

"I don't know what to think," Bonnie says. She eyes Coco as she points a finger around, her mouth moving a million miles a minute. "And naturally," Bonnie adds, "you've got the queen herself, dressed in a pair of pants so tight you can see her religion." There is disapproval written all over Bonnie's face as she watches Coco spin around in her white jeans and yellow tank top. "Acting like she's Vanna White out there, showing off *our* island to these strangers."

"Okay. Let's get our wits about us," Fiona says, moving away from the window as Coco walks in their direction. "Quick—she's coming this way."

Bonnie scampers away from the window in her backless sandals, the little heels tapping against the tile floor of the bistro. "What should we do? Get a coffee and sit down?"

"That's not a bad idea. We don't need to put Coco on high alert, but we need to watch her every move. Can you be our eyes and ears at the B&B?" Fiona slides into a tall chair at a table near the front of the coffee shop and Bonnie follows suit.

"Of course I can," Bonnie says, batting her eyelashes as she gets settled in her seat.

Ellen Jankowitz—Carrie-Anne's wife and the co-owner of Mistletoe Morning Brew—approaches them warily. "You two gonna order, or are you just here to stalk visitors through our window?"

Fiona is about to answer when the door to the coffee shop flies open. The bells on the handle jingle aggressively.

"And this is Mistletoe Morning Brew, where they serve the best coffee you'll ever find on a nearly-deserted island," Coco says, leading her guests into the shop. "The owners decorate with a different theme every month, and this month is...I have no idea." She presses her hands together and looks at the posters and decorations with a confused frown.

"It's Harry Potter month," Ellen says with awe, gesturing around at this very obvious fact.

"Oh, of course," Coco says, clapping her hands once. "Ladies, it's so good to see all of you!" she says with a warning smile. "And Cap, it's good to see you, too."

Cap folds his newspaper and sets it on the table. He stares back at Coco but doesn't say a word. Everyone in the shop is frozen in place: Carrie-Anne has paused midway through wiping down the front counter; Ellen is standing next to Fiona and Bonnie's table, eyeing the newcomers; and two of the triplets are sitting stock-still at their own table, cups of tea held in their hands.

It's Cap who finally breaks the silence. "Coco," he grumbles. The look on his face tells everyone in the shop that what comes next could go either way, and with Cap, you can just never tell. Everyone holds their breath. "It's been a while," he finally says, settling on civility.

Coco looks relieved. "Indeed it has. I'd like you all to meet our guests for the next few days. This is Mr. and Mrs. Killjoy—" Bonnie snorts and Coco shoots her a warning look that's pure venom, "and this is Holata."

"It's a Native American name that means 'alligator,'" the man dressed in prison garb says loudly, spreading his feet and adopting a strong stance. He clasps his hands in front of his groin and raises his chin proudly. "You can call me Gator."

"Yes, just Gator is fine," Coco says nervously, blinking a few times as she touches the hair on the side of her head.

"Welcome Gator, welcome Killjoys," Ellen says, breaking the silence. "Can I pour you a cup of coffee? First one is on the house."

"No, thank you, Ellen," Coco says, pulling the door open again and ushering her guests outside. "We're just taking the grand tour of the island right now. Maybe in the morning."

Everyone waits a beat after the bells on the door handle stop jingling again.

Bonnie gives a little chortle. "The Killjoys! I couldn't...I can't..." she's laughing now. "It's too much."

"That's the oddest group of humans I think I've ever seen around here," Cap says, leaning his elbows on the table and looking around at his neighbors in the coffee shop. "And I see you all at the Ho Ho nearly every night, so that's really saying something."

"What does Holly think?" one of the triplets asks, taking a sip of the tea she's been holding.

Bonnie and Fiona exchange a look. "Well," Fiona says. "We've been trying to call her." It sounds lame and she knows it.

"You mean she has no idea that her mother's here with Gator and the Killjoys?"

"It sounds like a sixties band, doesn't it?" Carrie-Anne says from the side of the shop where she's straightening the cream and sugar station. "Like, 'Live at the sock hop on Saturday night, singing sensation *Gator and the Killjoys!*'"

"With their Top 40 hit, 'I Wanna Steal Your Land.'" Cap picks his newspaper up again, shakes it, and then sets it down again, realizing how bad his joke sounds. "And that's not a Native American crack— that's because they're here to buy up the island."

"How about 'Coco's Got a Brand New Bag'?" Bonnie offers.

"Or, 'A Change is Gonna Come,'" Ellen says forlornly.

"You didn't make a joke with that one," Carrie-Anne points out.

Ellen shrugs. "Didn't need to."

A thoughtful silence falls over the coffee shop. The only sounds are of spoons clinking against mugs, of the dishwasher running in the tiny back kitchen, and of Cap's newspaper as he opens it once again.

"Well," Fiona says, sliding off the chair. "I should probably try to call Holly again."

"Right." Bonnie clears her throat and stands up next to Fiona. "And I need to close up at the B&B for the day. I'll shoot Holly an email while I'm there. That way she'll definitely get the message that something is going on."

"What's going to happen to us if Coco is able to convince Holly and Buckhunter that this is a good idea?" Carrie-Anne looks around at the rest of them. "Or maybe not this group, but maybe some other? What happens to us then?"

Eyes dart around the room, making contact and sharing a moment of sadness and concern.

"We stick together, that's what happens," Bonnie says definitively, pulling herself up to her full height. "We're a family, and we'll figure this out, you hear?"

Heads around the shop nod slowly as everyone agrees, but there is a hesitation—an ounce of uncertainty has crept into the room like an unwanted visitor.

As Bonnie and Fiona walk out the front door, Carrie-Anne starts humming Sister Sledge's "We Are Family" to herself, picking up empty cups and spoons and getting ready to close up shop for the day.

9

"Rise and shine, milady," River says, shaking Holly from slumber. They've been struggling with jet lag for the last couple of days, and Holly wants nothing more than to roll over and sleep for a few more hours. "Come on, come on." He shakes her again. "There's coffee to be had, but we have to get out there and find it."

"Is this part of the game where I have to say yes?" she grumbles.

"It's *all* part of the game."

Grudgingly, Holly climbs out of bed and walks over to the window to peer through the curtains. It's raining.

"What happened to the sun?" she yawns.

"First of all we're in London, not Florida, so the sun isn't a given. Secondly, it's only May—not even summer yet."

"Oh." Holly lets the curtain fall. "What should we do after coffee?"

"It's Monday morning and I think we should call your new modeling agency."

"Get out of town, O'Leary," Holly says, shuffling into the bathroom. "No way. I know I agreed to this whole saying yes business, but I don't want to waste these people's time just for a lark."

"Who's wasting anyone's time? *She* approached *you*, Christie Brinkley!"

Holly turns on the shower in the bathroom and leans in to examine her sleep-lined face in the mirror. "I notice that all the supermodels you're comparing me to are over fifty," she says flatly. "You could at least call me Gisele or something."

"I'll call you whatever you want me to," River says, poking his head through the bathroom door, "as long as you get your sweet ass in gear so that we can get your career in front of the camera off the ground."

Holly puts one hand on his shoulder and pushes him out playfully, shutting the door behind him.

They're out the door in under an hour, but Holly refuses to put on extra makeup or to dress in anything she wouldn't normally wear. While she'd showered, River had taken the opportunity to use the phone in the apartment and call the agency. The chipper girl on the other end of the line had asked them to drop by at three for a cattle call, but promised to make note of the fact that Holly had been approached by one of the agents.

"I still think this is dumb—I'm sorry," Holly says. They're wandering through Notting Hill in the drizzle of the morning. The air is crisp and refreshing in spite of the car exhaust and the other big city smells that tickle Holly's nostrils.

"It's dumb to come to Europe and do what everyone else does," River counters. "We can see Big Ben and the Tower Bridge and all that, but why not do some unexpected things while we're here?" He puts a hand on the small of Holly's back and guides her over a step and into a pub. River ducks through the short doorway of the old building, and they scan the room for an empty table.

"Got room for two over here, loves!" calls a harried waitress as she breezes past. Holly and River grab the table she's pointed at. They're just getting settled when the waitress is back with two menus. "Coffee? Tea? Full English?"

"Coffee is a yes—for both of us," River says, making comical wide eyes in Holly's direction as if he's warning the waitress of an eminent meltdown if they don't get coffee soon. "And what's a full English?"

"A full English breakfast, dearies. It's sausage, bacon, beans, tomatoes, an egg, and toast. Oh, and black pudding," she adds, nodding her head as she ticks off each item on the list.

"What's in the black pudding?" Holly asks, handing back her menu.

The waitress sighs. "Oatmeal, onions, pork fat, blood—"

"Nope," Holly says, turning to River. "This is not part of the 'yes' game. I'll never be able to eat oatmeal again if I taste it mixed with blood and fat." She looks back up at the waitress. "The full English breakfast for me, please, hold the black pudding."

"I'll take the whole kit and caboodle," River says, passing his own menu to the waitress.

"Got it. Back with the coffee in a titch."

"I can't decide whether you think you're British or whether you're ready to retire to Christmas Key and start hanging out with everyone there," Holly teases, reaching for the mug of coffee that the waitress sets in front of her. "Thank you," she says gratefully to the woman.

"Why?" River laughs, taking a sip of his steaming black coffee.

"Eating disgusting food like black pudding and saying stuff like 'kit and caboodle'—you're just funny."

River shrugs, holding his mug with both hands, elbows on the table. "I'm just being myself. But if I entertain you, milady, then so much the better."

"You do," Holly assures him. "So what are we going to do all morning to work off the pound of meat we're about to consume?"

River sets his coffee down and pulls a map from the pocket of his lightweight nylon jacket. "Well, let's have a look-see here, dearie," he says in a terrible British accent. "Shall we get a photo of you in a red phone booth and then take a tour of Buckingham Palace?"

"That sounds fun," Holly says, smiling at him over the rim of her coffee mug. The caffeine is finally hitting her, and she's starting to feel more human, jet lag be damned.

They eat as much of their full English breakfast as they can—

Holly gags at the black pudding as River takes a tentative first bite, then finishes it off, declaring it "not half bad"—and afterwards they hit the wet pavement again to explore the city.

The previous day's drama of being mugged and spending time in the local police station hasn't dampened the overall excitement of the trip at all. Her stolen credit cards have been cancelled, and even though not having her cash or cards puts Holly at River's mercy, he's promised her that he doesn't mind paying for everything while they wait for her new Visa card to arrive via FedEx.

They pass the morning looking for the famous red phone booths, and they watch the changing of the guard at Buckingham Palace along with a throng of other people. Holly picks up a few Christmas ornaments shaped like crowns in the gift shop, and they brave the Tube to get around the city, hopping off at Westminster to see Big Ben and appreciate the view of the London Eye behind them.

Holly and River get to the modeling agency just before three o'clock. It's still raining, and Holly ducks under a doorway and pulls her Yankees cap off of her head.

"Fix me," she laughs, pointing at her damp hair.

River looks her up and down. "Ehhh," he says, assessing the damage. "Well, you could pull that hair up into a bun and put on some lipstick or something, but the wet tennis shoes and wrinkled cargo pants aren't exactly going to scream 'MODEL' when you walk into the room."

Holly isn't even sure that she wants to scream MODEL when she walks into the agency, but as two tall, lithe girls with smooth skin and tight black clothes slither past them, her shoulders fall. One of the girls punches a button on the buzzer and the door clicks open for them to enter.

"Okay," Holly says, "this is ridiculous. Did you see those twenty-year-olds? I'm old enough to be their mother. Let's get out of here."

"You are *not* old enough to be their mother," River scoffs. "You're not even thirty-one yet."

"I look eighty-one today," Holly argues with a frown as she

catches a glimpse of herself in the window of the building. "And also a little like a drowned rat."

"Let's go," River says, grabbing her hand forcefully. He yanks her into motion before she can even ask where they're going.

"River," Holly protests as he leads them down the sidewalk. "I'll go in—seriously. If you want to keep doing this 'yes' game, then I'll go in, even looking like this." It seems like he's angry at her for pouting about her wet hair, and Holly feels bad about ruining his fun.

They reach the end of the block and turn right, where a tall building looms in front of them. In huge vertical letters on the corner of the building is the word HARRODS.

"We're going in," River says. They cross the street with the other pedestrians and walk under the little green awnings that line the sidewalk.

Inside, River takes Holly's hand and leads her up to the first store employee they find. "We need women's clothes, men's clothes, and make-up," he says, face serious. "We're on a mission."

"For MI6, I presume," the older man in the business suit says drolly with a twitch of his groomed mustache.

"Yes, naturally." River plays along. "We're agents on a highly classified mission who need to look like, oh, let's say we need to look good enough to pass as models."

The man's eyebrows shoot up as he takes in their rain-battered clothing. "Menswear and Beauty are on the Ground Floor," he says, "and Womenswear is on the First Floor."

"Thank you!" Holly is the one to pull River along this time as they head for the crowd that's funneling onto an escalator.

"Let's go to Beauty and Womenswear first," River says, stepping onto the moving staircase.

"Because it's going to take more work to make me presentable?"

"I wasn't going to say *that.*" River leans over to plant a kiss on Holly's cheek. "Hey," he says quietly in Holly's ear, "have I mentioned yet how glad I am that we're here?"

A warm feeling spreads through Holly's core. "Me, too," she says, squeezing his hand.

THE DOOR to the agency swings open at three-forty-five, and a chic couple struts into the all-white lobby. Everyone waiting looks up from their phone screens for a moment to gauge the competition. River is dressed in fitted jeans and a black leather motorcycle jacket, his hair combed to one side. Holly's black skirt hits her mid-thigh, and her new black boots end just below the knee, revealing a patch of tanned leg. She's wearing a body-skimming black turtleneck that's tucked into her skirt, and the woman in the Beauty department had slicked her light brown hair into a tight bun and quickly powdered, high-lighted, and enhanced her face with a palette of make-up that's left Holly looking put-together but not overdone.

"River O'Leary and Holly Baxter to see Louella James," River says, leaning over the counter to speak quietly to the receptionist as he holds a shopping bag full of their old clothes.

There's nowhere to sit, so they huddle in the corner near a potted plant, Holly holding onto River's arm nervously. "This is crazy," she whispers between gritted teeth.

"No, this is fun," River says, tipping his head toward hers. "At least until I get my credit card bill next month."

"I'll pay you back—I promise," Holly says out loud, forgetting that they're in a silent lobby as she remembers the numbers on the cash register at Harrods. She has no idea where she'll ever wear this outfit on Christmas Key, but the whole thing makes her feel like a glam-orous city-dweller, and she loves the square toes and chunky heels of the boots.

"I'm not worried about that," River says. "But we'll definitely be wearing these outfits for every fancy meal we go out to on this trip."

"River and Holly?" the receptionist calls out. They step forward. "Louella will see you now." The other would-be models in the lobby look at them with mild interest and a hint of distaste, obviously wondering how these latecomers are getting called into the office before them. "This way, please."

Behind a door is a long, white hallway that's lined with blown-up, framed magazine covers. The receptionist leads the way to an office with an open door and holds out her hand wordlessly to indicate that they should enter.

"Holly!" The woman behind the desk stands and walks toward them with her arms open like they're old friends. "You came!" The office has high ceilings and tall windows. The walls are brick, and a clear, Lucite desk and chair face the door. Louella pulls Holly into a light embrace and touches her cheek against Holly's. "And this must be your gorgeous boyfriend," she says, reaching out a hand and taking River's. "Stunning—both of you. Come in," she says, closing the door behind them and pointing to the two zebra-print covered chairs positioned in front of her desk. Louella walks back around and sits in her own chair.

There are poster-sized black-and-white images blown up and framed on Louella's walls. One is of a very recognizable supermodel in a dark bikini top, her cleavage and shoulders covered with grains of sand as she looks into the camera with heavily-lidded eyes. Holly can't help but wonder whether she's one of Louella's clients.

"You look like a grown-up version of the girl I met at Heathrow," Louella says, wrapping her bright pink cashmere shawl around her shoulders and holding it there. Her shawl and matching fingernails are the only pop of color in the whole office. Everything else—including Holly and River—is black and white. "And your man is simply dashing. I love the James Bond look," she says, waving a hand up and down at their new clothes.

"Thank you." Holly crosses her ankles under the desk demurely. Something about being in a modeling agency makes her feel like she should be standing up straighter, or walking around with a book on top of her head.

"I'm so glad you called, because I have something in mind for the both of you. Will you hear me out?"

"Absolutely," River says. "I think Holly was born to be a model."

Holly elbows him in the side without looking away from Louella.

"There's a client who wants a successful-looking couple in their thirties to do a shoot at a gorgeous residence in the Cotswolds. Have either of you been?" Louella arches her eyebrows expectantly.

"To the Cotswolds?" Holly asks. "No, never."

"It's lovely," Louella assures them. "Just lovely. Anyhow, my client is a luxury magazine based in Dubai. They want to do an editorial spread that showcases a posh country couple at home. It wasn't what I had in mind when I met you, Holly—in fact, I was thinking of something beachy and carefree and this is quite the opposite—but now that you're both here and this opportunity's come up...I'd like to submit you for it." She looks back and forth between River and Holly. "What do you say?"

"When is the shoot?" River asks.

Louella taps on the keyboard of her open laptop. "Wednesday. And the pay is ten thousand pounds for the couple," she says, reading the details from her email. "I'd need to take some quick pictures to send over to the client, but I think they're going to love you both. What do you say?"

There's a moment of silence as Holly and River look at one another.

"Well," Holly says, pretending to consider such a ridiculous sum of money. Her mind spins at the utter ridiculousness of her posing as a paid model. "I guess we have to say yes."

10

Coco shows up at the Jingle Bell Bistro with Gator and the Killjoys for dinner on the second evening of their visit and demands a seat on the patio.

"We'd like to see the water," she says to Iris Cafferkey.

"No one else has asked to eat outside tonight," Iris says, "but I can get a table set up if you give me five minutes."

Jimmy, Iris's husband and the bistro's resident chef, comes out of the kitchen with his apron and cap on. "Coco," he says in a loud voice, his Irish accent on full display. "What brings you to the island?"

"Hi, Jimmy," she says, taking a step back so that she won't be forced into an awkward embrace. "This is Netta and Brice Killjoy, and this is Gator." Jimmy thrusts out a hand to welcome each of the guests. "And this is Jimmy Cafferkey. He and his wife own the bistro and have lived on the island for—what? About twenty years now?" Coco asks politely.

Iris breezes past them with an armful of linens. "Twenty years in August," she says. "Emily was just a wee lass when we moved here." As if on cue, Emily herself emerges from the kitchen with a pitcher of water in her hands. Iris and Jimmy had moved from Dublin to Christmas Key with their daughter, determined to give their youngest child the richest life they could, and to raise a little girl with Down Syndrome in a tropical paradise. So far, they've been successful beyond their wildest dreams.

"Hi, Coco," Emily says. "Holly's in Europe with her boyfriend."

"Oh?" Coco's eyes go wide. "I didn't know she had a boyfriend."

"It isn't Jake," Emily says, shaking her head and smiling. It's not a terribly well-kept secret that Emily has a huge crush on the island's only police officer, though she'd been ridiculously happy for Holly when she and Jake were an item.

"As I mentioned," Coco says to her guests, turning to Gator and the Killjoys, "my daughter does a passable job of keeping things running around here, but clearly her priorities aren't always with the island."

"Now, wait just a second there," Jimmy says, putting both hands on his aproned waist. "The mayor loves this island more than she loves anything." His voice is defensive, his stance somewhat hostile. "She deserves a vacation every now and then just like anyone—"

"Your table is ready," Iris says, sweeping in and breaking up the potential showdown between her husband and Coco. "Follow me, please."

The group heads out to the patio that looks onto the beach, and as the door swings shut behind them, Jimmy grumbles to himself about Coco and her high-minded ways.

"Dad," Emily says, putting a hand on her father's back. "Be nice. She's Holly's mom." Emily is—perhaps above all else—loyal to her oldest friend in every way. "Maybe we don't like her, but we like Holly."

Jimmy puffs out an impatient breath, considering the wisdom of his daughter's words. "Indeed we do, lass." He watches as Coco and her guests get settled at the white linen covered table outside. "Indeed we do."

"But if you want to spit in her food," Emily whispers, leaning in closer, "then I promise I won't tell anyone."

Jimmy pulls his daughter in for a tight hug and plants a kiss on top of her blonde head as he roars with laughter. "Maybe I'll just put a dash of baking soda in everything I make for her —how's that?"

"That's a better idea," Emily agrees, nodding as her dad lets go of her. "I'm going to go and pour water now."

"You do that," Jimmy says, watching his daughter with pride. Everything is how they'd always dreamed it would be, and their little island is the perfect paradise. Jimmy narrows his eyes as he watches Coco gesturing with her hands and talking on the patio. There's no way they can let this woman sweep in and change it all—he won't let her.

"So they're here to look at the island? Like, to buy it?" Jake asks, holding his bottle of beer to his lips. The usual crowd has gathered at the Ho Ho Hideaway for a Sunday evening nightcap, and Jimmy Cafferkey is recounting the tale of Coco and her guests at dinner.

"That's what it looks like. I heard from Fiona that this Gator character is a Native American, but we don't know anything about these Killjoys."

"Love the name, by the way," Millie Bradford says, leaning in to the small group with a cup of coffee in her hands. "Isn't Killjoy a perfect name for these people?"

"Indeed," Jimmy agrees. "What's with the coffee, Millie? Couldn't get Sacamano to pour you a real drink?"

Millie glances down at the mug of cooled coffee in her hand. "No, I just want to be alert. Ray isn't feeling well, and I don't want to go home and fall asleep—he might need me."

"What's going on with the old dog?" Wyatt Bender asks as he joins the crowd. "He seen the doc yet?"

"He saw Fiona," Millie confirms. "She ran a few tests, but there's nothing conclusive yet."

"Well, let us know if there's anything we can do to help," Jimmy says to her, putting an arm around Millie's shoulders. "In the meantime, let's keep our eyes on Coco and keep our ears to the ground. Has anyone let Holly know what's going on around here?"

"Fiona and Bonnie have tried," Wyatt says. "But from what I hear, they haven't been able to reach her."

"That's odd. I can't imagine her being out of reach on purpose." Millie frowns and swirls the coffee and cream around in her mug. "I hope she's okay."

"I'm sure she is," Jimmy Cafferkey says, his arm still around Millie's shoulders. He gives her a gentle shake. "You just take care of that old husband of yours, and we'll work on tracking down the mayor."

"Maybe we should set up one of those group chat thingamabobs," Maria Agnelli says, materializing at Jimmy's elbow. At just under five feet tall, Mrs. Agnelli is a pocket-sized pistol full of sass and vinegar. "Keep each other posted on what we know."

Millie pulls her phone out of her pocket. "How do we do that?"

Cell phones are pulled from pockets and purses. The devices have more apps and capabilities than an island full of Baby Boomers knows what to do with, and everyone is quickly engrossed in punching buttons and trying to figure things out.

"No idea," Wyatt says, shrugging as he looks at his home screen.

"I've got you." Jake slides his own phone from the deep cargo pocket of his black shorts. He opens up a text and quickly taps in the names of everyone present. "I'll add Bonnie and Fiona, too," he says, creating the group chat in seconds. "And Buckhunter."

"Good idea," Millie agrees, staring at her phone as she waits for something to happen.

"There we go," Jake says. He types the word "hi" to start the group chat and hits send. "Voila—we're in a group chat. Now whoever hears from Holly first should send a message out to all of us."

"And any news on Coco and what she's up to can be shared this way, too." Jimmy holds up his phone and gives it a shake. "And Millie, if you need anything from us or if Ray gets worse, just shoot us a message."

"Perfect. We have a plan." Jake drains his bottle of beer and swallows. "And on that note, I'm going to call it a night. See you all tomorrow." He holds up the empty bottle in parting, setting it on the bar as he passes Joe Sacamano.

"Night, Officer Zavaroni," Millie says, waving at him.

Jake's police cart is in the lot next to the rustic looking bar, and he slides behind the wheel in the darkness, looking at the light of the moon as it dances on the ocean. The palm tree next to the Ho Ho is wound with twinkling Christmas lights, and the sound of music from the bar is in the air. Jake thinks about the ever-changing dynamics of the island, and about the very real and present threat that Coco poses. What will happen to everyone if she convinces Holly and Buckhunter to part with Christmas Key? Depending on the circumstances, they might all be able to stay, but would it ever be the same?

The Holly Jake knows wouldn't even consider letting go of her beloved island—after all, she'd chosen Christmas Key over him when he'd proposed to her the year before—but the Holly he knows wouldn't normally consider disappearing for three weeks and going totally incommunicado. Everything is up in the air, and the untethered feeling that's filled Jake for months is almost overwhelming. When his short-lived fling with Bridget had ended with her miscarriage and departure from the island, Jake had sincerely hoped that things would get back to normal. But now, as he sits here on the firm seat of his cart, wheel gripped in both hands, he's starting to wonder what normal even looks like. Is normal an island owned by the Killjoys? Is it him, forever alone and just waiting to see what Holly's next move will be? Or is it Christmas Key without Holly?

Jake exhales and runs a hand through his dark hair. A wave crashes loudly on the shore and he turns on his cart to drive home.

11

Holly tucks her cosmetic bag into the side pocket of her small duffel bag on Wednesday and turns around in a circle. Her other black boot is missing, and the last time she'd seen it was the day River tugged the new boots off after their trip to the modeling agency and pushed her back onto the bed.

She gets on her hands and knees now and lifts the duvet cover. The boot is wedged under the iron frame of the bed.

"You ready, superstar?" River asks, poking his head into the doorway.

Holly rolls her eyes. "Just about. So wait—what's the travel plan?"

"Train from Paddington Station to Swindon," River says, pulling a folded up piece of paper from his pocket. "And then we're meeting a taxi for the ride into...Fairford."

"And that's where the house is?" Holly yanks the boot out from under the bed and sits back on the floor so that she can pull both boots on over her black stretch pants.

"Mmmhmm." River is squinting at the paper with the instructions for their trip. "Says to take the taxi into town and then call when we get there. We're staying over tonight and then shooting all day tomorrow, and then they'll ship us back to London."

"Has it occurred to you yet," Holly says, tugging at her boot, "that this whole thing is insane?"

River folds the paper up and shoves it back into his pocket with a smirk. "What whole thing? Going out to some country house to have our pictures taken?"

"No," Holly says, zipping the boot over her right calf. "Saying yes to everything. We could end up on a boat to Africa, or in a hot air balloon over Italy."

"Oh, I wish!" River says, folding his arms across his chest. "That's the beauty of saying yes, Mayor. You give life a chance to take you places instead of trying to cram the whole of life into the little box you've created for it."

Holly reaches for the edge of the bed and pulls herself up, smoothing the long, sky blue shirt she's wearing over her hips. "Is that what you think I do? Cram life into a box?"

River shrugs and leans into the doorframe. "Kind of. Sometimes. Maybe."

Holly stands there for a second, looking at him in a different light. "I never knew you felt that way about me."

"I don't 'feel that way' about you—it's just an observation. You like things to be a certain way, and when they're not, you resist. You don't like change. You don't like to relinquish control."

"Does anyone?" she asks defensively.

River steps forward to take Holly's packed duffel bag. "Some people. The ones who sell everything they own and sail around the world for a year. The people who choose joy and adventure over knowing what's around every bend."

"But why is one way right and the other way wrong?" Holly follows him down the stairs, holding onto the railing as she walks carefully in her new boots.

"I never said it was," River says mildly. "I'm just telling you what I see."

At the door to the apartment, Holly pauses and waits. River sets her bag next to his own and turns to her.

"Some people would think that living on a tiny island and trying to turn it into something bigger and better than what it is *is* pretty exciting," Holly says.

"I'm not going to argue with that." River reaches out his hands and puts them on her waist, pulling her in closer. "All I'm saying is that there's adventure beyond the shores of Christmas Key, and if you never say yes, you never get to see what's out there." He bends forward and kisses her on the lips.

"I said yes to this trip, didn't I?" she asks, her mood mellowed by the touch of his hands and lips.

"This veered off in a direction that I really hadn't intended." River pulls away from her. "Listen, I think you're nervous about this photo shoot thing, and you really don't need to be. We have nothing to lose. And I know leaving the island for three weeks is way outside of your comfort zone, but all I'm saying is that it's a good thing. Either you'll fall in love with the world and want to see more, or you'll go back home knowing that you never need to leave again."

Holly stands in the marble foyer with the bags at her feet. Maybe River is right: her nerves are getting the better of her. After all, she's totally out of her element here, and in the past few days she's been robbed, offered a job as a model, and has agreed to give up contact with anyone from home until she gets back there.

She nods, forcing herself to look him in the eye. "You're right," Holly finally says. "Adventure. Life. See where the wind takes us. Got it."

River laughs. "Well, that's the condensed version, but yeah." He stoops to pick up their bags. "You ready to catch this train?"

Holly runs a hand through her hair and sighs. "Ready as I'll ever be."

They shut the door tightly and give it a tug to make sure it's locked, then River steps to the curb and flags down the first taxi they see.

∿

THE RIDE from Swindon to Fairford takes about twenty minutes, and

Holly watches the countryside roll by through the window in the backseat.

"First time in the Cotswolds?" the driver asks, making eye contact with her in the rearview mirror as he rolls to a stop in the village of Fairford.

"Yep, first time," she says.

"This is the High Street here," the driver says, stopping the meter. "If you want to call your people now, then this would be a good place to meet them. Town's not very big at all."

River pats his pocket and then looks at Holly sheepishly. "No phones," they say at the same time.

"Here, borrow mine," the driver says, passing an iPhone over the seat. River takes it and dials the number he's been given.

Five minutes later, River and Holly are standing on the curb with their bags when a Mercedes screeches to a stop in front of them. "Hop in!" a woman with a British accent, a huge mane of red hair, and an abundance of freckles says. Her window is down, and the radio is cranked up high, dance music pulsing from the speakers.

The driver's name is Allison and the house they're staying in is tucked down a quiet lane behind a school.

"We've got a big spread in the kitchen," Allison says over her shoulder as the wind blows through her hair. "Everyone is here already, and we're ready to start doing some set-up. You two have a room at the back of the house on the second floor. It's a lovely property—just lovely," she assures them, waving one hand around as she talks. "We just pop down this lane here," Allison says, swinging the car onto a narrow path that's lined with what look like cannon balls, "and then past the gardens here we find a hidden drive." As she narrates their every move, Holly takes a deep breath and reaches for her purse.

The rain clouds have broken up and rays of sunlight pierce the grounds, making the wet grass glisten in the afternoon light. The house is built of solid stone with trails of ivy clawing at its walls, and a tall hedge has been cut into an archway.

"That gate leads down to the river," Allison says, following Holly's gaze to the arch. "We'll do some shots down there as well—probably in the boathouse."

River is out of the car and gathering their bags while Holly looks around. The gravel crunches beneath her feet. This place is so different from Christmas Key, so far from everything she knows. There's a surreal moment where Holly contemplates grabbing her bag from River and demanding a ride back to the High Street so that she can catch a ride to Swindon, hop on the train, and head back to London. When she gets there, she'll pack her bags, catch another cab to Heathrow, and be on her way to Miami in no time.

"Hey," River says softly, coming up next to her as she inhales the fresh air. "You okay?" He looks concerned.

The moment passes for Holly and she remembers that she's here by choice. She wanted to leave the island and have a European adventure with River, and she agreed to his insane idea to say yes to everything. So here they are, posing as models in some tiny English village while she's got no way to contact anyone at home. Holly breathes in and out until her heart rate slows.

"I'm fine," she says with a weak smile, trying to muster some enthusiasm. River takes her hand and leads her through the heavy oak front door with its iron handle and knocker.

"Hello?" he calls out, ducking through the short doorway.

"Hello yourself," says a tiny brunette with what looks like a gun holster around her waist. But instead of weaponry, her belt is filled with make-up brushes, hairbrushes, and a clear spray bottle full of liquid. "Oh, don't mind me," she says. She's clearly American, this little spitfire who tosses her hair to one side and winks up at them both. "I'm not always fully armed and loaded." She points at the belt that Holly's staring at. "I'm Sarah, by the way." She thrusts a hand out to shake River's and Holly's hands in turn. "Thrilled to have some fellow expats on the crew."

"Where are you from?" River asks as he drops his duffel bag next to the stairs in the entryway.

"Washington," Sarah says. "As in state, not D.C.—that always throws people."

"Doesn't throw me at all," River says with a huge grin. "I'm from Oregon."

"Neighbors!" Sarah's face lights up like someone's just flipped a switch. Something about Sarah's bubbly attitude and the flirtatious thrust of her chest in River's direction is off-putting. Holly bristles.

"Seattle?" River asks.

"Mmhmm." Sarah nods at him eagerly. "And you—Portland?"

"Lucky guess," River says, pointing a finger at her. "Since that's the only major city in the state." They laugh together and Holly clears her throat.

"And what about you, Holly?" Sarah asks with slightly less enthusiasm.

"Christmas Key—just past Key West. I'm the mayor," she adds unnecessarily, as if this will impress a tiny, cute girl who's left home and is traveling the world with an arsenal of beauty gadgets dangling from a belt around her waist.

"Oh, cool. I love Florida," Sarah says. She looks at Holly like she's waiting for more. From the room right off the entryway, male voices debate the lighting in various accents, and the pop and flash of bulbs and lights fills the foyer with background noise.

"You know, I'd love to put my stuff somewhere and take about five minutes—do you know which room is ours?" Holly asks, putting special emphasis on the word *ours*. She has no idea why her defenses are up already with Sarah, who seems perfectly nice, but something about her youthful exuberance and neighborly camaraderie with River has set Holly's teeth on edge.

"Oh, yeah. Upstairs," Sarah says, pointing at the staircase, "last room at the end of the hall—it has the bathroom attached to it."

Holly nods her thanks and grabs both her own and River's bags.

"I'm just going to say hello and offer to help—I'll be right up," River says to her, already following Sarah into the kitchen.

At this point, Holly doesn't really care. Her bad mood has blossomed into a full-blooming cherry tree in spring time, filling her with floating pink petals of discontent. She has no idea why this whole adventure has her feeling the way it does, but she wishes with all her heart in this moment that she'd never taken Louella's business card at the airport, and she wishes even more that she'd never told River about the whole thing.

The stairs take a sharp turn and drop her on a landing that's filled with doors. She counts six bedrooms and a bathroom on her way to the end of the hall, one wall of which is a built-in bookcase that's completely filled with books. A skylight overhead casts a patch of light on the carpet beneath her feet.

The room next to the one she and River will share has its door ajar. It's got a single bed and a desk, and on the desk sits a computer monitor, its screen glowing enticingly. Holly's heart picks up its pace again and she tosses their bags carelessly into the room she'll share with River and rushes back to the computer. It's on. She looks around, peering into the other cracked doors. The voices are all coming from downstairs, and she can hear laughter and conversation from the kitchen below her.

It feels wrong and she knows it flies in the face of her agreement with River, but Holly tiptoes into the room anyway. There are no bags on the bed and no sign that anyone has picked this room, so Holly shuts the door quietly and pulls out the desk chair. The keyboard slides out from under the lip of the desk. Someone has logged into the computer already, giving her free access to the internet. In under thirty seconds, Holly is logged into her email.

12

The boat pulls up to the dock around four o'clock on Tuesday, and once again Bonnie and Fiona are watching from the coffee shop.

"This is insane," Bonnie says, looking through the window as three people disembark with the boat's captain. "We should be out there saying hello."

"I know, but I wanted to observe and see who was arriving before we threw ourselves into the fray."

"What fray, doll?" Bonnie turns to Fiona. "We're talking three humans, not a glut of aliens here to eat our souls and conquer our civilization. Let's go."

Bonnie yanks Fiona's hand, pulling her out the door and onto the sidewalk. She straightens her shoulders and approaches the tiny group as they sort through their luggage and look around.

"I'm just guessing here," Bonnie says to Fiona, leaning in closer as they walk, "but that older woman on the boat has to be related to Vance and Calista," she says, nodding at a black woman with regal posture. "And the other two must be related to Hal Pillory."

"Right! Holly did say that Hal's granddaughter and her son were coming down to stay with him full-time." Fiona pulls the sunglasses off the top of her head and puts them on so that she can check out the small group from behind her lenses.

"Hi, y'all!" Bonnie calls out, waving. "Welcome!"

A leggy, dark-haired woman puts up a hand to shield her eyes. "Hi," she says tiredly. "I'm Katelynn Pillory. This is my son Logan." Katelynn puts a hand on the shoulder of a tall, rangy teenager. He scowls at the horizon.

"Oh, honey," Bonnie says, throwing her arms wide and launching herself at the woman. "We're so glad to see you. Hal is just a dear, and we loved your grandma so much."

"Thank you," Katelynn says, extracting herself from Bonnie's clutches. "We're glad to be here."

"Speak for yourself," Logan says under his breath. The women ignore him.

"My uncle is ready to head back home to Ohio, so I'm here to take over my grandfather's care," Katelynn explains, shifting her purse from one shoulder to the other. Hal Pillory's daughter and son had been caring for him after it was discovered that Hal was digging holes all over the island without explanation and just generally acting out of sorts. It was a confusing time for the islanders who were baffled by Hal's strange behavior, and after discovering the real reason he'd been digging the holes (to find the ashes of his beloved late wife, Sadie, which he'd buried to keep safe from a storm), Fiona had run some tests and realized that Hal needed more care than they could offer him.

"We're really glad that you're here," Fiona says, offering Katelynn a hand rather than a hug, which felt more professional to Fiona as Hal's physician. "And it's nice to meet you, too," she says to Logan.

"Logan is going to finish his junior and senior year through an online school that the state of Florida provides," Katelynn explains. "And I'm going to be doing some freelance writing while we're here. This is going to be quite an adventure for both of us."

"Sweet Mary and Moses at Sunday brunch," the other woman says as she finally steps off the boat behind them. "The good Lord found it in His heart to get us here in one piece, and now I've got to stand around waiting to see my family, who aren't even here to greet me." Her head is wrapped in a yellow scarf, and ropes of amber beads hang around her smooth, mahogany-colored neck. "Idora Blaine-Guy," she says with her chin held high. "Mother of Vance, grand-mother of Mexico and Moritz." Idora holds out a hand with nails painted a shiny orange-red. Bonnie shakes it first.

"Well, I do declare," Bonnie says, looking the woman up and down. "Calista has told us so much about you."

Idora's nostrils visibly flare. She laces her fingers together and clasps them just below her large breasts. "I'm sure she has."

The boat's captain unloads boxes and bags from the cargo hold as an awkward silence falls over the small group. There's still no sign of anyone to greet the newcomers, so Fiona claps her hands together decisively.

"Now," she says, "let's get you all to where you're supposed to be. How about if I drive Katelynn and Logan so that I can fill her in a little on what's been going on with her grandpa, and Bonnie, maybe you can run Idora over to Vance and Calista's?"

Bonnie springs into action. "Got it. I'll just pull my golf cart up here," she says, already moving towards the B&B, "and we'll get you all loaded up and ready to go."

The new arrivals look a little baffled by the fact that they've been dumped on a dock on a strange island and left to fend for themselves, but the women smile gamely. Logan folds his arms and scowls again.

It takes about ten minutes to get both Bonnie's and Fiona's carts loaded with luggage, and then they're off to deliver everyone and everything to their desired destinations. On the way to Vance and Calista's, Idora clutches a large fabric purse in her lap and hums gospel tunes to herself. She watches the island roll by as Bonnie points out shops and landmarks. The triplets are standing in front of Tinsel & Tidings gift shop, which serves as the island's tiny grocery store, and they wave excitedly, identical smiles on their youthful faces.

"Oh my," Idora says, leaning forward in her seat so she can crank her neck and watch as Gwen, Gen, and Glen disappear behind them.

"I don't think I've ever seen triplets before in the flesh." She puts one hand over her heart. "The Lord does work in mysterious ways now, doesn't He?"

"Indeed He does, sugar," Bonnie agrees. "Indeed He does."

They turn up White Christmas Way and stop in front of the pink house with turquoise shutters that Vance and Calista Guy are renting with their twin boys, Mexi and Mori. Like most of the other houses on the island, the Guys have made a nod towards the year-round holiday decorations by wrapping the trunk of the biggest palm tree in their yard with Christmas lights. Idora takes this in with a frown.

"Mama!" Vance Guy says with obvious joy. "I didn't realize your boat was coming in so early!" He's been on his knees on the side of the house, pulling up weeds and tossing them into a growing pile in the grass. Vance slips his hands out of the gardening gloves he's wearing and strides over to where his mother is trying to push herself out of Bonnie's golf cart. "Here, let me help you."

"No need," Idora says, holding up a warning hand. "I might be almost seventy, but I've still got my wits about me, child."

Vance pauses and waits for his mother to stand and straighten her long, voluminous wrap dress.

"Grandma!" The twins come barreling out of the house, shoving each other as they trip over their own bare feet to get to their grandmother. "Grandma! Grandma! Grandma!" They launch their small bodies at their grandmother like missiles, wrapping their arms around her and burying their impish faces in her stomach.

"Hello, my loves," Idora says, cradling the matching heads of her twin grandsons. Their hair has grown and filled in since they arrived on the island earlier in the spring, and now their afros look like miniature versions of their mother's wild halo of hair. In contrast, Vance's hair is cropped close to the scalp, and small flecks of gray are visible above his temples. "Doesn't your mother work at a salon?" she asks the boys with a frown as she pats their springy curls. "Why hasn't she gotten you in for a haircut lately?"

"Mom," Vance interrupts, opening his arms so that he can hug his mother. "We're so glad you're here."

Bonnie is still sitting behind the wheel of the cart, watching this family reunion with a smile. "I can second that," she says, holding up a hand like she's taking an oath. "These boys are adorable, but a real handful."

Vance laughs quietly. "They've given everyone on the island a real run for their money." In his voice Bonnie can hear the memory of Mori's near drowning in the B&B's pool, and she knows that for Vance and Calista, the challenge of having his mother live with them will be outweighed by her ability to help keep an eye on two rambunctious six-year-olds.

"Well, Grandma is here now," Idora says soothingly, holding out her hands to pull the twins close again. They attach themselves to her sides obediently. "Everything is going to be just hunky-dory."

"Come see your room!" Mexi says, grabbing onto his grandma's left hand.

"Yeah, ith wight nekth to my woom!" Mori says with his trademark lisp.

"It's right next to *our* room," Mexi corrects, tugging his grandmother's hand. Idora abandons her bags and luggage in Bonnie's cart as she trails her grandsons into the house. She gives the pink exterior paint an appraising glance as they pass through the doorway.

"So," Vance exhales. "Test number one: total failure." He tosses his gardening gloves onto the mound of mulch that surrounds the base of a palm tree.

"Oh, sugar, what do you mean? Your mother seems," she pauses here, searching for a word that won't carry a tinge of Southern disdain, "lovely."

"Lovely is a stretch—especially since I know you've been talking to my wife," he says, wagging a long finger at Bonnie. "She's a handful. Eccentric, opinionated, and passionate about being right."

"So basically she's like every other woman on the planet and like every other old person on this damn island," Bonnie jokes.

"You do have a point there," Vance admits. "But I didn't show up to get her at the boat dock, and I'll never hear the end of that. I'm sure

Calista saw her through the window of the salon and ducked behind the front desk."

Bonnie shuts off her cart and climbs out, her struggle to move her backside from a sitting position to a standing one neatly mirroring the struggle Idora has just had. "Oh, I doubt that," she says, waving off the idea of a woman who might hide from her own mother-in-law, but remembering more than one time when she'd done the same thing to the late Ruth Lane during her marriage to Ruth's son. (A particular Christmas Day cigarette behind a horse stable at Ruth and Eli Lane's farm in rural Georgia when Bonnie's boys were little comes to mind...)

Pulling herself back to the present, Bonnie points at the items in the back of her golf cart. "Let me help you get this stuff moved inside," she says.

"Oh, no, Bonnie—seriously. You stay put. I've got this." Vance offloads the luggage in less than two minutes, piling everything near the front door of his bungalow. "I appreciate you running her over, and I'm sure Calista does, too."

"Tell her she owes me a free massage for taking on mother-in-law duty," Bonnie teases.

"She'd probably give you a year of free massages if you'd take over Idora duty on a permanent basis."

"That I can't do, but she's an interesting lady, so I'd love to take her for a cup of coffee once she gets settled in. You know, give her the low-down on the island and tell her what's what."

"That sounds...dangerous," Vance says with a laugh, running a hand over his short hair. "And I'm sure she'd love it. Thanks again, Bonnie."

Bonnie is almost back to the B&B when she realizes that the first thing she'd normally do in a situation like this is sit down with Holly and talk about the newcomers. It seems like things are changing on a daily basis at this rate, and the extra seven people who are currently on Christmas Key would be worth at least an hour or two of discussion over nachos and margaritas at Jack Frosty's.

Bonnie pulls into the B&B's lot and shuts off her cart. A dark feeling settles into the pit of her stomach, and an awareness that things just aren't right washes over Bonnie. It's as if she just realized the most obvious thing in the world, and now that it's hit her, she starts to panic. In the midst of all the hubbub and the comings and goings, she's forgotten to be really and truly worried about the most basic fact: that no one has heard back from Holly.

13

Dinner at the house in Fairford is going to be an outdoor affair, and Holly can hear the preparations below through the cracked window of the bedroom. The gardens of the house stretch down to a riverbank, and the back patio is a stone slab that's cracked and mossy in all the right places. Holly glances up from the computer screen in front of her and watches the activity on the ground floor as Allison and Sarah and two men she hasn't met yet drag a table and chairs into place for dinner. Sarah plugs in a string of clear fairy lights that are looped around the patio, and there's talk of roast chicken and side dishes. It feels like a summer barbecue.

On the monitor, Holly quickly taps in her password to her email account. In less than ten seconds, her inbox is staring back at her.

"One, two, three, four, five..." she counts sixteen messages from Bonnie in all, eight from Fiona, and a couple from her other neighbors. There's a rush of adrenaline as she clicks the very first one from Bonnie, sent late on Friday, May 12th. It'd probably come in as Holly and River had sat in the police station in Notting Hill.

Sugar—there's no need to worry...yet. Fee and I tried to call you from the beach tonight outside the Ho Ho, but no answer. Listen, Coco is coming to town. There's no way to put a candy coating on this lump of dung, so I'm just gonna say it. She called the B&B and then she called Buckhunter, and she's coming down with some people she wants to show the island to. I'll keep you posted, but please call me as soon as you get this! Love and kisses, Bon

Holly reads and re-reads the message, her eyes scanning the screen rapidly like a spy who might get caught riffling through the desk of a top government official. She commits the info to memory and moves on to the next one from Bonnie, sent on Saturday night.

The eagle has landed, sugar—or should I say the crow? (Haha—you know, because Coco is a bony old crow...okay, never mind.) Anyhow, Fiona and I were on hand to see her and her guests arrive today, and here's the skinny: a rich-looking older couple named the Killjoys (I couldn't make this stuff up!) and a Native American guy named Gator with no apparent sense of humor. They're staying at the B&B for a few days. We'll have to see how things go—after all, you can't tell much about a chicken pie till you get through the crust. CALL ME! Love, Bon

Holly pats her pockets frantically, automatically searching for her phone. Of course, there is no phone. She scans the room, but there's nothing. Skyping Bonnie isn't out of the question, but the noise it would make to call and talk to her is probably a bad idea.

"Hol?" River's heavy footsteps echo on the stairs. She logs out of her email without reading anything else and clicks off the monitor so that the screen goes black. "Holly—you up here?" It's too late to leave the room and step into the bedroom that she and River are sharing, so before he reaches her, Holly pushes in the desk chair, stands, and gazes out the window at the rolling grass and the water beyond the house, hands on her hips like she's pondering the view.

"Hey, is this our room?" River is standing in the doorway when Holly turns around with a placid smile on her face.

"This one? Oh, no, I was just coming back downstairs and I saw the view through this window," she says. "Beautiful place."

"Yeah, it is." A split-second passes between them where River is clearly gauging Holly's answer. His left eye narrows almost micro-scopically, and just as quickly, the moment passes. "Hey, do you want to go for a walk around the property before dinner? They kicked me out of the kitchen," he says, holding out a hand for Holly to take.

"Sure." She steps away from the window and takes his hand, grateful for the escape.

They wander through the tall grass all the way to a boathouse by the river, stopping to pick a few wildflowers as they talk about the crazy idea that they're about to be models in a real magazine. Holly laughs and smiles at River's jokes, high-stepping over rocks and following him up little hills and grassy knolls. In the distance the spire of a stone church that dates back to the 15th century is visible beyond the treetops.

A solid bridge with a gate at each end lets them cross back and forth over the narrow river. From where they are, Holly can see the outdoor lights twinkling over the patio on what has turned out to be a clear and beautiful evening.

"Should we head back?" River asks, turning to hand Holly another bunch of wildflowers.

As much as she isn't in the mood to have dinner tonight with a bunch of strangers, Holly knows it's time. She fills her lungs with air and nods. "Let's get this show on the road," she says with a forced smile.

Whether she wants to or not, it's time to put on her game face and try to push the emails from Bonnie out of her mind.

"So you two met on this tropical island?" Sarah asks, her eyes dancing between Holly and River as she searches their faces. "And it was totally random—just a fishing trip with the boys that turned into true love?"

"That's amazing," Allison adds, pushing back her chair on the patio and standing up to pour more wine into everyone's glasses.

Holly looks down at the table sheepishly. She isn't ready to address whether or not their initial meeting on Christmas Key was kismet or true love, and she's pretty sure that River isn't about to drop to one knee and profess his undying love either.

"Well," River says, drawing out the pause. They're just getting their footing again after so many months apart, and he jiggles his leg nervously next to Holly's under the table.

"Oh," Sarah says, her mouth staying in position after the small word. She turns it into a low whistle. "Sorry. That's none of my business."

"No," Holly says too loudly. "It's fine. We've had a couple of hiccups since we met, but we live three thousand miles apart. Long-distance relationships are hard." River says nothing, but reaches for his refilled wine glass, knocking his fork and knife off his plate noisily in the process. "And we're hoping that this trip will give us a clearer picture of what the future holds."

"How exciting!" Allison flings her bright red hair over one shoulder and blinks with wide eyes. "And romantic. Where are you going?"

River sets the wine glass down. "We're going wherever the wind takes us," he says, resting one strong arm on the back of Holly's chair. "We got mugged the first night we were in London, and Holly lost her phone and cash."

"No!" Allison and Sarah say, hands covering their mouths.

Holly looks at River's profile as he tells the story, feeling relaxed for the first time since they arrived at this country house.

"Yep. And we agreed that morning that we'd both get by for the whole trip without phones or any connection to home, and that we'd say yes to everything that comes our way."

"Pass the chicken?" Roberto, the editor for the magazine, holds out a hand as he interrupts the conversation. He and Heath, the photographer, have been eating and listening to the women with mild interest as they try to piece together Holly and River's love story. River picks up the platter of roasted chicken and baby potatoes and passes it down to Roberto. "Thanks, mate."

"So what have you said yes to so far?" Sarah spears a stalk of grilled asparagus on her fork and lifts it to her mouth.

"This photo shoot," Holly says. "I met a modeling agent at Heathrow and she gave me her card. River set up the appointment to meet her, and boom—here we are." She pushes her plate aside and leans back in her chair so that her shoulder touches the arm that River's still resting on her seat back.

"What if I told you that I'm working on a film set in Dublin in a couple of weeks and they need extras—would you say yes to that?" Sarah lifts an eyebrow.

"We might," River says without hesitation.

Holly is about to object, so she holds her tongue, focusing instead on the string of fairy lights winking against the sky that's smudged with darkness. Stars dot the various shades of blue like pinpricks. In the distance, the call of a lone bird pierces the evening.

"It's an action movie and it pays a per diem rate, but I could probably get you both in at the hotel where the extras are staying if you're interested," Sarah says, speaking more to River than to Holly, which Holly has picked up on and filed away for reference.

"Let's trade info and we'll touch bases," River says, putting his hand on Holly's shoulder and rubbing it with his thumb as he speaks.

"What info?" Holly turns to him. "We don't have phones."

"We could turn them on for that," River says. He lifts his arm from the back of her chair and leans forward, placing both elbows on the table on either side of his dinner plate. A soft wind rustles across the patio, lifting the edges of their napkins and blowing the women's hair around.

The only sound at the table is of silverware on plates as River's statement settles over Holly. There's been an unspoken friction between them all day, and River deciding without discussion that he's willing to turn on his phone for a call from Sarah irks Holly. She stands and starts gathering empty plates and glasses.

"Oh, don't do that," Allison says with a laugh that bubbles from her chest. "We don't make our models do grunt work." She stands on her side of the table and follows Holly's lead.

"I don't mind," Holly counters. "Really. I'm used to doing everything at my B&B. I can serve dinner, clean up after, run the office—you name it. I'm kind of a jack-of-all-trades."

"Impressive," Sarah says smoothly, leaning back in her chair. She doesn't offer to help clean up. "I admire a woman who can juggle so many different things."

Heath puts his salad plate on top of his dinner plate and pushes back his chair. "And I admire a man who doesn't let the women do all the washing up." His dark hair is coarse and rumpled, and over dinner, Holly's noticed the way his eyes always look like he's amused by everything that's going on around him. "Also, my wife would have my head if she heard I sat around and made the women wait on me, so let's do this, ladies."

In short order, Heath, Allison, and Holly have the table cleared and the kitchen cleaned. When the dishwasher is finally humming in the warm kitchen, Holly runs a rag over the long farm table that's been used for prep, swooping the crumbs into her open palm and dumping them into the sink. She doesn't even notice as Heath and Allison fade from the room quietly, replaced by River and his wineglass. He's standing next to the pantry door, his shoulder leaning against the wall as he watches her.

"You're mad," he says simply. "But I'm not sure why."

"I'm not sure why, either," Holly admits readily. "But I don't like being roped into something later on that I'm not even sure I want to do right now." The dishwasher clanks as water moves through the stacks of plates and forks.

"No one is roping you in," River says with impatience. "I thought 'maybe' was generous of me, when technically I should have said 'yes' to her."

Holly throws the dishtowel in her hand onto the counter and it lands with one end dangling into the oversized sink. "There is no 'technically' to this, River—we're making the rules up as we go." Holly pivots and stares out the window at the darkened garden beyond. "When we planned this trip, I thought it was going to be the two of us exploring Europe and seeing how this whole thing was going to work out between us—*if* it was even going to work out."

River pushes himself away from the wall and sets his wineglass on the kitchen table. He walks up behind Holly and wraps his arms around her shoulders, resting his chin on top of her head. They can see their own reflections in the window over the sink.

"And see, I think we *are* exploring Europe and seeing whether this thing between us will work out," he says softly, rocking her slightly as he holds her. "You know I like to have fun and be impulsive—who organized a game of baseball with coconuts on the beach in the moonlight?" he asks, reminding her of their impromptu game during his first visit to Christmas Key. "And if we're going to do this," he says, referring to their relationship, "then you have to accept that about me."

"And you have to accept that I'm a little less impulsive than you are," Holly says. "I like to plan and organize, and I like to have some control over my life. It's what I do—it's who I am."

They're both quiet for a moment as their words sink in with one another. "I don't think our differences are a bad thing," River says, letting go of Holly and turning her so that she's facing him. "But I would love to see you stop trying to live in two places at once, at least for a couple of weeks."

"What do you mean?" Holly wraps her arms around River's waist and puts her cheek against his chest. "I'm not living in two places at once."

River huffs. "You are *always* living on Christmas Key, at least in some corner of your mind."

Holly's kicked off her shoes and is standing on the warm terra cotta tiles of the kitchen floor in her bare feet. She tries to keep her mind entirely on the present: on the smell of River's cologne that fills her nostrils as she hugs him; on the feel of the smooth tiles under her feet; on the sound of the dishwasher that's filling the kitchen with heat. But she can't do it. The mention of the island brings Bonnie's emails back to the front of her mind, and the thought of Coco infiltrating Christmas Key raises her blood pressure and heart rate. She pushes back from River's embrace.

"You're right," Holly says with a weak smile. "I'll try harder." It's not terribly convincing, but it's what she can give him for the moment. "I think I'm going to turn in," she says. "I've never been a model before, but I hear they need their beauty rest. How about you?"

River looks away. "I think they're having dessert out on the patio, so I might join them and then come up. I'll try not to wake you." He plants a hasty kiss on the top of her forehead and walks away, picking his wineglass up from the table as he goes.

14

B onnie is sitting at the small table outside of Mistletoe Morning Brew on Wednesday morning with Katelynn and her son Logan when Holly's pink golf cart zips up to the curb. Coco is at the wheel.

"Let's grab a coffee," Coco says to Gator and the Killjoys, putting one foot on the sidewalk the minute the cart is switched off. She's wearing a pair of white shorts and a teal sun visor, her chin-length dark hair smoothed back from her face and tucked behind both ears. "I want to show you what I'm thinking and get your feedback."

Gator unfurls his long limbs from the back of the cart and follows Coco. Patience and calm ooze from his every pore, and his face is blank and stoic. Netta and Brice Killjoy look overheated and tired. Bonnie smiles at this. She isn't sure where they're from, but it's clearly not Florida. The heat of mid-May is getting to both of them, and Brice's golf shirt clings to his middle-aged chest, rings of sweat forming under his pecs like wet moons.

"I really like what we've seen so far," Brice Killjoy says, holding the door to Mistletoe Morning Brew so that the others can enter. He looks down at Bonnie and offers the slightest nod. She holds her cup of coffee aloft in greeting.

When the door closes behind the group and the bells on the handle have stopped jingling, Katelynn leans in closer. "Are those the people everyone is talking about?" she asks in a stage whisper.

"Those are them," Bonnie confirms. "Coco can already taste the money from the sale of this island."

"But she can't sell it." Katelynn frowns. "This is home for a lot of people. I remember visiting my grandparents here when I was a kid —and it's going to be home for Logan. I want him to know what it's like to grow up somewhere like this."

Logan grunts and jams the straw of his frozen hot chocolate between his lips. Bonnie looks at him directly, unwilling to hold back her thoughts, though she knows she should.

"Logan, let me ask you something," Bonnie says, folding her hands on the iron table top. The sun has been beating down on the metal and it's warm to the touch. "What was your life like back in... where are you guys from?"

Logan's eyes cut to his mom like he needs permission to speak. Katelynn leans back in her chair and just watches him.

"Cleveland," he says, swallowing hard. His Adam's apple bobs under the tight skin of his teenage neck. There's obvious discomfort in his hazel eyes as he becomes the center of attention at the table.

"Uh huh. Cleveland. And what was your life like there? Were you the captain of the football team? A straight-A student with a hot and heavy lady friend?" Katelynn's eyebrows shoot up at this last part, but she lets Bonnie run with this line of questioning. "Because I sense you don't want to be here, and I'm really curious about what you left behind."

Logan swallows again, his neck and ears reddening. "No, not really," he says quietly. "But my dad and his other kids live there, and my best friend Owen lived on my street."

Bonnie's heart seizes a little as she watches his eyes grow sad. She's miscalculated by just a hair, reading his belligerence for contempt when really he's just a kid who's bummed about leaving everything behind. But if there's one thing Bonnie knows from experience, it's teenage boys—after all, she's raised three of her own.

"Listen, sugarplum," she says, reaching across the table and patting his forearm. "Miles seem like lightyears when you're a kid, but people are pretty damn portable. You'd be surprised at how easy it is for you to ship off and head to Cleveland for a visit, or for Owen to come down here." Bonnie glances at Katelynn to make sure she hasn't just offered to have an off-limits friend come down to Christmas Key and wreak havoc, but Katelynn is smiling at her, so Bonnie continues. "This place is the most gorgeous home you'll ever have—mark my words—and there are people coming and going all the time. You might wake up one day and find that we've got a team of young Swedish figure skaters staying at the B&B, or a family with four teenage daughters who forgot to pack anything but bikinis—" Katelynn chokes on her coffee. "Just give it a chance, huh?"

Logan is staring at the tabletop, an irrepressible grin covering his smooth face. He runs a hand through his light brown mop of hair and nods, still not looking at Bonnie. "Yeah," he says. He picks up his frozen hot chocolate again.

Bonnie knows she's made her point, so she turns back to Katelynn and lets him off the hook. "Now, how is your grandpa doing?"

"He's okay," Katelynn says, her eyes softening as the smile dims just a bit. "My uncle is leaving this week, so it'll just be us taking care of Grandpa." She taps her nails against the paper coffee cup in front of her and glances at her son. "I guess I didn't really know what kind of work that would require, but it's going to be substantial. He can't be left alone for long, and he's pretty forgetful."

"Well, we're all here for you, doll," Bonnie says, and she means it. "Hal is one of us, and if you need respite care of any sort so that you can go out for lunch or take Logan to the beach for an afternoon, you just holler, you hear? One of us will swing by and give you a break."

"Thanks, Bonnie. That means a lot."

"Now," Bonnie says, changing gears. "You said you visited here as a teenager, right?" Katelynn nods. "Did you hang out with our feisty mayor much on your vacations down here to visit your grandparents?"

"Holly?" Katelynn laughs and her eyes crinkle at the corners.

"Absolutely. She's two years younger than I am, but we ran around together like a couple of mischief makers."

"What was she like?"

"As a teenager?" Katelynn turns her eyes to the blue sky like she's watching a movie that's replaying against the heavens. "Lanky. Tan. Smart in a way that a girl from a big city could never be. She showed me how to roam free on a wild island and how to make friends with anyone, no matter what their age, no matter where they were from. Good sense of humor, good taste in music, but a little...I don't know —reserved, maybe. Holly always had her eye on whatever her immediate goal was, whether that was finding the ripest coconut or making her grandpa laugh, and she wouldn't let anything distract her."

"And how many years has it been since you've seen her?"

Katelynn considers this. "Let's see, it was before I had Logan," she looks over at her son, "So probably sixteen or seventeen years."

"Based on your description she hasn't really changed much," Bonnie laughs. "You'll recognize her the minute she steps off the boat."

"Anyway," Coco's voice shoots out of the coffee shop as she pushes the door open with her shoulder. "I'd like to have one last look at the north side of the island before you all leave. I think that's our winning spot."

"Oh, Coco—I do, too." Netta Killjoy is holding an iced coffee in one hand, her long, French-manicured nails biting into the plastic cup. "I can see the lights along the shoreline now as the boats approach at night, and I can only imagine what a hundred or two hundred full-time employees would do for this economy."

"The housing alone and all the building that would have to take place would completely change the topography of the island," Brice Killjoy adds as the door to the coffee shop closes again. Gator is silent beside them, his dark eyes narrowed as he listens.

"Let me take you all over there again so we can talk through the obstacles we came up with last night." Coco climbs into the driver's seat of Holly's cart and sets her coffee in the cup holder near the steering wheel. She waits as everyone gets settled in the cart and then shoots Bonnie a look. "Hey, Bonnie," she says with a layer of frost in her voice. "I'm dropping my guests off at the dock around one, and then I'll be in to help out in the B&B office."

Bonnie's heart nearly stops. "No need," she says with the same cool tone that Coco's used on her. "I've got it all under control."

Coco lets the parking break out with one foot. "Oh, honey, I'm not going to leave you here high and dry," she says as the cart starts to roll away from the curb. "My daughter might have left you here to handle everything, but I plan on staying until she gets back. See you this afternoon." She punches the gas and pulls away.

"She's bossy," Logan says, offering his own unsolicited thoughts for the first time. He takes another sip of his cold drink. Katelynn shoots her son a warning look.

"Sugarplum," Bonnie says with a laugh. "Truer words were never spoken."

～

COCO DROPS Gator and the Killjoys off at the dock for their trip back to the mainland and rushes back to the B&B. She pulls Holly's cart into the sandy lot of the inn and shuts it off, gathering her purse and the can of Diet Coke she's been sipping all day. It's warm now, and she pours the stream of liquid onto the ground before using the back door of the building to let herself into the office.

"Bonnie?" she calls out, pushing her sunglasses on top of her head. "I'm here."

"Fabulous. Because things haven't been moving along just fine without you for Lord knows how many years," Bonnie says under her breath.

"Oh!" Coco stops short in the doorway when she sees Pucci staring at her from his dog bed in the corner of the room. "I didn't know that dog would be here."

Bonnie raises an eyebrow. Her slow, lazy blinks don't hide for one second how she and Pucci both feel about Coco's arrival. "He comes in here almost every day. Jake's watching him while Holly's gone, and he drops Pucci off here so that he doesn't get lonely while Jake's at work."

"Well," Coco skirts the edge of the room, avoiding the dog. "I'm allergic to him, and I'm pretty sure he doesn't like me." She drops her purse on the side of the desk where Holly normally sits and Bonnie cringes visibly. "Much like you."

"A rabbit knows a fox track same as a hound does," Bonnie says with a shrug. She turns her attention back to the email she's writing to Holly. There's still been no answer from across the pond, but it hasn't stopped Bonnie from calling her phone, sending her Facebook messages, and dropping an email any time something comes up. Her panic at Holly's radio silence hasn't reached the level yet where she's considered calling the American Consulate in London, but it's getting close.

Coco ignores Bonnie's barb and pulls out the chair across from her. "So. What are we working on?"

Bonnie's fingers slow to a stop, and the tapping of the keys peters out. She hasn't really considered the ramifications of Coco working in the B&B office with her until Holly's return, but now that she's here, it does seem possible that Coco will stay. After all, she owns as much of the island as Holly—well, one percent less, but that one percent won't do anything to slow down a destructive gale-force wind like Coco.

Bonnie gives in with a sigh. "I'm responding to emails, and planning for the wedding we're hosting here in October."

Coco makes a sound in her throat that's half disbelief, half derision. "A wedding? Small peanuts." She pushes the cup of pens and pencils to the opposite side of the desk and starts rearranging Holly's workspace. "I've been telling Holly for years that she needs to think bigger. Aim for the stars. Thank God I'm here."

"Indeed," Bonnie says. Her fingers start moving on the keyboard again.

Coco—visibly pleased with how she's arranged Holly's workspace to suit her own needs—folds her hands on the desk and smiles at Bonnie. "Now, how do I go about getting a village council meeting put together?"

Bonnie's eyes flit to the calendar on her own desk. The village council meeting *should* have been today, had Holly not left the island. "Uhhhh, very difficult process. Lots of work. And we would never have one without the mayor present."

"I'm calling b.s. on that, Bonnie Lane." Coco smoothes her hair with one hand, tucking it behind two lobes studded with diamonds the size of green peas. "This tiny little group of oldsters might take a day and a half to get over here for the meeting, but it can't be that hard to call it and put it together. I want to have a meeting," she demands.

"Any official gathering of more than twenty islanders must be approved and presided over by the mayor of the municipality," Bonnie says in what she hopes is an official-sounding voice. "It's in our bylaws."

"Like hell it is," Coco spits back. "I have a groundbreaking offer that I want to share—not that I need to, because the vote is ultimately up to me, Holly, and Leo—but I'd like to get as many people on board with it as possible. It can't hurt to have everyone's support."

Bonnie closes her laptop so that nothing separates her from Coco. "What—some multi-million dollar offer from that motley band of investors you just put on a boat? You think anyone around here cares what they have to offer? Most of us don't have long enough left to live to start dreaming about turning this island into a water park or a Southern outpost of the Florida State History Museum."

"Give me a break, Bonnie." Coco narrows her eyes. "You think I'd waste my time on offers like that? We're talking housing developments here. New residents. A broader tax base. Big money, huge investors, unimaginable revenue. And nobody would have to leave the island if they didn't want to."

Bonnie silently reminds herself to breathe: *in through the nose, out through the mouth*. She watches Coco's nipped and tucked face as she powers towards the crux of whatever plan she's about to hatch.

"All this time I've been trying to get Holly to sell this damn heap of sand and take the cash and run, but she won't. I feel like I'm fighting some uphill battle, and then one day—boom—an idea comes to me for how we can hit the fast-forward button on her big dream to develop this place. Get some big investors to come in here and turn Christmas Key into a mint. Throw up some houses, get more infrastructure. Build something that actually draws the tourists in year-round. We'll be printing money in no time."

Bonnie's stomach sinks as she envisions what Coco is trying to do. She knows that hitting the fast-forward button is *not* what Holly wants, and she can't imagine Buckhunter going along with this scheme either. The massive, instant development of an enclave like Christmas Key is nothing but a recipe for disaster.

"Now, I want a meeting," Coco says, standing up and looking down at Bonnie. "And if you don't make a village council meeting happen, then I will—in pieces. I'll gather nineteen people at a time so that there aren't more than twenty of us at once, and I'll pitch my idea to them that way." She picks up her purse and wedges it under one arm. "Hey," she says as though an idea has just come to her. "That might be better anyway. A room full of islanders might pick up some momentum and actually be able to put up a united front. Meeting in smaller groups means I can start to spread my ideas around like a bee spreading pollen." Coco walks to the doorway, sunglasses in hand. She pauses and looks back at Bonnie. "Actually, I kind of like that."

"More like a mosquito spreading malaria," Bonnie says to herself once she's alone again.

15

It rains all day during the photo shoot in Fairford. Holly smiles politely as Sarah touches up her makeup while she perches on a windowsill, water streaming down the glass behind her. Roberto, the magazine editor, is pleased with the slightly reserved look on Holly's face, but only River knows her well enough to know that it's because she feels like a fish out of water.

Allison drags a steamer over to where Holly stands, tugging at the electrical cord as she crosses the room. "Doing okay there, love? Need a sip of tea or water?" Holly shakes her head no. There are safety pins on the sleeve of one of Allison's arms, and she's wearing a roll of masking tape on her wrist like a bracelet. "Hold still just a tick, alright?"

"Sure, no problem," Holly says, standing stock-still as Allison brings the head of the steamer to the side of her wool pants. A loud gush of steam hits the pant leg, blowing the wrinkles out of the fabric.

"How do I look?" River asks, his chest pushed out theatrically. He's wearing a three-piece suit. Sarah's taken a pair of clippers to his hair, taming his sandy locks and making the whole cut look more triangular. He looks hipper than Holly is used to.

"Very handsome," Holly says, holding out a hand for him to join her. She's spent the morning getting her makeup done in the bedroom with the computer, and it took all her willpower not to ask Sarah whether she minded at all if Holly just popped on and checked her email.

"I think we're ready for Buckingham Palace." River steps into place next to Holly. They're standing beneath a huge light that's shaped like a dome. Heath tips a round disc that reflects silver onto their faces as he checks his light meters, clicking a small remote and making the flash pop each time.

"This is a real photo shoot," Holly says quietly. She leans in to River and puts her chin against his upper arm.

"Ah, ah, ah—makeup on the clothes!" Sarah shouts, rushing over to them. Holly pulls her chin away like she's just rested it against a branding iron. "Don't touch each other, please." Sarah brushes at the spot on River's navy blue coat with one hand where Holly's foundation has left a small mark.

"Sorry," Holly says, touching her chin reflexively.

"Don't touch yourself, either!" Sarah swats at Holly's hand.

Holly puts both hands in the air in surrender. "Okay, I'm just standing here like this until we're ready."

The actual shoot takes way less time than Holly would have imagined; it's the preparation that seems endless. When it's all said and done, they photograph eight different outfits with hairstyle changes for Holly, working until the light is nearly gone outside.

When they're done, Holly tears off the borrowed clothes and pulls on her own jeans in a large bathroom, scrubbing at her face with a washcloth as she digs through her duffel bag for a t-shirt. She can't wait to get out of there and back to London.

"You're sure you can't wait another hour and have pizza with us? Roberto will be back with it in a bit, and then one of us can drive you to the train later on." Sarah is pleading with River downstairs when Holly comes down in her Converse and with a totally clean face.

River glances at Holly with the "we have to say yes to everything" face, but one look at her seems to change his mind.

"We should really get back to our flat and pack our stuff, and we need to get some sleep. Our train to Amsterdam leaves first thing in the morning," River says, giving Holly a wink that looks like he's got something in his left eye.

Sarah and River trade phone numbers so that they can talk about the film shoot in Dublin at the end of the month, and then the taxi arrives, its wheels crunching on the loose rocks of the driveway.

"Thanks for everything," Holly says, perking up a bit now that she knows they're leaving. "It was fun." She shakes hands with Sarah and Allison and accepts a hug from Heath, who tells her she's a natural in front of the camera.

"She missed her calling," River says, smiling down at Holly with pride. "Though I think she makes a damn fine mayor, which is almost as exciting as being a supermodel."

They climb into the cab and sit close together in the backseat, Holly resting her head on River's shoulder in the darkness. It's late, and the day has been long and tiring. The driver starts the meter and pulls away, driving slowly down the long lane that leads to the High Street.

"Not your cup of tea, eh?" River asks, jostling his shoulder to rouse Holly as the car picks up speed.

"Cindy Crawford can keep her job, and I'll keep mine," Holly says definitively. "It was too much fussing and standing around for this girl."

River laughs. "Really? I kind of liked it. And the money isn't bad, either."

They ride in silence the rest of the way to the train station. Holly watches the windshield wipers move back and forth rhythmically, thinking about the way River had navigated the whole modeling thing with ease. He could talk to anyone on the set, charm them all, and then get in front of the camera and give them exactly what they wanted. It was almost unsettling to watch him in a role Holly had never imagined him in. She held onto his arm tighter as they drove, the same thought running in her head on a loop the whole way: *he's the one who's a natural.*

~

St. Pancras International train station is busy on Friday morning, and the first order of business is breakfast. Holly sits with their bags next to her on a bench while River gets in line at Starbucks to order muffins and coffees. She'd tossed and turned the night before, listening to the rain and to River's snoring as she thought again about the things Bonnie had emailed her. Coco being on the island has her worried and curious, and she'd like nothing more than to run to the nearest payphone and call home to see what's going on.

"Peppermint mocha and a chocolate croissant for milady," River says grandly, handing Holly her pastry and drink. He sits next to her so they can eat quickly before passing through customs and security.

"What the heck..." Holly is chewing a bite of her croissant when a cluster of uniformed officers descends on two men in soccer jerseys and leather jackets. They strip the men of luggage and coats, patting them down with efficiency as one of the officers takes their passports and begins to examine them and radio some unheard information on to someone else.

River takes a drink of coffee while he watches. "They're serious about security. I've seen more armed guards and police officers just roaming around this station than I've ever seen in my life."

"I think it's safe to say that I've never seen this much police activity," Holly says jokingly. "Even in Miami."

"We've got military presence, too," River says, lifting his chin at two men in dark green fatigues who are heavily armed and holding assault rifles in front of their chests.

"I'm not sure if it makes me feel better or worse." Holly tears off another bite of her croissant. "Like, are they protecting us, or are we in imminent danger?"

"Maybe a little of both," River says pensively. "Let's get through security so we can find our seats on the train." He stands up and tosses their garbage in the trashcan next to the bench. "Finish that coffee, girl—they won't let you get through security with it."

The ride to Brussels is slow and plagued with delays along the way, but Holly has a book to read and River's shoulder to lean against while they wait. The voice on the speaker that announces their stops and starts does it all in three different languages each time: French, German, and English, and when the man says that his name is Jean-Jacques, Holly repeats it to herself, letting the French pronunciation roll around in her mouth.

"Jean-Jacques says we'll be starting up again in about ten minutes," she repeats to River.

"So I hear," he says, looking up from the newspaper he'd purchased at the train station.

"Jean-Jacques says we'll be in Brussels by noon."

"Jean-Jacques is a really cool guy," River says, lifting one corner of his mouth in a half-smile.

"He does seem cool," Holly agrees. The train is warm and crowded and she's feeling drowsy. "I mean, if you can speak three languages and manage a whole train full of people who're trying to get somewhere, you'd have to be."

The train starts up again in a few minutes and rolls toward Brussels without further delay. As they pull into the city, graffitied walls near the train tracks pass by in a blur of color. The rain has started again, and the dreary gray concrete, gray skies, and big city feel of the graffiti overwhelms her. For a second Holly feels such a powerful sense of homesickness for blue skies and palm trees that her eyes well up with unshed tears.

In order to refocus her mind and shake off the helpless feeling of being far from home, Holly rereads Bonnie's emails in her mind. There has to be a way to call or respond—she needs to make contact somehow. If Coco is really stirring things up and bringing strangers to Christmas Key, she needs to be able to mitigate the effects, even from thousands of miles away.

"Here's your bag," River says, standing up and grabbing their things from the overhead bin as the train rolls to a stop. "Because of that delay, we've only got about five minutes to get to the other train, so I think we're going to have to run. You up for this?"

"We have to run?" Holly puts the straps of her duffel bag over her shoulder and stands up, ducking so she won't hit her head on the low ceiling above the seats.

Jean-Jacques comes on the speaker once again, giving his last words in German, then French, and finally English. "We apologize for the long delays," he says in a French accent so thick that Holly starts craving a baguette. "The connection for Amsterdam is going to be a short window of time. It will be challenging, but it *can* be done!"

"Yeah, it's going to be close. Take my hand."

"It will be challenging, but it *can* be done!" Holly parrots back to River in her impression of a French accent.

River pulls her through the throng of people and as soon as their feet touch the platform, they break into a flat-out run. Holly apologizes to people as she bumps them with her flying duffel bag and her loose elbows, and they push past people who are dallying at the bottom of an escalator. They're looking for the right platform to catch the train to Amsterdam, and when River spots it, he grabs her hand again and pulls her forward in one last burst of speed, yanking her up the step and onto the train just as the wheels start to move. They've made it. River looks down at Holly in breathless admiration as he pulls her close for a congratulatory hug.

"Nice hustle, kid."

The next leg of the journey is about two hours, and they pull into Amsterdam in the middle of the afternoon. This train ride is much smoother and without delays, and they exit the train with their bags and walk into a big, open station with shops and restaurants. People stream around them, and different languages flow past their ears as they consult a sign with a map of the city.

"The boathouse I rented for us is supposed to be really close to the station," he says, pulling a piece of paper out of his pocket. "I have the address here, and the directions."

Holly leans in and looks at what he's written. A woman with a baby in a stroller stops and looks at the map. She smiles at Holly and speaks to her little girl in Dutch. The words are unfamiliar to Holly's ears, but the tone is universal. Holly wiggles her fingers at the happy baby.

"We need to catch the ferry, which is across the street there," River points at the road just outside of the station, which is filled with pedestrians and bicyclists. "It's about a five minute ride, and then we walk for another five minutes or so."

Holly puts her hands into the pockets of her denim jacket and looks up at him. "You know what I think?" she asks, kicking his foot with the toe of her Converse.

"What?"

"I think it sounds challenging, but it *can* be done!" she says with her faux French accent.

"And you know what I think? I think you're a nut." River puts his hands on the sides of her waist and pulls her close. "Come here."

"Oh, hey," Holly says, taking her hands out of her pockets and wrapping them around River. "Right here in the train station, huh?"

"This is Europe, baby—anything goes." River smiles down at her, looking deep into her eyes. For the first time in a couple of days Holly relaxes and remembers why she took this trip with him in the first place. This is River—fun, easygoing, sexy, kind-hearted River. This is the guy who landed in her life during a tropical storm and helped her to keep it all together. He's the one who tried to help her through the last gasp of her feelings for Jake, but ultimately took a step back and let her figure things out for herself when she needed the space. And he's the guy who is here for her now, taking her on the adventure of a lifetime and looking at her like he wants to kiss her in the middle of the train station in Amsterdam.

And so, with a smile and a giddiness that momentarily erases her worries about what's going on at home, she lets him.

16

"I'd like to call this unscheduled village council meeting to order," Coco says on Friday at noon, lifting Holly's pink marble gavel and rapping it against the matching block that's resting on the podium. The B&B's dining room is filled with curious islanders, most of whom ignore Coco's request for silence and continue to chatter amongst themselves about the fact that Holly isn't there and is still unreachable by phone and email.

"Can I have your attention, please?" Coco pleads, banging the gavel loudly three times. "As a part-owner of this island, I have the right to call a meeting to order, and I deserve the courtesy of having you all sit down to listen." She tosses her head in annoyance, flipping her shiny bob over one shoulder with the movement.

The islanders slowly creak into chairs, some working their aging hips and knees into a sitting position in stages. Maria Agnelli takes her seat in the front row, settling her small, thin frame into a chair and folding her arms across her chest as she stares up at Coco. Jake leans against the wall, silently refusing to sit, and Cap Duncan and Wyatt Bender choose aisle seats across from one another, their legs spread wide so that their feet take up space in the aisle.

"I have several things I'd like to discuss with you all," Coco says too loudly as she tries to talk over the dying din. "But first I think we should introduce the newcomers, as I haven't even had the chance to acquaint myself with them."

"Well," Maria Agnelli pipes up, clearing her throat. "If you'd spent any time here over the years, you'd probably at least know Hal and Sadie Pillory's granddaughter, Katelynn."

Coco blinks rapidly. "I *have* spent time on this island, Maria— don't be ridiculous." A roomful of disbelieving faces stares back at her.

"Let's not mince words here, doll," Bonnie says, standing up at her seat in the third row. She isn't normally one to speak up at village council meetings, but with Holly gone, it almost feels like her duty to hold Coco's feet to the fire. "You have a grand scheme that you want to pitch to all of us, so let's just get down to it."

The triplets are seated a few seats away from Bonnie, and they lean forward in their chairs so that they can make eye contact with her. Gwen nods in support, winking at Bonnie when she gets her attention.

"Fine, if you want to dispense with the pleasantries," Coco says, her face flushed from the shock of being called out. "I'd like to propose a business opportunity to all of you that I think is a fabulous compromise. As you probably know, I've been trying to find investors for the island for some time now, and I've had my eye on selling Christmas Key to someone who might be able to fund improvements in a way that Holly, Leo, and I are unable to." Coco waves a hand in Buckhunter's general direction, though it's clear from the look on his face that he's as much in the dark as anyone else in the room.

Coco has made no secret of the fact that she thinks very little of having Buckhunter as a half-brother, and their discussions about island business have gone about as well as the ones that Coco has had with Holly. In fact, on numerous occasions, Holly and Buck-hunter have stood in a united front against Coco, directly blocking her from doing the things she wants—the things she feels are her right—to do with Christmas Key.

"I brought some guests here this week to show them around and let them get a feel for the island, and I think it went well," Coco says, trying to keep her eyes focused on the space just above everyone's heads. "Brice and Netta Killjoy are investors from Tulsa, and they're interested in partnering with the Seminole tribe to turn Christmas Key into a premier gambling destination." The essence of her plan falls on a silent crowd. Coco feels a jolt of panic as a shocked stillness settles over the room. No one says a word.

"We've been looking at the north side of the island," Coco continues, "and it seems like the best place to build a dock and hotel." There's a gasp from the center of the room at the mention of building a hotel. "Right now we're thinking about a two-hundred room resort with a fully-functioning, top-notch casino. That means restaurant, bar, spa, and five-star amenities."

"But we already *have* restaurants, bars, and a salon here," Maria Agnelli says, speaking the thoughts that are in the minds of everyone around her. "And think of what a bunch of new people would mean for the businesses we already have. Why would we want competition from some resort?"

"That's a good question, Maria," Coco says. She picks up the glass of water she's positioned on the podium and takes a drink to buy herself some time. She sets it down again and leans her elbows on the stand. "But a fully-staffed resort will have employees, and those people will need somewhere to live, shop, eat, and drink. So think of the increased business you'd have around here just from the new residents who'd live here full-time."

"No." Cap Duncan stands up and moves into the aisle. He jabs one large index finger in Coco's direction. "No way. This goes against everything Holly has been building towards. It goes against everything your father wanted, and it'll tear this island apart." Cap's brief run for mayor against Holly just six months before had been based on the fact that he wanted zero progress, so it's no shock to anyone that he's vehemently opposed to Coco's plan.

"Let's not bring my father into this," Coco says. She stands up straight again and slaps a palm against the podium. "He made enough of a mess when he was alive, and his wishes are not relevant when it comes to our plans for the future."

"The hell they're not!" Ray Bradford stands up and Millie reaches for his hand with a worried look on her face. "Your parents had a vision for this place that's been reinforced time and again. We all know what they wanted, and we're pretty much living their dream right now."

"Here, here!" Jimmy Cafferkey shouts. Iris whacks him on the arm with her hand, less out of embarrassment than from sheer habit.

"Anything Holly's done has been with the best interests of all of us in mind, and even that cockamamie reality show she brought here turned out to be pretty fun in the end," Cap says. "Except for Jake—sorry, buddy." He raises an apologetic hand at Jake, not quite meeting his eye. Jake tips his head in acknowledgment of the show that brought the short-lived relationship with Bridget into his life.

"But this," Cap goes on. "This casino goes against Holly's careful plans for expansion, and it threatens to bring in drunken, gambling riffraff. It'll also flood our community with strangers and their families who just want to make a living off of this casino."

"Where would we even house all these people?" Ray Bradford asks, still standing.

"Part of our discussion was the need for housing," Coco says, obviously proud that she's got answers to their questions. "The Killjoys are interested in funding a low-cost alternative to the casino workers in the form of a multi-unit condominium complex. There's plenty of room for that on the west side of the island, near the property my parents claimed as the family's private land."

"I can't tell whether I'm dying, or if my lunch is just repeating on me," Maria Agnelli says, putting one birdlike hand to her chest and making an unpleasant face. "Cottage cheese doesn't taste too good when it comes back up."

The crowd roars to life in front of Coco, anger and disapproval tearing through the dining room like someone's touched a match to spilled gasoline. Maria Agnelli is still thumping her chest and swallowing in the front row. She shakes her head.

Ray and Cap have begun a debate that consists mostly of insults that they'd like to hurl in Coco's direction, and Jake has one hand over his unshaven face as he imagines how Holly will react to all of this.

"What the hell is going on around here?" Katelynn Pillory asks Jake as she steps over the bare, liver-spotted knees of her grandfather, who had demanded to be included in the village council meeting, though he's been sitting there stonily for most of it, saying nothing. She reaches out a hand as she almost trips over her grandpa's foot and Jake catches her, helping her find her balance again.

"Coco," he says to Katelynn, folding his arms and nodding at the beast behind the podium. "Coco is what's going on, and it's not good."

Katelynn leans a shoulder against the wall next to Jake. Coco is talking loudly to the triplets, who've all approached the front of the room. The tendons in her neck are strained as she tries to talk over the three angry women whose faces are normally sunny and bright. As the owners of the only gift shop and grocery store in town, it would make sense for them to be in favor of some real expansion, but from the looks of it, they're just as opposed to Coco's plan as everyone else in the room.

"I take it Holly doesn't know about any of this," Katelynn asks in a low voice, the register of which feeds directly into Jake's ear canal, sliding in under the higher-pitched yelling of the rest of the crowd.

"No one has been able to get ahold of her since she left, so I don't think she has a clue," he says. Katelynn is standing close enough to him that their shoulders touch lightly when she moves.

"I know I probably don't have a right to even have an opinion yet, but this seems like a really crappy move." Katelynn watches Jake's face as his strong jaw and cheekbones flex and clench.

"It is a really crappy move," he says, meeting her eye. "Pretty much every move Coco makes is a crappy one." There's a long, intense look that passes between Jake and Katelynn, and the spark in her brown eyes turns them to chips of amber as he stares into them.

"Oh my God!" Millie Bradford yells from the center of the room.

Somehow, over the noise of the angry mob of islanders, her voice carries. "Ray!" she screams.

A hush falls over the crowd as Ray Bradford keels forward. He's still talking to Cap, and Cap reaches out and catches the other man's forearms in his large hands. He holds the bulk of Ray's weight as Ray falls to his knees, his face red and contorted in pain. As everyone watches, stunned into inaction, Fiona jumps out of her seat next to Buckhunter and steps up onto a line of chairs, walking across the seats in order to get to Ray as quickly as possible.

"Back up!" she shouts, stepping down onto the carpet from the chair and dropping to her knees next to Ray. "Ray? Can you hear me?" she asks loudly, helping Cap to lay him down on the dining room floor. "Ray, I need you to keep your eyes on me, okay?" Fiona finds the pulse in Ray's wrist and starts counting in her head. "Cap," she says calmly. "Do you have gas in your boat?"

"Always," Cap replies, watching Ray's face as his eyes go glassy.

"We're going to need a ride to Key West," Fiona says with a grim face. "Ray is having a heart attack."

17

The five minute ferry ride from the train station across the water in Amsterdam drops its passengers at a dock that's flanked by a restaurant and a few dessert carts. Holly and River have quickly made a habit of stopping at the carts so that she can get a pastry each time they walk from the ferry to the houseboat they've rented on a narrow road called *Buiksloterwag*.

"You think we should go to Anne Frank's house?" Holly asks around a bite of a pastry that looks like a toaster waffle and a rainbow sprinkle cupcake had a baby.

"We could do that," River says amiably, chewing a piece of gum as he walks down the pedestrian sidewalk next to her. Bikes whiz by them on the paved road that's reserved for cyclists only. "You're not worried about eating all these desserts?"

"Why should I be?" Holly looks up at him just as she's about to take another bite.

"I dunno, just wondering. You live in a bikini at home, so I thought you might be worried about putting on five pounds."

Holly frowns. Is this what he thinks of her? That she's the kind of girl who'd pass up dessert in a foreign country so that her bathing suit will fit when she gets back home? After thinking about it for a second, she takes another huge bite. "Nope," she says. "I'm not worried. Life is too short not to eat dessert."

River waves the waffle away when she holds it out to offer him a bite. "I'm chewing gum," he says, pointing at his mouth. "And I'm thinking ahead to that film in Dublin. The camera adds ten pounds, so I don't want to put on any extra padding." He pats his flat stomach as they walk.

His eyes focus on a spot in the distance as they walk, and Holly knows he's envisioning that the final 'yes' of their trip will be to a film shoot in Ireland. Rather than discuss it, she changes the subject.

"We've also got the van Gogh museum to see, and we can do a boat tour of the canals," Holly says, pulling the tourist map from the back pocket of her jeans and thrusting it at River.

The sun is out and most of the people around them are wearing lightweight dresses and short-sleeved shirts, but the sixty-degree weather feels chilly to Holly's tropical blood, and she's got a thick sweatshirt on over her t-shirt. River examines the map as they walk, and—feeling self-conscious about the waffle, though it makes her angry that she's even giving it a second thought—Holly tosses the remainder of her snack into a trash can and brushes the sprinkles from her hands.

"We could go to the top of that building there and check out the view of the city," River says. "There's a swing that goes over the edge of the building so it feels like you're floating over Amsterdam—it's the tallest swing in Europe."

"Nope," Holly says immediately and without consideration. "No, no, no. And a great big *hell no.*"

River laughs. "Are you kidding me? This is a once in a lifetime experience. And, may I remind you, the answer to anything on this trip is what?"

Holly inhales and exhales once, standing at the mouth of the ferry as they look up at the A'dam Lookout building to the north. "The answer to everything on this trip is *yes*," she says in a flat tone. "Except dessert. The answer to that is apparently no." She can't resist adding this last part, though she says it in a half-mumble.

"Oh, come on, Hol. You know I didn't mean it like that." River pulls her to the side to avoid being flattened by a Dutch woman in a skirt and clogs as she rolls her bike to a stop in front of the ferry. "Listen, we probably need breakfast—a real breakfast—before we do anything else. Let's go in here and get some grub, okay? Being hungry makes me grumpy, and living on sugar alone can't be good for your mood."

"Or the size of my butt," she adds unhappily.

They look both ways and enter a small cafe with views of the ferry and the train station on the other side of the ferry route. People stream by the windows as they take a seat in wooden chairs and order two full breakfasts with coffee. They wait quietly for the food to arrive, neither willing to acknowledge the strange turn their moods have taken.

The waitress sets toast, slices of cheese, hardboiled eggs balanced in little egg cups, and dishes of yogurt with granola on the table. River immediately tears off a hunk of bread and cheese.

"So what's going on here?" he asks, biting into the thick toast.

Holly dips a spoon into the bowl of yogurt in front of her, swirling the chunks of granola and the dab of honey around like she's stirring a pot of soup. She shrugs.

"Eat something, will you?" River reaches for the small silver pitcher of milk and pours some into his coffee. "I'm not kidding. I know you're the queen of feasting on whatever is closest and living off the remnants of your bare cupboards, but we've been on the go for a couple of days and all I've seen you do is snack. Here." He pushes her egg cup closer and nods at it. "Protein."

Holly says nothing as she peels the shell from her egg and dips the corner of her toast into its runny center. She takes a bite, then another.

"You're super-sensitive and I can tell you're not all here," River says carefully, looking down at his mug as he clinks a spoon around inside of it, stirring the milk and coffee until the liquid turns a creamy color. "I could tell you weren't into the modeling gig, and that's fine." He sets the spoon on the saucer and picks up his mug. "But that job is basically funding our entire trip, and it's all because we weren't afraid to say yes to something crazy. Can't you see that?"

"I know," Holly says, picking up her other wedge of toast. "I get that. The saying yes thing is kind of fun, but can I be honest with you?" This would be the perfect time to tell him about the computer at the country house and the emails she got from Bonnie. She could come clean with him and be free of the nagging voice in her head that's constantly reminding her about the fact that she's essentially lying to him. All it'll take is a few words—an honest admission about what happened—and then they can clear the air and go from there.

River pulls back slightly, a worried look on his face. "Of course you can be honest with me. I think you have to, or this is never going to work." He pushes his bowl of yogurt and granola to the side and focuses on the bread and cheese again.

Holly sighs. She's ready to tell him the truth. Maybe he'll laugh and say he knew it all along. Or maybe he'll feel some sympathy and offer to pull out his phone and charge it up in the boathouse for her so that she can make a call home. But most likely he'll be disappointed in her for being cagey and secretive. Her heart seizes up as the words stack up on her tongue, ready to spill over.

"I'm just...I guess I'm a little preoccupied about what's going on at home. I can't help it," she says lamely, not able to meet his eye. "When I'm there, it's all I do—you know that. I plan things, I worry about things, I fix things. And being so far away makes it really hard to know what needs planning, worrying, or fixing."

River is nodding at her from across the table, his hands laced together on the tabletop, mug of coffee at his elbow. "I get it," he says kindly. "Christmas Key is in your blood. It's not just a job for you. That's one of the things I love most about you." River's voice drops a notch or two. "Among other things," he says with a smile.

This makes Holly feel even worse. In an instant, she's avoided being honest with him, elicited his sympathy, and gotten him to say nice things to her. The guilt inside of her feels like salt rubbed into a paper cut. Unexpected tears prick at the back of her eyes.

"Hey," River says, reaching across the table and taking her hands in his. "What's wrong?" He gives a small, surprised laugh. "Don't cry."

His words are like a starter pistol firing into the air, and just like that, Holly's off to the races. The tears spill over and she pulls her hands from his, picking the napkin up from her lap and holding it over her face as if this will somehow hide her outburst of emotion.

"I'm sorry," she says from behind her napkin. "It's been a long time since I was away from the island for this long." Holly tries a casual laugh, but it comes out like a hiccup. "Maybe I'm just homesick. And I left some things on the burner when I went on vacation, so I'm feeling a little stressed."

"Don't be stressed," River says reassuringly. "Bonnie can handle anything in your absence. She's a totally capable woman." The waitress returns with a pot of coffee and a concerned look on her face. "Thank you," River says to her, smiling to let her know that everything is under control.

"I've just never been out of touch this long, and I'm worried that something might happen—"

"What could possibly go wrong?" River's voice hitches up and a hint of annoyance is evident. "It's not hurricane season, you don't have any major weddings or group visits planned, right?"

Holly shakes her head and dabs at her right eye with the napkin.

"When you get back you'll dive in headfirst and get back to real life. I promise it'll all be waiting for you the minute you set foot on Christmas Key."

Holly takes a deep breath and sits up straighter, giving her head a toss like she's putting it all out of her mind. "You're right," she says agreeably. "I know you're right."

River takes her hands again from across the table and gives them a squeeze. From the relieved look on his face, Holly can tell that he thinks he's dodged a bullet. Her guilt at lying to him by omitting the truth about her stolen computer time fades a bit when she realizes just how stubborn he's going to be about the whole staying-out-of-contact business.

They finish their breakfast amidst Holly's dissipating sniffles, and after they pay the bill and step outside, River points at the tall A'dam Lookout building again. "So?" he asks hopefully. "What do you think?"

Holly sucks on her teeth. "Well," she says, looking at the sky deck and the big red swing. "I think we should probably at least go up there and check it out." She's working hard to recover her footing after the unexpected emotional outburst at breakfast.

River reaches out and takes her hand in his with an amused grin. "That was a resounding 'yes' if ever I heard one. Let's go."

THE SWING IS TERRIFYING. The fact that it arcs out over the edge of an incredibly tall building as its riders take in the view of the city below is enough to make Holly feel like she's having an out-of-body experience. This is the kind of thing she'd never say yes to on her own, and the weightlessness she feels as she flies over a city that looks like Lego buildings below her is surreal.

Her legs are rubber for most of the afternoon as they walk from the Anne Frank house to the Van Gogh museum, and people on bikes blow past them noiselessly, startling her each time they get too close. River plays tour guide, his elation at having gone on the swing filling him with a jovial excitement that Holly almost shares. Almost, but not quite.

After a long day of sightseeing, they end up back at their houseboat around seven, and Holly sends River to the store for tampons and cookies. (Her tears at breakfast should have been her first indication that tampons and cookies would be necessary that day.) The minute he's out of sight, she slips out the side door of the tiny rental, the ground swaying slightly beneath her as the houseboat rocks with the movement of the tiny river they're situated on.

The owners of the rental also own a larger houseboat on the same property, and Holly covers the twenty feet between the two homes in seconds, rapping on the door of the main house with urgency.

A blonde woman about fifteen or twenty years older than Holly opens it. "Hello," she says with a smile. She's holding a lit cigarette in one hand, wearing jeans and a white shirt that buttons up the front. "How is your stay so far?"

Holly shifts her weight, trying to be patient. "Really good. The house is so cute."

"Not too small?" The woman's words are slow, her English lightly accented. She brings the cigarette to her lips, narrowing one eye as she takes a pull and then blows the smoke to the side. "Some people are frightened away by trying to live in a tiny house, but it really has everything you need."

"It does," Holly agrees. "Except one thing."

"Oh?" Her eyebrows lift elegantly and she runs her free hand over her smooth bun.

"Internet. I need to check my email."

"But the Wifi password—"

"Won't help me," Holly finishes for her. "See, the problem is, we got mugged in London, and I lost my cell phone."

"Oh, no!" The woman leans out to tap her ashes into the gravel next to the front door. "That's terrible."

"It was. And the worst part is that River—my boyfriend," Holly hooks her thumb in the direction of the rental house as if he's in there, "he wants to pretend like we have no way to check in at home for the whole three weeks of this trip, but I can't do that."

"He doesn't want to check in at all?"

"No! He's got this weird, romantic idea about saying yes to *everything* except to me," Holly goes on, growing slightly hysterical as she explains. "And he went to the store just now and I really need to check my email and let everyone know I'm alive." Weirdly, the tears Holly felt earlier at breakfast are threatening to return, but this time they feel more like desperation than defeat.

The woman tries to hush Holly, but it sounds more like "Tch, tch, tch." She looks both ways up and down the sidewalk in front of her property, then reaches out and grabs Holly by the forearm, holding her cigarette in the other hand. "Come in. Hurry, please." She closes the door behind Holly and leads her through a mostly white house that looks like it was decorated entirely from Ikea catalogs and by watching reruns of mod shows from the 1960s. A thick, white fur rug covers the space in front of a low sectional couch, and a huge pendant lamp dangles from a delicately arched silver stand, its base improbably holding the whole thing upright.

"The computer is here," the woman says. "And I am Eva."

"Holly," Holly says, extending a hand in a belated introduction. "Thank you for this. I really appreciate it."

Eva points at a spot on the couch and lifts the lid on the laptop. "It's all yours," she says, clicking on a tab and closing what she's been looking at.

"Thank you so much," Holly says. She sinks into the couch and starts tapping her log in information into the computer. She feels like the hero in an action movie with only seconds left to defuse a bomb as she fights against the clock to get the information from her email account before River gets back from the store.

Eva wanders over to the open kitchen area and stubs her cigarette out in a blue cut-glass ashtray, her eyes focused on the water just beyond the windows. "Men are funny creatures, aren't they?" she wonders. Her back is to Holly as she watches a bird swoop and dive into the water. "My husband once bought me a cat when I'd already told him that I didn't want animals in our house."

"Really?" Holly asks politely, her eyes on the computer screen.

"Yes. He thought I was missing something by not having a pet, but I swore to him I wasn't missing anything at all."

"They don't believe us, do they?" Holly asks distractedly, scanning her inbox for the most important looking messages. It's Friday evening, which means it's lunchtime on Christmas Key. Her last email from Bonnie is two days old, and all she talks about is Coco wanting to help out in the B&B office. Not that Coco meddling in B&B business isn't bad enough, but at least she hasn't opened an email to find an S.O.S. from Bonnie or a message informing her that Christmas Key has already been bought and paid for by some outside entity.

"It's not that they don't believe us," Eva goes on, oblivious to

Holly's eyes rapidly scanning the computer screen. "It's that they don't believe we already know what we want."

Holly finishes reading Bonnie's email about Coco rearranging her desk and demanding that she call an impromptu village council meeting. It makes her blood boil to imagine her mother moving her belongings around and answering the office phone, but the real panic sets in when she imagines Coco hearing that Holly is out of reach and hasn't been heard from.

"But maybe your man isn't trying to control you by forcing you to say yes to everything," Eva allows, tearing her eyes from the window so she can find her pack of cigarettes in the fading light. She switches on a lamp on the kitchen counter. "Maybe he really just wants you to see that the world gets, you know..." Eva waves her hand around like she's searching for words, a new, unlit cigarette already between her fingers, "...bigger. It grows when you say yes to things you otherwise would have said no to."

Holly pauses, considering this. "You're right," she says. "I have definitely said yes to things on this trip that I would have normally said no to."

"And have you learned anything? Does the world seem bigger?"

"It seems...scarier," Holly says. "It makes me want to go home right now and not leave my little island ever again."

"That's honest." There is admiration in Eva's voice. "But when you go home to this little island, do you think you'll do anything differently?"

Holly thinks for a second before she answers. "You know, I do." It shocks her to admit it to a woman who is, essentially, a complete stranger, but Holly knows it's true. "There are some things I could say yes to in my normal life that I would have just been stubborn about before." She nods, thinking of her life on Christmas Key and her plans for the island.

"Then that's something, isn't it?" Eva flicks her lighter and holds the flame to the end of her cigarette.

"I guess it is." Holly watches as Eva turns back to the window, then she opens up a blank email and addresses it to Bonnie.

Bon—I'm so sorry I haven't emailed yet! You won't believe everything that's happened, but I'm without a phone for the rest of the trip. I'll check email when I can, but I'm not sure when I'll have access to a computer again. I hope you're keeping Coco in line, and I want to hear everything I'm missing—EVERY. SINGLE. THING. I'll talk to you soon! xoxoxoxo Holly

Holly logs out of her email and gently shuts the lid to the laptop. "Thank you. I really needed this," Holly says to Eva. She means the use of the computer, but somehow she also means the female companionship and the supportive ear. Eva smiles knowingly.

"You're welcome. Enjoy the rest of your trip, huh? You're only young once, and there's something to be said about enjoying Europe —and life—without being tied to a cell phone."

Holly follows her through the open living space, pausing on the doorstep as Eva holds it open. The lights are still off in their tiny boathouse next door, so she knows River isn't back yet.

"Hey," Holly says, looking at Eva curiously. "Whatever happened to that cat?"

A smile spreads across Eva's face, and a map of fine lines creases around her kind eyes. "Our neighbors were moving to Norway," she says, pointing her cigarette at the tall row house across the street. "Their little girl always loved my cat, so I asked her parents if they could take him."

"Did your husband ever know?"

Eva looks heavenward with her eyes as she tips her head to one side, considering. "No, I don't think so. I told him the cat ran away. It made sense, because his name was *Avontuur.*"

Holly frowns, her next question written all over her face.

"It means *adventure,*" Eva says, winking at Holly before she shuts the door.

18

The wait is endless. No one sleeps after Cap's boat roars off into the open water with Ray, Millie, and Fiona on board, Ray's lifeless body lying prone on the bottom of the boat as Fiona tends to him.

Bonnie and a handful of the other women gather in the B&B's kitchen as they do during every emergency. They'd used it as their home base during the tropical storm that had hit the summer before. It'd been the place to gather when an unfortunate accident had led to Jake and Bridget's miscarriage, and everyone had cooked and waited during the touch-and-go time when Mori Guy, one of Vance and Calista's six-year-old twin sons, had fallen into the pool at night and nearly drowned. So now, again, they wait—they cook, and they wait.

"My rosary hasn't gotten this much work in years," Maria Agnelli says, one hand wrapped in the white beads as proof. "This is the same one I used during the war," she says softly, looking at the beads. "And when my kids were sick, and when Alfie was dying..."

"We're all praying for Ray," Gwen says, leaving her identical sisters at the counter where the three of them are chopping vegetables for a salad. She walks over to Mrs. Agnelli and puts her arms around the shorter woman. "This is just unthinkable," Gwen whispers, holding her elderly friend in an embrace. "And poor Millie."

Bonnie says nothing as she watches the scene around her, but purses her lips and stirs the batter in her mixing bowl with fervor. She's making drop biscuits to go with everything else that's cooking: roasted chicken, sweet potato wedges, and the triplets' salad, but she's not talking much.

Her late husband had died of a heart attack. A completely sudden, out of left field, who'd-a-thunk-it, kind of heart attack. They'd been having a wonderful afternoon the day it happened, shopping for dinner makings after their oldest son's baseball game when Ed had fallen to his knees in Aisle Seven at the Publix while "How Deep Is Your Love" by The Bee Gees played over the speakers in the store. He'd been gone by the time the medics arrived.

And he'd looked almost exactly the way Ray had looked that afternoon.

"Bonnie, how long till the biscuits go in?" Heddie Lang-Mueller leans across the steel counter of the B&B's kitchen. "I've got the buffet table set up, and Cap is moving tables and chairs so that we can all sit and eat together."

Bonnie reels herself in, the memory of the Gibb brothers' smooth voices, and the cold, shiny linoleum floor beneath her bare knees fading away as she comes back to the reality of the B&B kitchen.

"They're going in right now. Give me ten minutes, and you'll have hot biscuits." Bonnie smiles at Heddie and blinks a few times, pushing the tears away that spring to her eyes every time she remembers her beloved Ed spread out on the ground next to the shelves of Cheerios and Frosted Flakes.

Heddie reaches out and wraps her long fingers around Bonnie's soft hand. "Everything is going to be okay," she says softly. "Even if it's not okay, we still have each other." She's mistaken Bonnie's teary eyes for concern about Ray. Bonnie *is* worried about Ray—and Millie—of course, but her salty tears as she preps cheesy biscuits for the oven are for Ed.

She keeps her memories and her worries to herself and smiles at

Heddie again. "I know, Heddie. We'll get through this, no matter what happens."

The door to the kitchen swings open as Coco rushes in. "I called the hospital in Key West, and they won't tell me anything," she announces, stopping short of a foot stomp that would announce to everyone just how unused to being denied she is.

"Patience, young lady." Maria Agnelli is stern and disapproving. She shoots Coco a look that's full of venom. "We'll know more when it's time for us to know more." She totters over to the doorway and hands Coco a cup full of silverware. "Now go and put this on the buffet table so we can eat something before midnight."

Like an obedient (if slightly offended) teenager, Coco turns heel and walks back through the swinging door.

"I swear..." Bonnie shakes her head but doesn't finish her thought. She doesn't need to; everyone in the room is thinking the same thing. They need Holly back, and they need Ray to be all right. They need Coco to disappear, and to take her half-cocked ideas about a casino and an island full of service workers living in clapboard apartment buildings with her.

People start to filter out to the dining room with stacks of plates in hand, hot dishes held on trays, and pitchers of water and iced tea. Bonnie waits in the kitchen for the biscuits to rise and turn golden brown. When she's finally alone, she allows herself a few, private tears. Some for Ed, some for Ray, and some for the fact that she's scared of what's going to happen if Coco gets her way.

It's late when Bonnie gets home, but she checks her email before turning in, like she does every night, hoping for a message from Holly. And like magic, this time she's got one.

"Hallelujah!" she shouts in the living room of the empty house. Without kicking off her shoes, Bonnie sits on the couch with her laptop and opens the message.

Bon—I'm so sorry I haven't emailed yet! You won't believe everything that's happened, but I'm without a phone for the rest of the trip. I'll check email when I can, but I'm not sure when I'll have access to a computer again. I hope you're keeping Coco in line, and I want to hear everything I'm missing—EVERY. SINGLE. THING. I'll talk to you soon! xoxoxoxo Holly

A wave of happy-sad emotion floods Bonnie's tired body. She's happy that Holly still sounds like Holly—somehow far away and unreachable, but still Holly—but sad that she's going to have to tell her about Coco's casino plan and Ray's heart attack. A phone call would be a better way to break some of this news, but for some inexplicable reason, Holly's got no phone on this trip. So Bonnie puts her fingers to the keyboard and lets the words tumble around in her mind as she starts to type.

Hi, sugar! I miss you so much—she writes, then pauses. She looks around her living room at the throw pillows and at the photographs on her wall that her son took and then blew up and framed for her. The lamp is on in the corner of the room, glowing warm and yellow against the dark night beyond her windows. Bonnie sets the computer on her coffee table and stands up to close the curtains and turn on the porch light.

She's about to sit down and find a way to deliver all of the island news to Holly in writing when her phone rings from inside her purse on the couch. Bonnie digs it out and silences the ringer as she brings the phone to her ear.

"Bon?" Fiona says. She sounds tired.

"Fiona. What's happening over there? How is he?"

Fiona pauses. The sounds of a busy hospital are audible in the background, and a nurse's voice on a distant intercom comes through the receiver as Bonnie waits.

"Ray didn't make it," Fiona says, her voice betraying more emotion than a doctor's should. "We did everything we could, but it was too late by the time we got to Key West. I've got Millie here, and we're making some decisions about what happens next. I'll call you when I know more, okay?"

Bonnie's hand is over her mouth, her eyes wide. This is not the news she wants to hear. Ray was a wonderful, funny, gregarious man, and the thought of Millie walking down the lonely path that Bonnie already knows well from her own experience as a widow pushes her over the edge.

"Okay," she sobs. "Give Millie our love."

"I will. And would you let everyone know? I think it's best if we don't come back and have to spread the news ourselves."

"Of course," Bonnie says, nodding. One hand covers her open mouth as she stands there in the quiet living room.

She's still in shock as she hangs up the phone and sits down in front of the laptop again. This isn't the time to compose an email to Holly. She can't tell her about Ray like this. So instead of finishing the message she's started, Bonnie closes the laptop, sets it on the coffee table, and turns out the lights.

19

H olly has stepped out of line briefly to find a cup of coffee, and as she walks back to the boat ramp where they've been told to wait, she can see River making conversation with the people in front of him.

"This guy has a good suggestion," River says. He puts one hand on the small of Holly's back as they wait in line to board the boat for a tour of Amsterdam's canals on Saturday morning.

"Hi," Holly says politely to the two men in spotless white Converse and fitted jeans. She sips her coffee, preparing to hear about whatever these guys have suggested to River that will now dominate her afternoon. Her talk with Eva the night before has given her a new perspective on this trip, and she's feeling almost sanguine about the notion of saying yes to a helicopter tour of Sweden with the Royal Swedish Army, or scaling the Eiffel Tower to make a Youtube video of herself hanging off the top observation deck so that some kid can post the video and go viral. At this point, she's resigned to hear whatever comes out of the mouths of these two clean-cut guys who've been talking to her boyfriend.

"We're giving away our tickets," says the shorter of the two guys, "to a really small, underground concert." He's got a British accent and a two-day beard that looks scruffy against the pink and green polo shirt he's wearing. "They only have room for about fifty people, and you have to be open to hearing their new stuff—you aren't allowed to shout out requests for their oldies."

Holly snorts. "They're so famous that I'd know their oldies?" She looks up at River with curiosity. "You're into this?"

River's eyes twinkle. "You know what I'm going to say," he goads her, knocking her arm with his elbow playfully and accidentally sloshing her coffee around. "Oops, sorry."

The guy who hasn't spoken yet looks at Holly from under the brim of a black baseball hat with no logo that matches his black t-shirt. "You'll know them."

"Who is it?" Holly asks the next obvious question.

The guys look at River. "Not telling," River says. "But you have to trust me on this one."

Holly sighs. The boat is anchored and tied up at the dock, and the tour guides are starting to take tickets and assist people as they step into the vessel for a ride through the city. "Okay," she says. "Why not?"

"Here you go," says the guy with the black hat. He slides two tickets out of his wallet and hands them to River, who immediately puts them into his own wallet, being careful not to let Holly have a peek at them.

"Thanks—this is going to be amazing," River says. "She's going to love it."

"Have fun. Wish we could've hung around another day to see it ourselves," the short guy says wistfully, watching as River puts his wallet away.

As they board the boat, River is humming a familiar tune. Holly leans her shoulder into his. "Who is it? You can tell me. I already said yes," she chides, rubbing her cheek against his upper arm the way Pucci rubs against her legs for attention.

"I could...but I won't," he says with mischief in his eyes. "Here, let me hold that." River takes Holly's coffee and helps her into the boat.

They choose a bench right behind the boat's captain. It's a bright, sunny morning, and Holly digs through the purse she bought after hers was stolen in London, coming up with a pair of sunglasses.

"You're mean," she says, holding her hand out for her coffee. "It better not be something horrible. I'm not trying to spend my last night in Amsterdam listening to Shania Twain prepare for a comeback."

"You don't like Shania?" River asks, recoiling in mock horror. He sings a few words of "Man, I Feel Like a Woman" while Holly gags and makes faces.

"No! I do *not* like Shania Twain. Never have. But if she's your cup of tea, then more power to you."

River laughs.

"Sit back and enjoy the tour today," the captain says into a hand-held speaker, using lightly-accented English. "We're taking a ride through the most beautiful part of Amsterdam. You'll see historic buildings, charming bridges, and lots of people on bicycles." Everyone on the boat chuckles. "Feel free to take as many pictures as you like, but please stay seated and keep all your belongings inside the boat."

"Is it Vanilla Ice?" Holly asks when the captain clicks off the scratchy speaker and puts the boat in gear. The engine roars to life as he carefully backs the boat away from the dock.

"I don't think Vanilla Ice needs a comeback, does he?" River turns his head to look at Holly. "I thought he had some remodeling show on HGTV or something?"

"You know way too much about Vanilla Ice for my comfort level," Holly teases. "So who is it? Come on, come on, come on," she says, bouncing around in her seat, "you can tell me!"

River shrugs and looks out at the water as the boat cuts through it, leaving a wake in its trail. "Eh. I'd rather wait and see your face when we get there." He's got something that Holly wants, and he's clearly enjoying it, reveling in the fact that she's acting like herself for the first time in days.

"Huh," Holly huffs, leaning back into the hard bench seat. "I can wait. In fact, I don't even care that much." She tosses her brown hair over one shoulder and puts her coffee cup to her lips. "It's whatever."

"We're passing under our first bridge here," the captain says, his speaker crackling to life again. "And if you duck your heads, we might make it under this low clearance." Everyone chuckles politely.

"It might be whatever," River says to her, "but you're going to be flying *high*. You've never had *a night like this*."

Holly rolls her eyes. "You know," she says, changing subjects. "Without our phones, we're missing the chance to take photos of this trip. Neither of us even brought a point-and-shoot camera."

"I'm missing nothing," River says. "If I spent time behind the camera snapping photos of you in front of everything, I'd miss it all. I just want to remember it."

"So we're just going to go home and have no pictures of us in Europe?"

"We've got a least a few photos of us pretending to be the Lord and Lady of the manor in Fairford."

"Oh. Right. Those pictures." Holly rolls her eyes. "I'm buying a camera today, just FYI."

"That's cool." River gives her an easy smile as she leans her head against him. They watch the buildings that run parallel to the canal as the boat glides by, and the slight breeze blows their hair. "Isn't this *just like heaven*?" River asks without looking at her.

"I guess." Holly frowns. "I mean, if heaven had a red light district and smelled like marijuana." She gives him a puzzled look. "But Amsterdam is a cool place. I guess heaven could be worse."

River's body shakes as he laughs to himself. He starts to hum again, a tune that tickles at the back of Holly's brain as she tries to place it. Instead of bugging him for hints that she knows he won't give, she sits quietly for most of the tour, sipping her coffee and listening to the boat captain's humorous tidbits on the history of the famous red lights of Amsterdam.

∾

THE CONCERT STARTS LATE that night, and they don't leave the houseboat until after ten o'clock. River's convinced Holly to wear the black outfit he bought her at Harrod's with the knee-high boots, though she'd rather be in jeans and comfortable shoes. "Trust me," he'd said. "This is the kind of event where you should wear black." So she'd showered and dressed, blowing her hair straight and zipping the black boots over her calves tiredly.

The crowd standing in line in front of the brick bar called Maloe Melo is all in black.

"You were right," Holly says, looking up at River. "Everyone is in black." He puts an arm around her shoulders. "Are we seeing Johnny Cash?"

"Johnny Cash is dead."

"Metallica?"

"This is a pretty small space," River says. He tries to look through the front window of the bar, but dark curtains cover the glass from floor to ceiling. "I doubt Metallica could jam in here without shattering some windows."

The front door opens and the crowd starts to move forward. "Do you have the tickets?" Holly pokes River's side.

"Yep." He pulls his wallet out and slides the tickets from a fold behind his collection of euros, British pounds, and dollars.

The woman at the door is wearing a piercing through her septum that looks like it weighs five pounds. It's dragging her nose down slightly with its heavy metal, and her eyes are ringed in smoky liner and shadow. "Tickets?" she asks them, holding out a hand that's covered with a fingerless glove.

In exchange, she hands River a small program that looks like a pamphlet.

"Lemme see!" Holly stands on the toes of her boots as they enter the bar. She tries to catch a glimpse of the program over River's shoulder, but he blocks her and she laughs, feeling excited for whatever is about to happen. It could be something lame, and Holly knows this is still a real possibility, but her chances of it being amazing are even better.

A group of middle-aged guys with thinning hair and clean shirts wedges in next to Holly and River. They're speaking French and laughing loudly at each other's jokes. Behind them, two women dressed much like the ticket-taker at the door are examining the glowing screens of their cell phones and speaking Dutch to one another whenever one of them comes up with something worth sharing. Holly turns to the stage and watches as the men who are working up there rearrange a microphone stand and drum kit.

It's only when the larger of the two men moves to one side that she can see everything. There, on the front of the bass drum, is the name of the band.

"Shut up!" Holly says in a loud, disbelieving voice. She swats River's arm. "No way...is this for real?" She looks at him, eyes wide as she waits for him to admit the whole thing is a ruse.

River lifts a shoulder and smiles at her. "It's for real."

Holly's head whips back to the front of the room and she stares at the men as they put the finishing touches on the tiny stage. "We're actually going to see The Cure?" she asks in an awed whisper.

When she turns back to River, he's watching her with twinkling eyes. "Yes, my little closet Goth girl, we are. Are you happy?"

Holly has no words. Is she happy? Of course she's happy. One of her favorite bands in the world is about to come on stage in a tiny club in Amsterdam and sing new songs. Remembering the program, she reaches out and slides it from River's hand. Inside, it lists the songs they're going to perform, and there's a web address for concertgoers to visit and share their thoughts on the new music.

"I can't even," Holly says, shaking her head slowly as she processes everything. But she doesn't have time to think about it too much, because the lights dim and a hush runs through the crowd. The band members walk single file through a door behind the tiny stage. Holly hands the program back to River and watches as the drummer takes his spot, followed by the keyboardist, guitarist, and bass guitarist, and then—finally—Robert Smith.

He's wearing a long, black shirt over black jeans and heavy boots, his trademark mane of hair teased into a rat's nest around his heavily made-up face. He looks out at the small crowd through the tangle of hair over his eyes, his lips red and smeared as he smiles shyly.

"Thanks for coming," he says into the microphone, his British accent evident in even the simplest words. Without further ado, the band launches into the opening song of the set. The sounds of the instruments fill the small room completely, and Holly is totally lost in the music. The entire concert is a blur to her, and she alternates between listening with rapt attention, looking up at River with a happy smile, and swaying along to these new songs. At the end of the set, they play a couple of old favorites, much to the delight of the mostly middle-aged crowd.

When it's all over, the street outside is quiet and nearly deserted. Holly and River catch a cab back to their houseboat, cuddling in the backseat while Holly happily recounts her favorite songs. She's lost in that after-concert haze that happens when you see your favorite band —the one where you relive it all and marvel about the fact that you've just been *in the same room* as one of your favorite performers—and her giddiness overlaps with tiredness, making her overly chatty.

"Wait, wait, wait," Holly says, sitting up and pulling her shoulder out from under River's arm. "Now I get it!"

"You get what?" River's head is leaned back against the bench seat, his eyes at half-mast.

"All the things you were saying earlier today: 'A night like this' and 'just like heaven'—you're sneaky," she says, leaning back and folding herself under his arm again. He'd been slyly referencing titles of songs by The Cure.

"Don't forget 'high'—I slid that one in, too." River's head tips in her direction as they round a corner too quickly. "But I'm glad you had fun."

"It was amazing," Holly confirms, resting her own head on the back of the seat and looking at River so that their eyes and lips are just inches apart. "The best thing I've said yes to in a long time."

The tall, narrow houses along the streets are dark and quiet, and the streetlights flicker across Holly's bare knees as they drive towards the train station. There's still a short ferry ride to get across the water, and a five minute walk to their houseboat that will take all the energy Holly has left.

"Hey," River says in a voice that's barely audible. "You know what the best thing I've said yes to is?" Holly's eyes crinkle at the corners as her lips pull into a dreamy smile. "A fishing trip to some hot, unpaved island off the coast of Florida. And you."

River scoots his head closer and kisses her. Holly's heart races; this is the feeling she's used to having in his presence. A warm happiness spreads from her chest to all the extremities of her body as River's lips part suggestively.

"We're here," the cab driver says in English, halting at the curb. River pays the driver and they rush through the train station, huddling together near the window on the ferry to continue their kiss. There are only a handful of other people at this hour, so Holly and River carry on as if they're the only people there.

It feels like the perfect evening to Holly. Her arms are around the thick, strong torso of a beautiful man who cares about her; a cool breeze is whipping through the front of the ferry, tickling her bare thighs under the black miniskirt and keeping her awake; and she's just been within spitting distance of one of her favorite bands. Can it get any better than this?

The low horn of the ferry blows into the dark night as they glide to the dock. Holly presses her cheek against River's chest, listening to the steady beat of his heart. There've been a few moments on the trip so far that leave something to be desired, but *this* moment is close to perfect. And yet, even though most of this major European city is asleep and it feels like the stars and the water and the cobbled streets belong entirely to them, and even though they'll be traveling to Paris in the morning (*Paris!* Holly thinks, the very word filling her with excitement), something still feels off.

The thought sobers Holly. What's not right? What could possibly put a damper on the way she's feeling in this moment? As the deckhand ties the boat to the dock and opens the gate for passengers to disembark, the silly grin she's been wearing all evening melts away, leaving behind the simple truth that's been nagging at her for days: something is happening at home. And whatever it is, it isn't good.

20

There's a pall over the whole island that extends to even the youngest residents of Christmas Key. On Saturday afternoon, Logan is walking down Main Street behind his mother, carrying three overstuffed bags of groceries and provisions in his arms. He doesn't say a word as she points at the golf cart silently, indicating that he should load them in the back. Mexi and Mori are a few steps ahead of their grandmother as Idora gives firm directions about where they should and shouldn't go, and for once their faces aren't the least bit impish or mischievous.

Cap is standing in front of his cigar shop with Wyatt Bender and Buckhunter, all three men conversing in low tones. Their arms are folded as they discuss Ray's fall at the meeting on Thursday, disbelief over the fact that he's really gone forcing them to replay the events for clues of a disaster that they never saw coming.

"You say he wasn't feeling well?" Cap lifts his chin at Buckhunter.

"Fiona had seen him a few days before because he was under the weather. That's about all I know," Buckhunter says, recounting what his girlfriend had shared with him.

"Damn." Wyatt moves a toothpick from one side of his mouth to the other. "Just goes to show you never know what's lurking around the corner."

"There's real truth in those words." Cap reaches up and offers a broken cracker to Marco, who's perched on his shoulder. Marco takes the chunk of saltine from Cap's strong fingers, pulling it into his beak with a single bob of his colorful head.

"We need to do all we can to rally around Millie when she gets back," Wyatt says. "I'm sure the women will coordinate meals, but the rest of us can step up and help her out, too."

"I'm happy to mow her lawn and take care of anything she needs around the house," Buckhunter says, holding up a hand. "I'm sure Jake can pitch in if I need any help there."

"How about with anything else?" Wyatt looks back and forth between the two other men.

"Uhhhh," Cap says. Buckhunter's face tells them both that he's drawing a blank as well.

"You talking about emotional stuff?" Buckhunter's forehead creases. "Like, sit with her and help her call relatives?"

"Probably ought to let the women guide us on that," Cap decides, holding up another piece of cracker for Marco.

"Yeah, good call." Wyatt nods seriously. "I guess that means we just take their lead on pretty much everything when Millie gets back."

"Wouldn't be the first time we let the hens peck us in the right direction," Cap says with a broad grin.

"And it won't be the last," Buckhunter agrees.

"You all!" Bonnie calls out from the sidewalk on the other side of Main Street. She's standing outside the B&B, her fiery red hair flaming in the afternoon sunlight. "I heard from Holly!" Bonnie looks both ways before she crosses the street, her short, curvy body swaying in a walk that's half strut and half scurry. "She's alive and well," Bonnie says as she approaches the knot of men. "But I didn't have the heart to tell her what's going on around here—at least not in an email."

"Probably best," Cap says, reaching out a hand and touching Bonnie's upper arm. "How are you holding up, kid?"

Bonnie's eyes fill with involuntary tears. "It's hard," she says, putting a hand beneath her nose and taking a moment. "It reminds me way too much of when I lost Ed."

Wyatt springs into action, stepping up beside Bonnie and placing one of his palms on her back. "I'm so sorry, Bonnie," he says quietly. "It ain't easy, and you never quite get over it, do you?" His voice is soothing.

"I know you understand, Wyatt." Bonnie locks eyes with him and they exchange silent sympathies. Annabelle Bender's passing had been the catalyst for Wyatt's decision to spend half the year on Christmas Key, and while he doesn't speak of his wife often, everyone on the island knows that she was the love of his life. His fondness for Bonnie is also common knowledge, but even that flirtation pales in comparison to his love for Annabelle.

Cap clears his throat. "We were just talking about what we can do for Millie when she gets back."

"We've got meals under control," Bonnie says, wiping at the corner of her eye. "And we're thinking about the logistics of a service in the chapel, if that's what Millie wants. Otherwise we'll help her make the arrangements and deal with relatives who want to visit and whatnot."

"See? I knew the women would spearhead this effort," Cap says as an aside to the other two men. "Okay, so just tell us what we need to do," he tells Bonnie. "If the service is here, I'm happy to lead it. Buckhunter says he'll help her out around the house. And the rest of us are on call for anything else you can think of."

"Much appreciated," Bonnie says, making grateful eye contact with each of them.

"When do Fiona and Millie get back?" Wyatt asks.

"I talked to Fee last night," Buckhunter says. "She said they were due back around six this evening."

Cap checks the watch face that's attached to his thick wrist with a worn leather strap. "Bout four hours we got here," he says, mentally calculating. "What should we do?"

Bonnie glances at her own watch. "Here's what I think," she says, tugging the hem of her shirt down over her round hips. "The thing I hated most when Ed passed was coming home to my house and finding his half-empty coffee cup from breakfast still in the sink. I hated seeing his toothbrush in a cup on the sink and having to decide what to do with it." The emotion starts to well up in Bonnie again, threatening to spill out through her eyes. "And I couldn't stand that my neighbors didn't know. The man across the street came over that afternoon and wanted to talk to Ed about the hedge clippers he'd loaned him, and the first thing I did was fall to my knees at the mention of Ed's name."

"Well, we've got the neighbor thing covered," Cap says gruffly. "Everyone here knows, and no one will be knocking on her door asking for Ray."

Buckhunter puts a rough hand to his scalp and runs it over his hair. He's gotten used to his gray-blonde buzz cut and is thinking of keeping it shorter now that the weather is heating up for summer. "I'm not sure that I'm up for moving a man's toothbrush..."

"I've got that," Bonnie assures them. "Calista has been spending the most time with Millie lately, so she and I are going to head over now and see if we can't tidy up in the tiniest ways possible and at least move some of the most obvious reminders."

"Good plan." Wyatt gives Bonnie's back a gentle pat, removing the hand that's been resting there. "Call if you need anything, you hear?"

"Will do," Bonnie says. She steps back into the street and crosses back to the B&B to get her golf cart from the lot.

There really isn't much to say, so the men nod at one another gravely, silently acknowledging the subtle shift in their life on the island. They've lost one of their own—a man they all genuinely liked —and now they'll have to do their best to help his widow pick up the pieces.

COCO PICKS up her iced tea from the bar at Jack Frosty's, making her way to the seats that look out onto the street from inside her half-brother's open air bar. She's been privy to the comings and goings of the islanders all day as they prepare for Millie to arrive back on the island, but she hasn't volunteered herself for any of the cooking or housekeeping duties.

She puts the straw between her lips and takes a long drink as she squints out at Main Street. Things are happening, and some of it is definitely to her advantage. Having a new teenager and two new women arrive at the same time certainly shakes up the island, and with each person who arrives on Christmas Key, the residents are going to be forced to admit that new blood and fresh ideas are the only ways to keep moving forward. At least she and Holly can agree on *that* vision for the island.

But more than that, Coco hopes this cluster of old-timers and recluses can see that taking a different tack will revitalize what she sees as a dilapidated amusement park for Baby Boomers. Her parents had bought this place with some grand vision of making it a retirement paradise full of walkers and non-stop bingo games, but their passing had left it in the semi-capable hands of her daughter, who—in Coco's humble opinion—can't see past the end of her own nose to get beyond the ticky-tacky weddings and B.S. treasure hunts she wants to put on for day trippers. There's so much more that could be done with this place, and Coco fully intends to monetize and capitalize on its potential.

"More iced tea?" Buckhunter asks, passing by with a sweaty pitcher that he holds aloft.

"Sure." Coco slides the nearly empty glass across the slab of wood that serves as a counter, staring out at the hot street with a bored expression. "Hey, Leo," she says. As usual, she's refused to refer to half-brother by his last name, as all the other islanders do. Buckhunter cocks an inquisitive eyebrow. "We need to talk about the casino. You and me. Before Holly gets back."

Buckhunter tips the pitcher over her glass and watches the amber liquid splash over her melting ice cubes. He gives a quiet chuff and finishes pouring. "About what?"

"Come on," Coco says, slapping a palm against the wood. "You see the potential here, don't you? I want to show you some numbers and figures that I got from Gator and the Killjoys. We're talking serious money here."

Buckhunter sets the pitcher down and pulls out the stool next to Coco's. He sits next to her, facing the street and not looking her in the eye. "You know," he says with a sigh. "I don't think that matters much to anyone but you."

"Being financially solvent doesn't matter to you?" Coco rears back, staring at Buckhunter's profile. "The man who left you and your mom to rot up in Savannah your whole life leaves you something that could change your destiny, and you just want to squat on it and serve margaritas to liver-spotted grandparents until you die?"

Buckhunter's laugh is a loud, surprised bark. "You do have a way with words," he says, shaking his head. The lines at the corner of his eyes deepen as he lets the vision that Coco's painted form in his mind's eye. "But your dad didn't leave us to rot. We were happy, and he sent money. You know all that," Buckhunter says dismissively. "Besides, I've got no hard feelings. It is what it is, and when he asked me to come down here a few years ago, he gave me a gift I didn't even know I wanted. And I'm not talking about some stake in this place, I'm talking about a family. The people on this island are my family."

It's Coco's turn to laugh in disbelief. "These people all *have* families, Leo," she says meanly. "You're just their bartender."

Buckhunter pushes back his stool and stands up slowly, lifting the pitcher of tea off the counter. "My mom's been gone for years, and being an uncle gave me a purpose again. Even when Holly didn't know she needed me, I was there." He looks down at his half-sister, his eyes searching hers. "And if you spent more time here you'd know that we *are* a family. Not just me and Holly, but all of us. And I'm not willing to sacrifice that for some casino."

"Don't think about the casino, think about the *money*," she implores.

"I don't want the gamblers, I don't want the cheap laborers, I don't want the slot machine coins and cigarette butts that will wash up on our shores. And Holly won't either. Guaranteed." Buckhunter pushes the stool under the rough wooden counter with his foot and walks away.

It's just like everyone around her to be so short-sighted. Coco picks up her fresh glass of iced tea as she watches Calista Vance move around inside of Scissors & Ribbons across the street from Jack Frosty's. A hot breeze blows off the street, cooling the sheen of sweat that feels ever-present to Coco.

She's bored. Bored on this quiet island. Bored up in New Jersey, where she's the trophy wife of a successful man who tolerates her demanding nature because all her hours at the gym keep her taut and youthful. Bored with her life. In her heart, Coco knows that this island could really be something, and having a project like a casino to build would fill her with a sense of purpose that she hasn't had in years...or maybe ever.

She takes a long drink of her cold tea. Holly will be back in ten days. That means she has ten days to come up with a compelling reason to make this happen. Ten days to get this floating lump of sand and wrinkled flesh on board with her plan. Coco jabs her straw into the shards of ice still in the bottom of her glass, watching as people start to trickle down Main Street towards the dock. She leans forward and looks down the street: a boat is approaching in the distance. It has to be carrying Millie and Fiona, and it looks like everyone is rushing to meet them.

Step one of winning these people over is blending in and commiserating with them, and Coco has every intention of doing just that. She pulls a five dollar bill out of her wallet and tosses it on the counter to pay for her iced tea.

"See you later," Coco says to Buckhunter as she breezes past his bar. "Millie's back." With no further explanation, she's down the stairs and walking under the hot sun, following Bonnie and Iris Cafferkey as they make their way to the dock to offer their condolences.

She'll just have to call Alan and let him know that she won't be home for a couple more weeks. There's still way too much work to be done here on Christmas Key.

21

Paris is basking in the glow of a warm, clear Sunday afternoon. The parks are filled with people eating baguettes slathered in butter and stuffed with ham and cheese, and the carousel near the Eiffel Tower spins merrily under a blue sky, children hanging from the horses and laughing happily as they rotate beneath one of the world's most beloved monuments.

Holly and River stroll hand-in-hand around the Trocadéro, stepping over the mechanical toys for sale by street vendors, and ignoring their pleas in accented English to check out the tiny Eiffel Tower statues and wind-up dogs displayed on long sheets of fabric.

"You want a coffee?" River asks, tugging lightly at Holly's left hand.

"I want to go to the top first." Holly looks up at the majestic tower in the distance, turning her shoulder so that she won't bump into a woman pushing a stroller. "I'm dying to see the city from nearly a thousand feet in the air."

"Are you sure? We could get a snack first—our tickets are for two o'clock and it's only one now," River offers, leading her through the throngs of tourists wielding selfie sticks and fancy cameras.

"Let's go down and see how long the wait is," she says.

The line to get into the tower is long, but Holly isn't unhappy as she waits. She watches the armed guards circulate around the base of France's most popular tourist spot. A man in front of them is speaking rapid Italian to his four young children, offering cookies to the smallest one as they wait to be searched by security. Holly opens her backpack in preparation for the checkpoint; she's already grown used to the necessary step of having a stranger paw through her belongings and look at her appraisingly before she boards a train or enters a building.

The ride to the top is fast, and even the jammed elevator doesn't quell her enthusiasm.

"We're going to see everything from up here," she says in River's ear. "The Arc de Triomphe, the Champs Elysées, Notre Dame." Holly's feeling rhapsodic at the classic view that awaits them, but she notices River's hand tightening around her own as they ascend, and he's staring at the floor like he needs to reassure himself that it's still there. "You okay?"

River shakes his head, not looking up. "No. But I will be," he says tersely.

"Wait, is this scaring you?" Holly can't believe it. Mr. Adventure, Mr. Say Yes to Everything is actually looking pale and slightly clammy. "River, we're fine," she promises.

"I think we should go back down," he says.

Holly laughs incredulously. "Are you kidding?" she asks, knowing that he's not.

"No. This feels weird."

"We don't have to do this," Holly says, pulling him out of the way of human traffic. "But I wish you would have told me before we came up that you didn't want to." They huddle next to the center of the structure and River places his back against the cool metal, watching anxiously as people scamper over to the railings to peer out at the City of Light.

"Can't say no." River sounds like he's short of breath. "Gotta say yes to everything."

"Look, we can go back down. It's cool. I can say I've been up here,"

Holly says gently, holding his hand again. People are walking by, shooting the occasional glance at River. Holly watches the families in matching berets, the children wearing shorts and summer dresses as the mothers tiredly wave people into formation. They hold their cameras in place, no doubt trying to capture Facebook-worthy shots of their trip to Paris.

"No, let's hurry up and see the city," River says, looking less convinced than he sounds.

"But we're at the top of the Eiffel Tower! I wish you weren't in such a hurry to get back to the ground. It's kind of a downer," Holly says. "What feels weird about this? You went on that swing in Amsterdam like it was nothing."

River inhales through his nose, holds it for a second, and then exhales. "I think it's the security everywhere," he says, nodding. "Yeah, it's making me a little nervous. And the dudes with the machine guns on the ground just set me on edge."

"So it's not the height?" Holly takes his hand and starts walking towards the view of the city that's spread out all around them in muted shades of beige and stone, punctuated by patches of green.

"No," River says definitively. "I'm not afraid of heights." The words are barely out of his mouth when a shove from behind sends him plowing into Holly, knocking them both to their knees. The people around them make startled noises, some giving sharp barks of pain as their bare skin hits the patterned metal floor.

"What—?" Holly raises her head, hands and knees still planted on the ground. Her backpack has slipped from her hands and River is crouched on top of it.

Two men in black pants and black t-shirts rush through the crowd of fallen, frightened people, shouting in an unfamiliar foreign language. The woman next to Holly whimpers to herself as one of the men steps on her fingers with a heavy black boot. There is a feeling of chaos and uncertainty as Holly peers up at the men and at the shocked faces of everyone around her.

A siren sounds from below, and a rush of uniformed guards spreads through the confused crowd, fanning out with their heavy artillery. River reaches over and puts an arm around Holly protectively.

"*Descendez, reste en bas!*" shout the armed guards. "Get down, stay down!" they repeat in English. Even in the middle of the confusion, people obey.

Near the railing that looks out over the seventh arrondissement below, a guard pins one of the men in black against a thick beam. His face is pressed to the metal, hands behind him as the guards chase after the other man. Holly watches from under the shelter of River's strong arm, heart racing. It's all happening at lightning speed, but the seconds pass by in a way that feels like time has slowed to an interminable crawl. In these weird seconds and moments, the entire trip so far spins through Holly's brain like a movie: the flight across the Atlantic; getting mugged (that feels like years ago!); going to the modeling agency by Harrod's; seeing The Cure in Amsterdam and sending off an email to Bonnie during the stolen minutes while River was at the store. *Bonnie!* Her mind reels as she thinks of home. She'll need to email Bonnie again—or, better yet, call her—as soon as she can. River will just have to deal with her breaking the rules of their game. And after this fiasco, how could he not understand her need to reach out and touch Christmas Key in any way she can?

The thoughts that fill her head feel lucid and linear, but as the guards capture and pin the other man, Holly realizes that she's in shock. She's watching people with machine guns, actual *heavy artillery*, as they apprehend suspects, and the only thing she can think of is Main Street. The light posts wrapped in tinsel for the holidays. The front window of Mistletoe Morning Brew painted to reflect whatever is going on inside during any given month. The way people slow in their golf carts to chat with each other outside her office window every day.

"We can get up," River croaks, sounding a little out of it himself. He gets to his feet stiffly, offering Holly a hand. The people around them look this way and that, making sure the coast is clear before they stand. A new wave of confusion winds its way around the top deck of the tower as people who speak a multitude of different languages try to figure out what's happening and what just went down.

"What are we supposed to do?" Holly asks, reaching down for her backpack. "I don't understand."

River takes her hand and laces his fingers through hers with urgency. He's holding her tightly and watching the guards for an indication of what happens next.

"I think they'll have us clear the tower," he says. Holly's not sure whether he's overheard this or is intuiting it, but she nods mutely, leaning into his arm for physical and emotional support.

The two men in black are hogtied and lifted from the ground by their bound wrists and ankles like they're made of foam, and the guards surround them both as they spirit them away. The remaining guards assume positions near the elevators and start to shout orders in English.

"Line up, single file here, please," says a woman in fatigues with a severe bun and a rifle strapped across her chest. Her English is precise and barely accented. "We will be taking the elevators down immediately and evacuating the tower as quickly as possible."

"Stay calm, please do not panic," says a male guard. He paces through the crowd, eyeing each of them warily. "Please be aware of your surroundings, and do not leave anything behind."

Holly and River trip through the line behind everyone else, waiting their turn to step into the elevator. It's a surreal feeling. Everyone around them looks just as stunned as Holly feels.

They don't speak on the way down to the ground level, and when they step off the elevator, River grabs Holly's elbow and guides her through the line of people waiting to exit the monument. On their way out, guards search their bags once more and they're forced to show their identification and to write down contact information in a log book.

The streets around the tower are shut down to both pedestrian and automobile traffic, and there's an eerie quiet as they walk back up to Trocadéro, taking long steps to get themselves away from the tower as quickly as possible.

"What the hell just happened?" River finally says, stopping in his tracks. Holly stops and turns to face him, hands looped through the straps of her backpack. "Who were those guys?" Several different layers of understanding and confusion are peeled back behind River's eyes as Holly watches him.

Holly thinks for a moment. "I don't know," she says. "But it was terrifying." Her chest tightens with a feeling that's as solid and undeniable as concrete. Without another thought, she realizes what she already knows in her heart to be true. "I want to go home."

"Yeah, let's get back to the apartment and just grab something to eat so that we don't have to leave again today." River holds out an arm so that Holly can tuck herself beneath it.

She stays put. A certainty builds inside of her that she hasn't felt in a while. It's the certainty that saying yes to everything can't be right. Saying yes to *some* things is good, but there's a time and a place to tap the brakes, and for Holly, this moment is it.

"No, I mean *home*. Christmas Key. I'm ready." She stares up at him, unblinking.

"But we still have a week and a half." River frowns at her.

Holly shakes her head. "I need to get back."

A dark cloud passes over River's handsome face in stark contrast to the blue skies overhead. "You *need* to get back, or you *want* to get back?"

Holly shrugs and looks around as people stream past them and away from the tower. "Both, I guess."

River stares at a spot just beyond Holly's right shoulder. "So we have one scare and you go running back to the island, huh? Is this how it's always going to be?"

"One scare, River?" Holly asks incredulously. "In addition to being robbed, we just got caught in some sort of terrorist nightmare at the top of the freaking Eiffel Tower," she spits, pointing at the iron pyramid in the distance. It stands proudly against the late Spring sky, its solid countenance giving no indication that anything is amiss.

"We don't know that," he argues. "It could have been two protestors who got out of hand."

"*You* were the one who didn't even want to go up," Holly points out. "You said it felt wrong."

"So maybe we should have gone to the Louvre first." River makes a face that belies the shock Holly had seen in his eyes as they'd waited to come down from the top of the tower. "Listen, Hol—life is short. We can't keep pushing things away just because we feel a little fear. Do you really want to be stuck on an island with one paved road for the rest of your life?"

The blood in Holly's veins runs cold. *This again*. But this time it's not from Jake—it's from River. "I'm not *stuck* on Christmas Key," she says plainly.

"You know that's not what I meant."

"But it is," she says, feeling a calmness that she hasn't felt since before she buckled herself into her airplane seat in Miami. "Why do people think I have to choose? And why is it so wrong if Christmas Key is what I really want? It's always one or the other—with everyone."

"If you're comparing me to Jake, then you can stop right there." River holds up a hand.

"I'm not comparing you to Jake," Holly assures him. "That's apples and oranges. But I'm tired of being made to feel like the *real* adventure is somewhere else when the only adventure I really want is fifty miles from Key West in the middle of the Gulf of Mexico."

River's jaw tightens and he looks at the concrete beneath their feet. He nods slowly. "So this is it. Again. Only this time you aren't choosing another guy over me, you're choosing an island."

"I'm happy not to *have* to choose," Holly says, shifting her heavy backpack on her shoulders. She takes a step back and walks in a circle, her frustration evident as she paces. "How did this go from a trip to the top of the Eiffel Tower to us having this conversation right here?" Her nostrils flare angrily.

"You're just rattled, and you're taking it out on me," River says. His voice has grown firm again, and the discomfort he'd felt at the trip up the tower has been erased.

"Rattled? Yeah, a near-death experience will do that to a girl."

"Don't exaggerate," River scoffs.

"Look, you can call it what you want, but I'm done. I want to go home. I'm tired of this game where I can't call home, or check my email, or talk to Bonnie about work. All of that is a huge part of who I am, and that's what's been eating away at me—I'm missing a piece of myself."

River takes this in. "Okay," he says, weighing her words. "How about if we find a way for you to check in every day or two?"

"I'm not looking to compromise on this, River." The indignation that's been blooming behind Holly's ribs suddenly wilts. "This has been a good experiment, and I've gotten everything I need from it."

"An 'experiment'?" He gapes at her. "Coming to Europe with me was nothing more than an *experiment* for you? Huh." River's eyes glaze over as he looks at the tower behind Holly. "When did this train jump the tracks? Because I think I missed it."

"It didn't jump the tracks," Holly says. "There've been some really amazing things that have happened on this trip, and there've been some not so amazing things, too."

River takes a step closer and Holly can smell the perspiration mixed with the musky scent of his deodorant. "I guess I need to ask which parts have been so bad."

"Like I said, not being in contact with home. The *idea* of saying yes to everything without hesitation is a good one, but the reality is much...harder. I can't fly by the seat of my pants like you do. It's not who I am."

"But you tried," River says drily. "Or at least you tried harder than when I came to see you at Christmas."

"That's not fair." Holly's cheeks go pink like he's just slapped them.

"It's not fair for you to bail out like this in the middle of a trip just because you don't know who booked a weekend trip to Christmas Key. It's not fair of you to throw in the towel on an adventure where we've seen The Cure in Amsterdam and gotten an offer to be extras on a movie set in Dublin. It's not fair of you to lose it after two weird dudes trigger a military response in Paris. It's not fair to just give up on the rest of the trip."

"Oh, we're doing the not fair game?" Holly lowers her chin and raises her eyebrows at him. "How about this: it's not fair that you get to infringe on me running my business and that you pass judgment on where I want to spend my life." River opens his mouth to protest, but Holly plows on. "It's not fair that I lost my phone, but you still had yours handy to put Sarah's number into. It's not fair that you've called all the shots on this trip, from us going on that swing over Amsterdam, to telling me I was eating too many desserts."

River closes his eyes with exaggerated patience. "I knew you were going to throw that back at me. I was kidding, Holly. That was supposed to be a joke. And I only took Sarah's number so that we could follow up about going to Dublin."

"Whatever. The point is that you want me to be things that I'm not, and in the end, that's totally unsustainable."

River has no comeback for this. It's like he knows he's lost both the battle and the war, and so he just stands there, letting Holly continue to lob grenades at him.

"So is this what I think it is?" he finally asks.

Holly shrugs. "I'm not sure. I think we should take this trip for what it is and assess the damage when we get home."

River's face is awash with regret and disappointment. "Wow," he says. "And here I was thinking that this trip was pretty fantastic. I had no idea you felt imprisoned."

It's a decent description of how Holly's been feeling, even though she hasn't thought of it in those exact terms. "I'm sorry, River."

"No, I'm the one who should be sorry," he says, holding both palms out to her. "Clearly my idea of a fun adventure is your idea of unwilling captivity. I can't..." He runs his hands through his hair, shaking his head. "I'm kind of at a loss for words here, Hol. This conversation totally veered off course."

They're both silent as they stand there. Sirens fill the air in the distance and police and military vehicles move in on the Eiffel Tower, its patrons still streaming away from the monument and disappearing into the city streets beyond.

"Let's go back to the apartment," Holly says softly, moving into River's personal space. Without being invited, she puts her hands on his hips and looks up at him. "This isn't what you think it is," she assures him. "The whole thing just took a sharp left for me when we had to hit the deck up there and try not to get trampled. All the things that haven't been working for me kind of snowballed and I realized that I'm at that point." Holly tugs at the sides of his t-shirt with both hands as she gazes at the firm set of his jaw. "It's just time for me to go home."

After what feels like an hour, River looks down at her face. There's a distance in his eyes that makes Holly feel cold. River takes a step away from her, forcing her to let go of the grip she's got on his shirt. "Then I guess you need to go. Let's head back and change your ticket."

22

Millie's gray countenance and the look of shock in her eyes has everyone on edge. Ray's loss has been a very real reminder that even in paradise, there's no such thing as immortality. As planned, the women are busy cranking out meals in the B&B's kitchen and keeping Millie company as she readjusts to a life without her husband of forty-two years.

"I'll just run this dish out to Millie's and be right back," Iris Cafferkey says to no one in particular. She slides a tray of mini-quiche off the steel countertop in the kitchen and uses her backside to bump open the swinging door.

"I've got a right mind to email Holly again and tell her what's going on," Bonnie says to the other women. She wipes her forehead with the back of her hand and rests her hip against the counter. "I can't imagine how she's going to feel coming back to this and not knowing about Ray before she sets foot on the island."

"Still can't understand how she could leave us for more than two weeks and just go incommunicado," Maria Agnelli grumbles. "Doesn't seem right."

"She did email me back once," Bonnie admits. "But all she said was that she lost her phone or something and would check back in as soon as she could. I didn't bother to use that group text thing that Jake set up to tell you all because there wasn't all that much to share."

Quiet up until this point, Coco sees her entry into the conversation and pipes up. "Now, Maria," she says indulgently. "She's just trying to do what she thinks her grandfather would want her to do. She was always a bit of a granddaddy's girl. And while I admire her for trying to play mayor, I think she's out of her element."

"You've made that quite clear," Bonnie snaps, swinging around to face Holly's mother. "You don't miss an opportunity to tell us all that she's just a kid—which, at thirty years old, she is most definitely not —and that it's time for her to hang it up and let you make the decisions."

"Bonnie," Coco says in a soothing tone. "I'm not asking her to hand everything over to me. I don't mind if she still wants to run your little meetings and sit there at her desk," she points in the general direction of the B&B's back office, "presiding over you all like the Queen of Main Street, I just think it's high time she get some counsel from someone who sees the bigger picture."

The women in the kitchen all studiously look away from this exchange, busying themselves with refrigerator organization, counter cleaning, and ingredient prep while still carefully listening to every word that's being exchanged.

"Coco," Bonnie says. Her exasperation has finally reached its boiling point. "I'm going to be honest with you, and you can thank me for it or not, but here goes: Nobody likes your damn ideas, and nobody wants you here meddling in our lives. So why don't you just head on out?"

The sound of minor kitchen activity is the only noise in the room as Coco and Bonnie stare one another down. Coco's nostrils flare, the mental calculations of her next move apparent on her face.

"She speaks the truth," Maria Agnelli says, putting one bony fist on her hip. "You're too young to be this much of a sour-faced prune, Coco, and none of us like it much when you come around and stick your nose in our business like a dog sniffing at the mailman's crotch."

Calista snorts from the other side of the room. "Sorry," she whispers as several sets of eyes turn to her.

Coco's mouth opens and closes a few times. "Well," she says. "I know you're all loyal to Holly—some of you to the point of insanity —," she shoots Bonnie a meaningful look, "but I was hoping that you'd be willing to hear the voice of reason and to consider looking after your own best interests."

"Coco," Gwen says, closing the refrigerator door. Her identical sisters are at the counter next to her. "We've just lost someone we love this week, and one of our own is hurting. Would it kill you to back off for a bit and just let us grieve and attend to Millie?"

Coco and Bonnie narrow their eyes at one another for a few seconds more. Finally, with the air of someone who is giving in but not entirely giving up, Coco tosses the spatula that's in her hand onto the counter.

"Of course," she says in an overly gracious tone. "I can wait for Holly. In fact, I'll just take my stuff out to her house now and set up camp there so that I stay out of your hair."

As she storms out of the kitchen, there is an audible sigh of relief from everyone except Bonnie. Her goal had been to shut Coco down and get her off the island for good, *not* to send her over to Holly's to mess with her belongings and sleep in her bed.

"Let's get back to work, ladies," Bonnie says. She reaches for Coco's discarded spatula and sets it upright in the container that holds cooking utensils. "Millie needs us right now."

AND MILLIE DOES NEED THEM. She's all but fallen apart at the sudden loss of her husband, and her ability to take on even the most basic tasks has faltered. Fiona and Calista are tag-teaming in order to make sure that someone is always with her or in close proximity, and Fiona has offered to write her a scrip for sleeping pills if she needs them.

"I'm fine, girls," Millie says tiredly, her eyes telling them that she's anything but. "It just takes time to get over the shock. Wait—how

much time *does* it take?" She turns to Fiona, obviously hoping that
her medical expertise extends to matters of the heart.

"I don't know, Millie," Fiona says honestly. "Everyone is different.
The symptoms of emotional shock can vary in each person, but a
psychological trauma can be really overwhelming."

"We need you to lean on us, okay?" Calista bends forward in her
chair to look Millie in the eye. "However long this takes. In fact, if you
need me to stay here at night for a while so that you aren't alone, I'm
happy to leave my mother-in-law in charge of the boys," she offers.

Fiona throws her a look. Calista's made no secret around the
island that adjusting to Idora-ble the Horrible being in her home has
been a less than smooth transition. But her offer to stay with Millie is
sincere—if a little self-serving—and so Fiona merely gives her a
flicker of exasperation when their eyes meet.

"I think I'm okay," Millie says slowly. "I like having you ladies
around—and everyone else, too—but at some point I'm going to have
to figure out how to do this alone." She pushes herself up from the
couch and stands in the middle of her living room, looking around.
Everywhere are signs and reminders of Ray. His favorite chair with
the impression of his large frame pressed into the cushions; the
remote on the coffee table that he always seemed to clutch as he
dozed in front of the television; the curtains he'd lovingly hung for
her as she'd stood in the middle of the room, directing his every
move. A sob escapes her.

"Oh, Millie," Calista says, opening her arms to wrap her friend in
a tight embrace. "What can we do?" The question is almost rhetori-
cal, as they all know that there's nothing to be done. Nothing, really,
that will quell the pain of losing the man she's spent forty-two years
sleeping beside. Nothing that will ease the heartache of realizing over
and over again each day that he's gone. Nothing that will bring
Ray back.

"It's okay, it's okay," Millie says, giving Calista a firm hug and
releasing her. She wipes at her eyes and shakes her head. The gold
hoops she always wears sway on her lobes. "I need to ride the waves
of emotion and also start being practical at the same time."

"Don't force yourself into practicality too soon," Fiona says. "That's what we're here for. We'll deal with the practical."

"You've all been so kind to help me with phone calls and arrangements," Millie says, holding out a hand to each of the women. They take her hands in theirs. "But I still have a business to run. I can't just let the salon go—Ray helped me to make that happen. He wouldn't want me to curl up in a ball and just give up."

Calista tugs on Millie's hand. "No one is expecting you to give it up, but no one is expecting you to get over there and open up for manicures and mustache trims, either. Give this time, Mill. Honestly."

"Calista is right," Fiona agrees. "The business isn't going anywhere. I'm sure you and Holly can work out the financial details of the space and all of that..." Fiona's voice trails off as she notices Millie's face crumpling. "Oh, Millie—no," she begs. "I'm so sorry. Was that too much practicality all at once?" Fiona puts a hand over her mouth in horror—she had no intention of bringing Millie to tears.

"No, no, no," Millie waves a hand at her. "It's just that Ray dealt with all the business stuff and I got to have fun with the salon itself. Now I need to figure out how to do it all."

"Okay, let's worry about that later. I promise I won't bring it up again, but let's just agree to table all of the details until Holly gets back, okay?"

"Oh!" Millie says urgently. "Holly! We can't have the service until Holly gets back."

Fiona and Calista exchange a look. They still have about ten days until Holly's return, and the general consensus on the island is that the service for Ray should happen sooner rather than later.

"You want to wait until the first week of June?" Fiona asks gently.

"I...I don't know. I guess so. I mean, we can't do this without Holly—that would be wrong." Millie's eyes well up with unshed tears. Holly being gone is just one more thing to handle, and at the moment, it seems like it's the straw that's threatening to break the camel's back.

"Let's talk about the date later," Calista says soothingly, slipping an arm around Millie's shoulders. "Why don't we go take a walk on the beach or something?"

"We could do that," Millie agrees. "Just to get out of the house."

"Okay, why don't you two do that and I'll check in with Bonnie and see if she's heard anything from Holly lately." Fiona picks up her purse from the couch and slips the strap over one shoulder.

The women agree to touch bases later, and Fiona heads toward Main Street in her golf cart, her thoughts on the memorial service and the things that need to be accomplished in order to pull off the type of ceremony Ray deserves.

At the corner of Main Street and Holly Lane Fiona nearly plows into Coco, who is standing in the middle of the street with her phone held in the air. Fiona skids to a stop, her tires grinding against sand at the spot where the paved road of Main Street meets unpaved Holly Lane.

"What the hell are you doing?" she shouts, putting her cart in park and climbing out. The sun is bright, and the glare has nearly blocked her view of Coco.

Coco puts the phone down with annoyance. "I was videotaping."

"Videotaping your own demise?" Fiona is several inches shorter than both Holly and her mother, but that doesn't stop her from squaring up to Coco like she's got the goods to back it up. "Listen," Fiona says. "We've got a lot going on around here and a memorial to plan. I get that you're going to stay at Holly's until she gets back, but I think the less people see of you, the better."

"Let's hear how you really feel, Dr. Potts," Coco says drily.

"I'm not going to mince words with you." Fiona lifts her chin, flipping her long, wavy hair over one freckled shoulder. "I know your plan is to just stick around and grind us all down to the point that we give in and do what you want, but you have to know Holly well enough to know that that'll never work with her."

Coco shrugs and holds her phone up again. She taps the screen to start videotaping. "This is the corner of Holly Lane and Main Street, which is ripe for development. If you continue on down Holly Lane, there's plenty of room to add a two or three story apartment complex, which could house casino workers on a temporary or permanent basis," she says to an unseen audience. "I think this is a solid answer to the issue of where the influx of residents would live."

"Coco," Fiona says loudly, interrupting the video. "What are you doing?"

Coco steps around the cart that Fiona's left parked in the middle of the road, walking down Holly Lane toward the Jingle Bell Bistro. "I'm making a video to send to other potential investors," she says breezily, not pausing to turn back. "And if we head down Holly Lane, I think there's the potential to add a small store and maybe another business or two to support the needs of our new residents..."

Fiona watches in awe as Coco's toned backside sways in her yellow shorts. She points her phone's camera at sand dunes and undeveloped plots of land, explaining her vision for the island to the Killjoys or to whomever else she might be trying to sell off her chunk of paradise.

With a shake of her head, Fiona climbs back into her cart and drives on, parking on the street right in front of Poinsettia Plaza. It's Sunday and she doesn't normally open her office unless someone needs to be seen urgently, but it seems like the only place to go and think without the distractions of being at home or sitting with Buckhunter at Jack Frosty's.

Fiona is sitting at her computer with the blinds drawn, splitting her time between updating her notes on the past week's visits with patients and putting together a timeline for Ray's memorial service. From the notes she's got to write up about the small lump she's found in Maria Agnelli's left breast, to the considerations of how best to give a proper send off for a friend and neighbor, the darkened office seems like the appropriate place to hide out from the piercingly joyful afternoon sunshine.

She's been lost in her tasks for almost two hours when the cell phone on her desk rings. It's an unfamiliar number and area code, but Fiona answers anyway, thinking it might be one of the many friends or family members she's left messages for calling her back about Ray and Millie.

"Hello?" she says, sliding off her reading glasses and setting them on the keyboard of her laptop.

"Fee?"

"Hol?" Fiona stands up, shoving her chair back with her legs as she does. "Where are you?"

"I'm in Paris. Listen, I don't have a lot of time—"

"Wait, is this River's phone?" Fiona holds the phone away from her ear and looks at the number again.

"Yeah, it is. But Fee, I'm coming home."

"Wait—now?" Fiona walks to the window and twists the handle on the blinds so that they open to reveal the quiet sidewalks of Main Street. "You're coming home before the end of your trip?"

"Tonight," Holly says. "We're back at the apartment here and I'm packing. I take off in about four hours, and I land in Miami tomorrow morning. If I go directly to Key West and catch a boat, I can be on Christmas Key by late afternoon."

"I have questions," Fiona says. Her mind is racing. "But I'm guessing you aren't going to answer them now."

"You guessed right." Holly's tone is grim. "I need to finish packing, and River and I have a few things to discuss."

"Wow."

"Yeah. And listen—if you see the news, don't freak out. We were at the top of the Eiffel Tower when it happened, but everything is fine."

"When what happened?" Fiona leaves the window and rushes back to her laptop. "What's going on?"

"Don't worry about it unless you see it. But I need you to do me a favor."

Fiona sits down in her chair and puts her reading glasses back on. She types CNN into the search bar at the top of her screen as she listens. "Anything, Hol. What is it?"

"I need you to tell Bonnie that I'm on my way, but I'd rather not have it be a big deal. I'm going to be jet-lagged and I'm kind of in a weird space, so I'd like to just get back to my house as quickly as possible and deal with everything the next day."

Fiona chews on her lower lip as she thinks about the stuff that

Holly's coming home to. "Holly..." She needs to let her know that Coco is staying at her house, otherwise her best friend is going to get home expecting a chance to get back on track in peace and quiet at her own bungalow. "I don't know how to tell you this—"

"Don't tell me yet," Holly interrupts. "I don't think I can take anything else right now. Seriously. Whatever it is can wait until I'm home."

Fiona wants to disagree, but in the end she knows Holly is right. "Okay. Let me know when you're leaving Key West so I know when to expect you. Have a safe trip."

"See you tomorrow, Fee."

They end the call and Fiona turns her attention back to CNN. There, at the top of the page above a picture of the Eiffel Tower, is the big, bold headline: TERROR AND CONFUSION AT THE TOP OF THE TOWER. Fiona scrolls down and clicks the link, scanning it for details. Her heart races as she sees the words *unidentified nationalities; possibly armed;* and *unknown motives.* She has no idea what's going on with Holly and River, but the idea of her best friend somehow landing in the middle of a terrorist plot—one that was foiled or not—sends a cold, prickling fear up and down her spine. The most important thing right now is the fact that Holly is coming home.

23

"So," River says, watching her pack as she sets his phone back on the dresser. "This is it? I can't change your mind? Maybe convince you to give it another day or two?"

Holly rolls up her jeans and shoves them into one corner of her suitcase. "Nope," she says, walking across the creaky, uneven wood floors of the ancient building. She flips on the bathroom light and scoops up the bottles and products on the counter that belong to her. "I need to get back. I could tell that Fiona had things she wasn't telling me, and I'm ready to get to the bottom of it."

It's mostly true, but not entirely. The other part of her has already started transitioning from the mindset of being on vacation and being with River, and in her head she's envisioning herself back in her own bed, hogging up as much of it as she wants and sharing her house only with Pucci. She's ready for the comfortable familiarity of her own life again.

"Holly," River says on a sigh, sinking onto the corner of the stiff IKEA bed. "I want this to work somehow. It feels like everything was great, and then you got this wild hair about going home."

"It's not a wild hair." She folds two t-shirts together and rolls them lengthwise like a long salami. "It's time. I've had fun, but I'm ready to be back at home, and you're ready to move on to Dublin and hang out with Sarah again."

"Don't make it about that, because it's not." River's voice sounds angry and tired. "It's about your inability to say yes to things in life—including me."

Holly would have been more angry at that blanket statement, but she knows it isn't true, so instead she just smiles. "I have learned some things about saying yes, whether you realize it or not."

River inhales patiently, giving her a disbelieving look. "Okay," he says. "I'm listening."

"I realized that I say no way too often in my life to things that could change me for the better. But I also discovered that being able to say no is a privilege that's important to me. I need the option of saying no."

"Okay, so say no to me and to us," River says, standing up from the bed. "Say yes to the island and forget about everything else." He puts his hands in the air in exasperation. The apartment has grown dim in the evening light, and neither of them has made a move to switch on the lamps that are scattered throughout.

"I wish it was that simple." Holly drops her zipped makeup bag into the suitcase and walks over to River. The wooden floor buckles under her weight as she stands on her toes and puts her hands on his shoulders. "But if you're going to understand me at all, then you have to understand this: I can't completely give up control of my life. I tried it, and I don't like it. And I have a responsibility to Christmas Key and to the people who live there. That's all." She's standing in front of him, head tipped up in the perfect position for him to lean down and kiss her tenderly. But he doesn't; instead River removes her hands from his shoulders and steps around her.

"Got it," he says. "Let me call you a cab so you get to the airport on time."

Holly lets her heels touch the floor again, her hands falling to her sides. She feels like she isn't doing a very good job explaining to River what's going on in her head, but she isn't even entirely sure herself what prompted the urgent need to get back to the island immediately.

If she knew, she'd tell him. It isn't as simple as the Eiffel Tower incident shaking her to her core, and it isn't as complicated as their intricate game of saying yes to everything sending her into an existential tailspin. It's some combination of everything woven together with the deep, ingrained understanding that she belongs at home. Now.

From the small front room, Holly can hear River calling for a cab, speaking in choppy English as he gives the address twice and repeats the time that he needs the car to arrive. She carefully places her black boots from Harrods into the suitcase, crossing them so that the heels are at opposite ends of the bag, and then sits down on the bed to put her Converse on her feet. Her Yankees cap will be the final touch, but instead of putting it in on her head, she slips it into her shoulder bag and zips the purse, then clicks the latches on her suitcase and sets it on the floor. She's ready.

THE FLIGHT to Miami is uneventful. Rather than being seated next to a nervous flier who needs to be talked down from the ledge, Holly is sharing a row with a dapper older man in horn-rimmed glasses and a navy blue v-neck sweater. He reads the *Le Parisien* newspaper from cover to cover without saying a word, then uncrosses his legs, sets the paper on the empty seat between them, unlatches his seat belt, and stands.

Holly looks out the window into the darkness. All she can see is the blinking of the light on the plane's wing. The low, steady hum of the engines lulls her. This flight is as full of anticipation as the one that had taken her to London, but in a different way. Now her excitement is for the return to familiarity. She can't wait to feel the sand under her feet as she steps from the boat dock, can't wait to see Mistletoe Morning Brew on her right as she makes her way down Main Street, and she's nearly giddy at the thought of Pucci bounding toward her when he realizes that his mistress has returned.

There's a lot to think about and a lot to do when she gets there, and Holly doesn't want to miss a beat. Throughout this trip with

River, layered over the discomfort and unease of never knowing what was around the corner and of having no control over what they would be doing next, was the growing understanding that she needed more of the unknown in her life. She knows now that she needs more opportunity—beyond the one time leap into the world of reality shows—she needs more possibility, and (maybe most importantly) the island needs her to treat it like it's being run by a woman who's seen the world and knows what's out there.

The man in the v-neck sweater returns and sits in his seat again. He gives Holly a mildly-interested, appraising look over the frames of his glasses and then punches the call button overhead.

"*Pourrais-je obtenir un verre de champagne, s'il vous plaît?*" he says to the flight attendant when she arrives. He turns to Holly as an afterthought. "Champagne?" he asks her.

"Champagne?" Holly repeats, blinking a few times. She hadn't expected him to acknowledge her. "Yes, please. I'd love champagne. *Merci.*"

The flight attendant delivers two glasses of champagne and disappears again, and the man holds his out to Holly so that they can touch the rims together in a casual toast. "*Santé,*" he says, bringing his glass to his lips.

"*Santé,*" Holly says, letting the bubbles tickle her nostrils as she watches the winking red light of the plane again. *Cheers to home,* she thinks, *and to knowing when to say yes, and when to say no.*

24

The sight of the island in the distance is maybe the best thing Holly's ever seen. She stands at the front of the boat, wind whipping through her hair as she watches Christmas Key grow closer as they approach. Everything is just as she remembers it: the palm trees around the dock; the curve of the island as it wraps around and turns into December Drive in both directions; the way the sky looks as it hangs over the most precious piece of land that Holly's ever known.

Within ten minutes, they're pulling up to shore and docking. As promised, Fiona is there to greet her with Bonnie by her side. They both cast furtive glances around to make sure no one is watching (but someone is always watching—Holly knows this) and as soon as Holly's feet are on terra firma, there's a manic scramble to see who gets to hug her first. In an effort to avoid squabbles and hurt feelings, she opens her arms wide and pulls both Fiona and Bonnie to her at once.

"I've missed you both so much," Holly says into their ears as she holds them close. "You have no idea."

"We've missed *you* so much," Bonnie says. "Don't leave us again, sugar. It ain't right!"

"Didn't we find out recently that leaving the island is a bad idea?" Holly asks, pulling back and looking into Bonnie's eyes. "Apparently I didn't learn anything from your adventure in Clearwater."

"Oh, let's not even mention that nonsense!" Bonnie scolds her, swatting away any talk of her ill-fated, short-lived plans to live near Tampa with the weekend pirate she'd met on Christmas Key. He'd turned out to be not only a dud with a flair for the kinky, but his swashbuckling pirate act had been a total misrepresentation of the facts. The women exchange an eye roll as they remember the situation.

"Bonnie and I need to talk to you." Fiona takes a step back and looks at her best friend. "I know you wanted to go home and just sleep it off for a night, but there are a few..."

"Issues," Bonnie offers. "We got issues, sugar."

"And they can't wait until tomorrow?" Holly lets go of the handle of her suitcase and looks at her watch. It's almost five o'clock, but it feels like ten at night. That—combined with the two hours of sleep she'd gotten on the plane the night before and the thick humidity that she's swimming through once again—makes her want nothing more than the cool darkness of her own bedroom.

"It can't," Fiona says. "And to start with, you can't go home."

"What do you mean I can't go home?" Holly frowns at both of them, panic ripping through her. Has her bungalow burned down? Flooded? "What's wrong with my house?"

"Coco's there." Bonnie presses her lips together apologetically. "We tried, but she wouldn't budge. Stubborn old mule."

"What the hell is my mother doing at my house?"

"Well," Fiona says, looking at Bonnie.

"Yes...well," Bonnie says, staring back at Fiona. They're clearly buying time and trying to avoid the inevitable.

"Spit it out. One of you."

"She wants to build a casino."

"What?" Holly's voice blooms like condensation in cold winter air as it leaves her mouth. "Are you freaking *kidding me*? I'm gone for one second, and she's down here trying to build a *casino*?"

"And it's not just the casino," Fiona says. "She's looking at a much bigger picture."

"Okay, I'm listening." In spite of her bone-deep exhaustion, Holly folds her arms across her chest.

"Let's go to my place, sugar," Bonnie pleads. "I've got my guest room set up for you, and Pucci is even there waiting. We tried to get Coco to leave, but she said she was staying until you got back, and we didn't want to tell her that you were coming back today."

Holly does a quick inhale-exhale loop as she runs through a vision of her mother camped out at her house. It doesn't do much to calm her. "Okay," she says. Let's go to your place, Bon."

"We know you're tired," Fiona says, reaching out and putting an arm around Holly's shoulders as they walk toward Bonnie's golf cart. "But there are a few other things we need to talk about before you fall asleep."

"Yeah, doll. You've been out of touch for way too long, and there are some things we need to talk to you about. By the way," Bonnie adds, "never do that again, okay?"

"Never leave you and not check in?" Holly laughs at Bonnie's emphatic tone. Even in the middle of her exhaustion and her fears about what else her friends have to tell her, Holly is elated to be home. "You got it. That's a deal."

BY TEN O'CLOCK, Holly is exhausted and all cried out. Pucci had worked himself into a full-on frenzy at the sight of his mistress, but is now lying calm and happy at her feet. Bonnie and Fiona hadn't been sure whether to tell her about Ray first or all about Coco's plans. In the end, they'd started by letting her know that Katelynn and Logan had arrived safely, and that Idora Blaine-Guy was completely installed at Vance and Calista's house on White Christmas Way. They'd given her the scoop on Gator and the Killjoys' strange visit to the island, and about Coco's plans for a casino, and had let her cool down from that piece of news before finally telling her about Ray's heart attack.

Holly's first response had been to jump up from Bonnie's couch and demand to be taken to him immediately. "Is he back home now? Fee—did you guys take him over to Key West to be seen by a specialist? No offense," she said in a rush, "it's just that you're a general practitioner, and he needs a heart doctor—"

"We rushed him to Key West immediately," Fiona had assured her, "but it was too late, Hol. He died before we got him there."

Holly sits between her two closest friends now, head in her hands, elbows on her knees. Her eyes feel puffy and closed up. "I'm speechless." She shakes her head. "I was only gone for eleven days."

Fiona and Bonnie exchange a look over the top of Holly's head.

"Let's get you to bed, sugar," Bonnie says, running her hand up and down Holly's back soothingly. "I'm sure Calista has Millie settled in for the night, so going to see her won't do anything but get her riled up again, and since Fiona couldn't convince your mother to get out of your house—"

"I tried!" Fiona says defensively. "After I got the call from Holly yesterday I drove over there and told her some story about how Holly wanted us to flea bomb the place, and she didn't buy it. She told me she hadn't seen a single flea, and she wouldn't be leaving until Holly showed up to kick her out herself."

"It's okay. I'm happy to stay here." Holly puts one hand on Fiona's knee to calm her. "I just need to sleep. I'll figure everything out tomorrow, but right now my head feels like it weighs a thousand pounds and I have to crash."

The women stand up and Fiona hugs Holly for a full minute, holding her in a tight embrace. "I'm glad you're back," she says into Holly's ear. "Get some rest."

As Fiona lets herself out, Bonnie leads Holly to the guest room, which looks almost more inviting than her own bed. The top cover is folded back to reveal clean, mint green sheets, and Bonnie's brought Pucci's dog bed over and set it on the floor next to the dresser. The overhead fan is on, and the room feels cool and safe.

"You need anything else, you just holler, you hear?" Bonnie stands on her tiptoes and plants a kiss on Holly's cheek. "Sleep tight, sugar. Sure good to have you home again."

All Holly can manage is a "Thanks, Bon," before she slips out of her clothes and into the bed. She doesn't shower, doesn't brush her teeth, doesn't do a single thing before sleep overtakes her.

Bonnie closes the bedroom door softly and leaves the hall light on.

25

The word is out that Holly's home, and speculation is running high about her shortened trip and about her lack of contact during her absence.

"I thought they were going to elope," Iris Cafferkey tells Carrie-Anne and Ellen as they make a fresh batch of coffee at Mistletoe Morning Brew. "Paris is very romantic, you know. It's where Jimmy proposed to me."

"Ellen proposed to me over beers at her daughter's Fourth of July picnic," Carrie-Anne says fondly, winking at her wife.

"While my daughter's cocker spaniel threw up on the floor next to us because she was scared of the fireworks," Ellen remembers.

"If not terribly romantic, then that was at least memorable." Iris picks up the wand that Ellen and Carrie-Anne have left out near the cash register as part of the Harry Potter decor. "Anyhow, I'll have a Butterbeer Latte for myself, and a Muggle Mocha for Jimmy—both to go, please."

"As you wish," Ellen says grandly, ringing up the order while Carrie-Anne starts to make the drinks.

"So this is where we're all gathering to dish the dirt," Maria Agnelli says, coming in on the heels of Cap and Wyatt.

Iris turns around to greet everyone. It's still only seven in the morning, but most of them have been awake for hours. "Didn't you hear, Wyatt? It's almost June."

"I heard," Wyatt says. The sun isn't even high in the sky yet, but he already looks overheated in the crisp Wranglers that he insists on wearing everyday, despite the humidity.

"Shouldn't you be back in Texas now, or are you sticking around for the summer to guard your favorite Southern belle and keep her safe from invading pirates?" Iris cocks an eyebrow at him. Everyone knows that Wyatt hadn't taken too kindly to Bonnie leaving the island with the cantankerous Sinker McBludgeon—weekend pirate extraordinaire—and the fact that he's there past his usual expiration date of April thirtieth is no real surprise.

"Thought I might stick around for a while and see what kind of trouble you all get up to come summer," he drawls.

"Of course." Iris gives him a knowing look as she takes the two to-go cups that Carrie-Anne has set on the counter for her. "You should stick around for the mosquitoes and for hurricane season—loads of fun to be had there, lad."

"Oh, leave the boy alone, Iris," Cap says. "He's a little lovesick, but it's nothing we haven't all been through, right?"

"I haven't been lovesick since 1942," Mrs. Agnelli offers. "His name was Giuseppe, and he worked at his father's salami shop in my village. Beautiful boy." Her eyes glaze over as she remembers. "Nice salami, too." With a cackle, Mrs. Agnelli elbows Cap conspiratorially, though their difference in height means she really just jabs him on the hip.

"Good morning," Heddie Lang-Mueller says, walking through the door of the shop. The small crowd parts as she steps up to the counter to join them. "Can I assume we're discussing Holly's return?" Heddie's gray-blonde hair is swept into a sleek, low bun as always, and she's the only one of the group who appears to be untouched by summer's humidity. She pauses next to Cap, her ballerina-straight posture and improbably smooth skin standing in stark contrast to the signs of time that her fellow islanders and seventy-somethings carry around like badges of honor.

"Of course, love," Cap says, putting a hand gently on Heddie's lower back. It's a small gesture, but it doesn't go unnoticed by anyone. Heddie and Cap have been quietly carrying on with one another for several months, and any time he gently ushers her across Main Street or someone catches them casually speaking in German to one another, smiles and secret looks are exchanged.

"And what's the verdict on her getting back so soon?" Heddie asks, looking up at Cap.

"We don't know. Bonnie wasn't sure about emailing to tell her about Ray, so I can only assume she got back and found out last night. I drove past Bonnie's around nine, and Fiona's cart was parked there, too," Cap says.

"Coco's still at Holly's place," Ellen says from behind the counter. "I heard she wouldn't leave until Holly got back and forced her out."

"I almost forgot we had Coco to deal with." Wyatt leans an elbow against the tall glass case that covers the muffins and scones. "What about that business with her and the casino? Are we done with that yet?"

"Not by a long shot." Cap shakes his head. He's known Coco far too long, and there's no doubt that she'll stick around and stir up trouble for as long as possible.

"It wouldn't hurt for us to have—"

"A village council meeting?" The door to the shop swings open, and Holly steps in. Her hair is still wet from her quick shower at Bonnie's, and she's wild-eyed and desperate for coffee.

"Holly!" Maria Agnelli yelps, tottering over to her with her arms thrown wide. "You're back!"

"Hi, Mrs. Agnelli," she says, letting the older woman rock her back and forth as she hugs her. "Hey, everyone." She waves behind Mrs. Agnelli's back, smiling at Cap and Wyatt, Ellen and Carrie-Anne, at Iris, and at Heddie. "It's so good to see your faces."

"We missed you," Heddie says in her crisp German accent. "It's good to have you home."

"I'm *so* happy to be back," Holly says truthfully, patting Mrs. Agnelli and letting her go. "You have no idea."

"What was that nonsense that happened in Paris while you were gone?" Cap growls, his bushy white eyebrows knitting together. "That Eiffel Tower business—were you in France?"

"I was there—at the Eiffel Tower that day," Holly says as she accepts a hug from Iris.

"No!" Carrie-Anne gasps. "What happened?"

Holly fills them in on the brief but dramatic incident, leaving out the details about how she'd immediately told River she wanted to come home. "And so I just realized that I'd had enough adventure for the time being, and that home was where I needed to be," she sums up neatly.

"Home is where you *belong*," Mrs. Agnelli says, giving a hard nod of her head. "We missed you."

"I missed all of you. And apparently I missed a lot here."

"Ray," Iris says softly, her eyes welling up. "We're all beside ourselves."

"I know." Holly's own eyes fill with tears again, and there's a moment of silent reflection in the coffee shop as they all remember Ray and reabsorb his loss again. "I'm so sorry I wasn't here. And that it happened at all. I still can't believe he's gone."

"We're taking good care of Millie," Cap says. "The womenfolk have everything under control, and the rest of us are on call for anything she needs—anything at all."

"I didn't doubt for a minute that you'd all pull together and help her." Holly wipes under both eyes, giving them a sad smile. "I need to get over to see Millie, so I thought I'd stop and get some coffee and take it to her."

"She'll be happy to see you," Heddie says. "I heard she didn't want to have Ray's service until you got back."

A huge wall of emotion smacks Holly in the face and her eyes overflow again in an instant. The thought that Millie had been concerned about *her* in the midst of her own sadness is almost too much to bear.

"I'm so glad I made it back sooner," Holly says hoarsely. "I can't imagine how she must be feeling."

"Let's get you those coffees." Ellen wipes at her own eyes and starts fixing two drinks. "And maybe a couple of blueberry scones, huh? You can take them over to Ray and Mill—" She catches herself. "I mean over to Millie's."

Holly leaves the rest of the group at the coffee shop and heads out to Millie's bungalow with the steaming coffees in the cup holders of her hot pink golf cart. As she bumps along over the sandy, unpaved roads she takes it all in: the tall palm trees; the cute little houses strung with Christmas lights all year long; the faces of the people she's loved her whole life. This place is *home*.

Millie's curtains are still drawn against the bright morning sun, and Holly knocks tentatively with her knuckles as she holds the coffees and the bag of scones. Millie pulls the door open slowly, her face lighting up when she sees who it is.

"Holly!" She throws the door open wide. "You're home!"

Holly steps into the house and sets everything on the table in the entryway so that she can hug Millie.

"I don't even know what to say," Holly sobs, bending forward slightly so she can embrace her friend. "We all loved him so much."

"I know, honey, I know." Millie shushes her gently. Her own tears have come and gone so many times since Ray's passing that she's surprisingly dry-eyed this morning.

"I didn't know until last night, Mill...I got in and Bonnie and Fiona told me everything. I'm so sorry I wasn't here."

"Wouldn't have a made any difference, sweetheart." Millie steps back from Holly and puts both of her hands on the sides of Holly's face. With her thumbs, she wipes away Holly's tears. Her own eyes well up in response to her young friend's tears, and she drops her hands to her sides decisively. "Now, I smell coffee. Did you bring me coffee?" Millie laces her fingers together under her chin, the gold rings on both hands clinking together as she does.

Holly nods. "Ellen and Carrie-Anne sent scones, too."

"Then let's go out on my lanai and have breakfast before it gets too hot to be outside."

For the next hour, the women pick at the scones and sip their coffee at the little breakfast table out back, sharing stories about Ray and discussing the island, how much it's changed over the years, Millie's plans for the salon going forward, and the memorial service. They laugh, they both cry a little, and Holly's resolve strengthens.

Whether she likes it or not, life is going to change. The island is going to change—it has to. She just needs to stay ahead of it so that she can be the one who says yes or no to whatever is coming down the pike.

~

"OH. YOU'RE BACK." Coco steps into the office of the B&B later that morning, her hair smooth and flat-ironed to hold up against the humidity of late May. Her face is perfectly made-up.

Holly spins around in her desk chair so that she's facing the door. "I'm back," she says simply, her smile tight and not terribly warm. "How was my bed last night?"

"I'm sleeping in the guest room. You can come home and have your bed." Coco eyes the hooks by the door and sees that both Bonnie and Holly have used them for their own bags. She drops her purse onto a chair against the wall. "Nobody is stopping you."

"I'd like my house back. We can get you set up here at the B&B," Holly says, opening up a reservations screen to pick a room for her mother. "Where's Alan?"

"He's at home. Working." Coco stands in the middle of the office awkwardly, watching as Bonnie and Holly tap at their respective keyboards. There's really nowhere for her to make herself at home now that both sides of the desk are taken. "How was Europe?"

"Fine. But I'm glad to be home."

"And River?" Coco folds her bare arms across her toned midsection. She's dressed from head to toe in a white spandex workout suit that shows off her dark hair and the hint of color she's gotten while on the island. On anyone else white spandex might have been a tragic fashion choice, but Coco's pilates and yoga-toned body looks like a million bucks in the stretchy fabric.

As always, Holly is acutely aware that her mother is still in her forties and that she's probably the living definition of the crude acronym "MILF." She tears her eyes away from Coco and looks at the computer screen.

"River is fine. He had a few more things he wanted to do in Europe, but the Eiffel Tower scare was enough for me."

Without even inquiring about the Eiffel Tower incident, Coco moves on to the next topic. "Why couldn't anyone track you down? I stuck around here to keep things running smoothly while you were gone, but we were worried."

"I'm sure." Holly catches Bonnie's eye over the top of their laptop screens, which are situated back-to-back on the desk so that the women face one another. Bonnie's wisely stayed mum throughout this exchange so far. "I lost my phone and was out of touch. It was no big deal."

"It was a very big deal," Coco says, arms still folded. "Ray died."

"I know."

"And I had big island stuff to share with you. But you were nowhere to be found." Coco's look is accusing and petulant.

"Sorry. I lost my phone and was out of touch," Holly repeats. "It was no big deal."

"Did you find your phone again?" Coco nods at the shiny phone at Holly's elbow.

"I stopped in at the Apple store when I got to Miami and bought a new one. Problem solved." She picks up the phone as proof and then sets it down again.

"Well, you're here now, so we need to talk. I have some big news and a huge opportunity to share with you. You've probably heard all about it," Coco says, giving Bonnie an accusing look, "but I want to sit down with you and Leo and tell you both about it myself. Especially since this decision is ultimately between *the three of us*," she emphasizes.

Bonnie's eyes are plastered on Holly's face from across the desk.

For a beat, no one is sure that Holly is even going to respond, but then she turns her head to her mother and blinks twice slowly. "Okay. How about lunch at Jack Frosty's?"

It's Coco's turn to blink repeatedly. "Really?" She obviously expected more pushback from Holly, or some sort of flat-out refusal to listen. "Lunch?"

"Yeah. Noon at Jack's." Holly reaches for a stack of papers and starts shuffling them loudly.

"Okay. I'll run by and tell Leo." Coco picks up her bag and puts the strap over her shoulder. "Is it still fine for me to be using the B&B's golf cart?"

"I don't care," Holly says casually. She clips the stack of papers together and sets them back on her desk. "Oh, but Mom?"

Coco turns in the doorway, eyebrows raised.

"I want you moved back into the B&B before lunch. I've been gone for a while and I want my house to myself." Coco is clearly about to argue when Holly adds, "I'm bringing Pucci home this morning."

Everyone knows that Coco hates Holly's sweet old dog, and these are clearly the magic words to flush Coco out of her house. She sniffs the air and gives Holly a haughty look. "Fine, then I guess I'll have to leave. You know how allergic I am to dogs, Holly."

She's already out the door and stepping down onto Main Street when Holly grins at Bonnie wickedly from across the desk. "Yes," she says. "I know."

26

L unch feels like a showdown. It's high noon when Holly steps up into the open seating area of Jack Frosty's, and Coco is already there, standing at the bar as she waits for Buckhunter to direct them to a table.

"Coco," Holly says with a nod. "Buckhunter."

"Hey, kid," Holly's uncle says with a lift of his chin. "Welcome home."

"Thanks. Where do you want us?"

There's the scrape of a chair across the wood floor and Holly's eyes flick across the bar. It's Jake and a teenage boy Holly's never seen. The table has two empty drink cups on it and two burger baskets with a few leftover french fries.

"Mayor," Jake says, approaching. "Good to see you back."

Holly feels only the slightest flutter in her chest as Jake's eyes lock in on hers. This is good, she tells herself—barely any physical response to his nearness—this is an improvement. Maybe her time away did more than show her Europe; maybe it also dulled her feelings towards her ex even more.

"Hi, Jake." Holly looks at the tall, lanky boy standing just behind Jake's shoulder. He's got short hair and a hint of red to his skin that will soon turn into a deep brown tan. His teeth are straight, and his elbows and knees seem just a touch too big for his youthful limbs.

"This is Logan, Katelynn Pillory's son." Jake turns around and claps a hand on Logan's bony shoulder. "Logan, this is Holly Baxter, our mayor."

Logan's eyes widen just slightly, and though it doesn't seem possible, his skin reddens another shade. "Hi," he says in a voice that somehow breaks on the single syllable. Jake and Buckhunter hide their amusement. Logan clears his throat and tries again. "Hey."

Holly puts out a hand to shake his. "It's nice to meet you, Logan. I've known your mom since we were teenagers." Logan pulls his lips over his teeth self-consciously and gives her a close-lipped smile and a nod. "How is she?"

"She's good." Logan looks at Jake for reassurance. "She's taking care of my great-grandpa right now."

"I'm so glad you two could come down here. How are you liking Christmas Key so far?"

Logan shrugs. "It's pretty quiet. And everyone is..."

"Old?" Holly finishes for him. Buckhunter and Jake laugh while Coco runs a hand over her already smooth hair.

"Yeah. I mean, kinda." Logan puts his hands into the pockets of his shorts and lets his shoulders fall forward. His discomfort is so tangible that Holly feels for him.

"What are you and Jake up to?"

"I convinced him to help me clear up the mess from that spot on December Drive," Jake says.

"Oh, the one where the palm tree is falling apart and blocking the road?"

"That's the one," Jake confirms. "In exchange I told him we'd have lunch and then Cap would take him out on the boat for a bit. It's not easy being the only teenager on the island."

"With no cute girls," Holly says, shooting Logan a sympathetic look. He blushes furiously under his sunburn again.

After an awkward pause that everyone but Holly notices, Jake steps up to the bar and hands Buckhunter a twenty to pay for lunch.

"We'll see you later," Jake says, making eye contact with Coco and Holly and taking his change from Buckhunter. He and Logan head back out to Main Street and cross over to North Star Cigars to meet up with Cap.

"Should we just sit anywhere?" Coco glances around the empty bar.

"This is good," Buckhunter says, tossing two cocktail napkins onto the counter. "We can talk while I clean up back here."

"I was really hoping for your full attention." Coco pouts at him. "Not half your attention while you wipe down tequila bottles and organize your glassware."

"So the island has some new blood," Holly says, hoping to change the subject. "We've got Vance's mom here to watch the twins, and Katelynn and Logan here to take care of Hal..." she trails off, looking out at Main Street. "It's amazing how different it already feels."

"And it could feel even more different." Coco jumps in with both feet, seeing her opening. "Different isn't always bad, Holly. With a few tweaks, we could have this island running like a well-oiled machine. New people, new revenue, new opportunities for exposure."

Buckhunter pours two iced teas and listens from behind the bar. This tug-of-war will be between his half-sister and his niece, and—if anything—his job is to play mediator and tie-breaker.

Holly chooses her words carefully. "I don't disagree with that." She slides the iced tea closer and jabs the ice with a straw. "I had a lot of time to think on my trip, and I do agree that we're missing out on some opportunities because of my stubbornness about change."

Coco visibly pulls back. For a moment, she's speechless. Even Buckhunter stops what he's doing to watch Holly's face, which gives away nothing.

"The reality show was fun and we got some crazy exposure from that, but an influx of tourists—particularly if they're only seasonal— isn't necessarily going to keep us afloat."

"Have we had that much of a reaction?" Coco asks, holding her iced tea in one manicured hand.

Holly nods. "Yeah, we've had tons of activity on social media, and

Bonnie says there are some bookings through the end of the year that are a direct result of *Wild Tropics*. I missed a lot by being gone and not having my phone handy, but she says we get calls and emails almost daily from people who want to come to Christmas Key."

One side of Buckhunter's mouth curls into a smile as he watches his niece hold court with her mother. "Good work, kid," he says quietly.

"Thanks." Holly smiles at him and they exchange a look. Their alliance is strong, and they both know that their votes will outweigh anything that Coco throws at them if need be. "So, let's hear all about whatever it is you're cooking up now." Holly turns to face her mother.

"I've got investors ready to bring a casino to the island, and we've already done the hard work."

"Such as?" Holly lifts an eyebrow.

"Scouting a location, surveying the island to see where we could expand and grow, looking into the kinds of utilities and services we'd need to support that kind of growth."

"And?" Holly sets her feet on the rungs of the barstool and prepares to hear all the ways her mother wants to dismantle her island.

"Casino on the north side," Coco launches in. "New apartment-style housing on the south side near the Jingle Bell Bistro. There are plenty of spots that could be developed with new stores and businesses, and we'd need a newer, bigger dock to support arrivals and departures."

Holly nods. "Who are the investors?"

Buckhunter scratches his bare arm as he leans against the bar. Still, he says nothing.

"Netta and Brice Killjoy would be the financial backers—"

"What do they do that they have that kind of money?"

"Investments, I think. And dot-com money."

"Ah." Holly takes another drink of her iced tea. "Go on."

"We had a representative of the Seminole tribe here to talk about using the land for a casino, and he's willing to come back to talk to you about how we'd work with the tribe to build and run the whole thing."

"Huh." Holly is intentionally keeping her thoughts in her head for the time being, though she has plenty she'd like to say. "Well, I think it would be best to sleep on this for a few days and then reconvene after I've had a chance to go over some pros and cons. Should I call you at home when I'm ready to talk about it?"

Buckhunter intentionally steps away from the women, turning his back so that Holly can process what he already knows is coming.

"I'm not sure I'm headed back up there anytime soon," Coco says. She crosses her legs under the wooden counter of Buckhunter's bar. "I've been feeling a little restless in New Jersey, and I think it would be good for me and Alan if I stepped away for a bit and got my head together."

"At a spa," Holly adds. The patient façade of neutrality drops. "You need to step away and get your head together at a *spa*, not on my island."

Coco's jaw drops. "I have every bit as much right to be here as you do, Holly. And this isn't *your* island."

Holly holds her tongue. Coco is right: Christmas Key isn't technically just her island, but in her heart it is.

"I have some ideas of my own," Holly says. "But I need a little time to get my thoughts together. Since I missed the last village council meeting, I'm thinking of calling one here soon." She stands up and smooths her shorts over the tops of her thighs.

"So that's it?" Coco shakes her head, looking back and forth between Holly and Buckhunter. "Holly isn't ready to decide, so we all sit on pins and needles while we wait for her to catch up. That's all there is?"

"That's all there is for now," Buckhunter says. His eyes dance playfully as he watches the firm set of his niece's jaw. "Give the girl a chance to re-acclimate to island life, and then we'll get the scoop. I promise."

~

HOLLY IS TAKING big strides as she walks the beach with Pucci at her side that evening. The sun has just started to set and the humidity in the air is finally retreating. Getting over her jet lag after coming this direction has been no big deal, and the walk is both invigorating and good for her mind.

The waves tear across the sand and lap over Holly's bare feet, covering them with the warm Gulf water. Of all of the people and things she missed on her trip, she has to admit that it's probably the beach she missed the most. And Pucci. And her bed. Oh, and Bonnie and Fiona and...well, she's missed all of it.

"Here, boy!" Holly whistles for Pucci as he takes off down the sand. It's not that she's worried he'll get lost or into mischief, but more that she's missed him and wants to see him at her side, brushing against her bare legs as they walk. "Want me to throw your ball?" she calls out. Pucci doubles back eagerly, his pink tongue hanging from one side of his mouth. Holly wings the yellow tennis ball into the surf and watches as her dog bounds in after it, the water slicking his golden fur to his body. She smiles at his wagging tail.

Having her mother here is going to be interesting, and not necessarily in a good way. She's going to have to get to the bottom of this nonsense about Coco needing to take a step back from her life with Alan; in fact, maybe a call to her stepfather is in order here to see exactly what's going on. Calling him isn't her first choice, but if she has any hope of getting Coco off the island, she's going to have to start digging a little.

Her cell phone is in the back pocket of her pink shorts. Holly slides it out and presses the button to turn on the screen. There are several notifications from Instagram and Facebook (people who watched *Wild Tropics* still follow and comment on Christmas Key's social media daily, and Holly makes a mental note to do better about commenting and responding to everything). There's also a missed call from River, which surprises her. She presses the voicemail button and puts the phone to her ear.

"I hope you got home okay. I hate that you left." There's a muffled noise as he shifts the phone around, and Holly can hear voices in the background. "Anyway, we tried, right? We took this thing off the island to see if it would float, and I guess it didn't. If you ever feel like talking, you know where to find me." There's more background noise and chatter, and she can picture him in a pub somewhere, making this call after a pint or two. The message ends, and she listens to it again.

Hearing River's voice has taken the wind out of her sails a little bit in terms of calling Alan, but it still needs to be done. With a sigh, she scrolls through her contacts until she finds her stepfather's cell number.

"Holly?" Alan answers after two rings. "Is everything okay?"

"Hey, Alan. Everything is fine." She takes a step into the water and stops there, looking out at the orange glow on the horizon. Pucci trots over to her and drops the soggy tennis ball next to her right foot. "I just wanted to call because I got back from a trip and found my mother here."

"Uh huh."

"And she's been talking about extending her visit a bit—"

"Yes," Alan says. She can picture him nodding and making a serious face on the other end of the line, his glasses resting on the bridge of his nose as he sets the evening newspaper on one knee. Her mom and Alan have been married for a number of years and Holly actually really likes him, but there's an awkwardness about calling him to pry into the state of his marriage to Coco that isn't lost on her.

"Anyway, I wasn't sure if there was something going on. Something I could help with." It sounds lame even as she says it, but Holly isn't sure what else to offer.

Alan exhales. "Well. She's a real ticket, your mom."

Holly gives a short laugh. "Understatement of the year."

"I know you two don't always see eye to eye, so it probably won't surprise you that she and I don't always agree either."

"I haven't fainted from the shock yet," Holly assures him. "Go on."

"Hol, she just isn't happy up here. She's got her yoga and the gym, and sometimes she goes out with girlfriends, but she says something is missing in her life."

Pucci nudges her calf with his cold, wet nose to remind her that she's got a job to do, so Holly bends over and picks up the tennis ball. She throws it into the sand this time.

"She has everything. I can't imagine what's missing." Holly watches Pucci trot off after the ball again.

"Well, *you're* missing, for one thing."

"Me?" Holly squints into the setting sun. "I'm right here—where I've always been."

"Yeah, but you're not in her life. Not the way she wants you to be."

Holly snorts. "You're kidding, right?"

"Now, just listen." Her stepfather's voice is smooth and calm, and she knows that—as always—he'll aim to be the voice of reason between Holly and Coco. "Your history is between the two of you, but I know most of the details, and I think she's always regretted the way she acted as a young mother."

"As a young mother? How about the way she acts now, Alan?" Holly ignores the ball this time when Pucci drops it at her feet. He pants and waits for his mistress to chuck it into the water again. "Her single solitary goal in life is to remind me that I'm a complete burden to her and that she will never support anything I say or do."

"Hol, you know that's not—"

"I know that's not what, Alan? True? I'm supposed to know that's not true?" Holly's voice skips octaves as she climbs the ladder towards hysteria. "And her being here—that can't happen. You two need to make up or go on a cruise to rekindle your romance or something— whatever it takes. Because she's down here trying to turn my island into a floating Golden Nugget. Next thing I know she'll be trying to convince me that no casino is complete without strippers."

Alan says nothing for a moment after Holly finishes her rant. "I think you're overreacting. She just wants to be involved," he finally says.

Holly folds one arm across her chest and holds the phone to her ear with the other. The beauty of her surroundings fades away as she seethes about her mother intruding in her life on a long-term basis.

"How about you give her a chance?" Alan goes on. "It would be a personal favor to me, Holly."

Holly isn't sure she owes Alan any personal favors, but he has kept her mom occupied and up North for the past fifteen years or so. He probably does deserve a medal or something for that. She sighs.

"Fine. I'll give her a chance. But the second she starts meddling in my personal life or trying to sell off chunks of this island to NBA stars who want to build McMansions, she's packed and on the next boat."

"Fair enough," Alan says. There's a tinge of sadness to his words. "I want her to be happy, you know." Holly nods, though of course Alan can't see this. "And if what she needs to do right now is be there with you and find some purpose to her life, then so be it."

"Yeah, so be it," Holly agrees, but with far less enthusiasm. They end the call with the agreement to stay in touch, and Holly's gaze refocuses on her surroundings. It wasn't exactly what she'd hoped to come home to, but what would her life on Christmas Key be without a few hurdles to clear?

"Pucci!" Holly calls, whistling to call him back from the sand dunes. "We've got our house back, boy—let's go home!"

27

"Mayor! Mayor, I'd like to speak with you!"

Holly slows to a stop on Main Street on Thursday morning and turns to see who's calling for her. Mistletoe Morning Brew is just ahead, holding its promise of coffee and happiness just out of her reach. Idora Blaine-Guy bustles across the street after a golf cart passes, waving her hand impatiently to hurry Maggie Sutter along and out of her way.

"I need a word with you, Mayor Baxter," she says commandingly.

Holly hasn't spent much time—none at all, really—with Vance Guy's mother since returning from Europe, but she's exchanged a pleasantry or two and she made sure to officially welcome her to Christmas Key the first day she got back.

"Good morning," Holly says, waiting for Idora to catch up. "I'm just headed in for coffee. Want to join me?"

"Love to," Idora says, her breath coming in little puffs as she pauses in front of Holly. She's short and round, but there's a layer of steel behind her eyes and a no-nonsense demeanor about her that reminds Holly of a strict school teacher who's seen it all and isn't afraid to march a child down to the principal's office.

Inside the coffee shop, Carrie-Anne and Ellen are having a heated debate while they work, their words ringing through the shop.

"We did that theme in 2014," Carrie-Anne says. She's on her hands and knees next to the front counter, picking up the ceramic shards of a broken coffee mug. "People will know that we're recycling ideas."

Ellen rolls her eyes as she rings up Cap and Heddie's coffee order. "No one will care. Plus we already have all the nets and beach glass in the storage shed."

"Morning, Holly," Heddie says, taking her steaming mug of coffee over to the counter on the side of the shop to doctor it up with cream and sugar. "And to you, Idora."

"Good morning," Idora says, nodding and holding her small purse in front of her stomach with both hands.

"Just coffee?" Holly asks Idora, stepping up to the counter. Idora nods.

"Two with room, please." Holly takes out her wallet and pays for the coffees. The women follow Heddie's lead at the cream and sugar station and then pick a bistro table by the front window.

"I've been wanting to talk to you, but I know you've only been back on the island for a couple of days," Idora says, pulling herself up onto the tall chair and moving around until she's comfortable.

Holly puts the mug of coffee to her lips and closes her eyes for a moment, anticipating the first hit of caffeine. "Is everything going okay so far? I know Vance and Calista really appreciate you coming here to help out with the boys."

"Of course they do," Idora says. "They needed me. Lord help us all if that doctor hadn't found my grandson in the swimming pool when she did." She shakes her head back and forth, her eyes turned to the ceiling like she's sending thoughts of gratitude up to heaven. It had been a stroke of pure luck the night that Fiona had decided to take a swim and discovered one of Idora's six-year-old twin grandsons in the B&B's swimming pool, and the impishness of the boys had ultimately driven the Guys to call Idora into action.

Holly smiles behind the mug. She knows that, while grateful that her mother-in-law is willing to help, Calista is less than thrilled at the prospect of sharing her house with her husband's mom.

"What I really want to talk to you about is my son." Idora picks up her own mug of coffee and blows on the steam.

"Oh?"

"Now, I know Vance has spoken to you about the empty space here on Main Street, and told you that he wants to open a bookshop." This much was definitely true; Vance and Holly had spoken at length and had even looked at the empty space together before her trip to Europe. "Anyhow, I hate to see my son down here on this island just drifting like he's lost at sea—he's a brilliant writer, but I've seen the novel he's working on, and honey, it isn't much. At least not yet."

Holly nods diplomatically, though she really wants to smile at Idora's plain assessment of her grown son's life and pursuits. "Yes," she says, wrapping her hands around the warm coffee mug. "We did talk about it a while back."

"Well, I'd like to go ahead on it. Where do I sign for the lease?"

Holly takes a deep breath. It's still early, and the first few sips of her coffee haven't entirely woken her up yet. "Oh, I had no idea we were talking business here."

"Somebody has to," Idora says, her mouth turning up on one side in a wry smile. "Otherwise these kids are just going to hang around here talking about yoga and giving massages," she waves a hand in the direction of Scissors & Ribbons, "and letting their kids run wild while a bunch of retirees try to pitch in and teach the boys the things they *should* be learning in a school."

Holly pauses as she digests what Idora is saying. She's actually been really proud of her neighbors as they've come together to help guide the rambunctious boys and to fill their days with fun things that double as educational activities. Having two children on the island has been a huge change for everyone to adjust to, and Holly's personal opinion is that they're doing an amazing job of integrating the kids into their island lifestyle.

"So," Idora continues, "I want to see my son pursuing something worthy, and if he's not going to pull the trigger on this bookshop, then

I will. I'll pay the monthly rent, and you and I can handle all the business dealings. I just want him out of the house and away from that computer. He stares at the same words on the screen all day long, and frankly, I'm tired of it."

"Huh." Holly stalls for a second by reaching for a stir stick in a cup on the center of the table. She sticks it into her coffee and drags the liquid around slowly. "So Vance doesn't know that you're taking the lead on this?"

"Not yet," Idora confirms. "But he'll be grateful. Men always think they know what's best, but let me tell you something: my late husband would've put his socks on his hands instead of his feet every day if I hadn't been there to tell him what to do."

Holly can't help herself—she actually laughs out loud at this vision.

"That's true, Mayor. I don't know if you've ever been married, and Lord knows I'm not asking, but if I know one thing about men it's that they're pigheaded and they'll follow a bad idea all the way to the bottom of a well."

"More coffee for you two?" Ellen appears at the table with a pot of coffee in one hand, ready to top them off.

"Not yet—thanks, Ellen," Holly says, putting one hand over her cup. Ellen nods and moves over to the next table.

"Anyhow, I'm ready to sign the papers and start getting that space ready for business." Idora tugs at the sides of her short sleeved shirt, pulling it down over her midsection firmly.

"Okayyyyy," Holly says, dragging the word out. "But I still think it's a good idea to sit down with Vance and talk about the terms and what his vision is. You know, just to make sure he's still on board with the whole thing."

"He will be." Idora squares her shoulders and lifts her chin. "I know my son."

Holly is hesitant to set up the terms of renting the space without more discussion with Vance, but in an effort to move things forward, she holds up her coffee cup like it's a mug of beer. "Then cheers to going into business, Idora."

Idora lifts her own mug and clinks it against Holly's. "Just tell me where to sign and where to send the check every month."

If only it were as simple as an autograph and a check each month. Going into business on Christmas Key is a lot of work, and the fluctuation of visitors definitely plays into a shop's success or failure. Something like a bookstore will probably do just fine with the locals, but there are a ton of details that will need to be figured out. However, rather than bringing all of it up now, Holly simply smiles at Idora and takes a sip of her coffee.

~

THERE ARE STILL plenty of emails to sort through from Holly's absence, so she spends most of the day behind her desk with Pucci resting at her feet, his soft fur pressed against her leg reassuringly. He's refused to let her out of his sight since her return, and having Pucci follow her everywhere doesn't bother Holly at all.

"We've got a wedding party to set up for October," Bonnie says. She's standing at the filing cabinet in the corner, dropping hard copies of vendor receipts into a standing file. "The bride has some really specific requests. Seems like kind of a bridezilla, if you ask me."

Holly smiles and wiggles her toes so that they rub Pucci's side. "Is this the one who had her assistant call you while I was gone?"

"That's the one." Bonnie shuts the drawer with a click. "Gave me some runaround about how this wedding has to be top secret."

Holly rests her hand on her chin and looks over at the big calendar on their whiteboard. "Have you written the dates down yet?"

Bonnie walks over to the whiteboard and flips a few pages on the calendar. "We're only at the end of May now, so we still have all of June, July, August, and September." She picks up a pen and writes something across a block of squares in October. "I can only imagine dealing with this gal for the next four months while she plans her top secret island wedding."

"We can do this, Bon. If it's going to be this big of a deal, then think of the money she might be willing to spend to make it exactly what she wants it to be."

"And think of the extra trips to Scissors & Ribbons that I'll have to make in order to get my gray hairs covered." Bonnie pats her red hair protectively.

"Oh! How is Millie doing?" Holly's been home for just a few days and has already completely immersed herself in the island and in work. A guilty flush creeps up her neck as she remembers that Millie needs her now just as much as some wedding in October requires her attention.

"Fiona and Calista are still taking turns keeping her busy, and last I heard, the triplets are managing the flow of food that's being dropped off. One of them is always around at mealtime to make sure she eats something."

Holly's heart seizes again as she thinks of Ray. "When is the memorial? Did she decide on a date?"

"This Sunday," Bonnie says, sitting down in her desk chair again. "Cap and Wyatt are planning the whole service, and I didn't think you'd mind, so I offered up the B&B's dining room for the gathering after. It's a potluck."

"Of course I don't mind!" Holly closes her laptop and puts her elbows on her desk, letting her face fall into her hands. "I can't believe how quickly I got sucked back into Coco and work. How come no one's looped me in and asked me to help plan?"

Bonnie smiles at her from across the white desk. "Well, sugar, you came back like a whirling dervish, ready to take on the world. I think we all just figured you should do what you do best, and that we'd handle the rest."

Holly lifts her head and her light brown hair falls around her shoulders. She hasn't stopped since setting foot on Christmas Key on Monday night, and by not stopping, she hasn't had to spend much time dealing with the stew of emotions inside of her. Now, as Bonnie looks into her eyes, she finally feels it all come to a slow boil.

"It's always like this, isn't it?" she asks hoarsely. "I mean, me—*I'm* always like this, right?"

Bonnie smiles at her patiently. "You're a wonder, sugar. I wouldn't have you any other way."

"But I can never see past the end of my own nose!" Holly argues, standing. She paces the length of the window that looks out onto Main Street. "It's always island business or B&B stuff. I can't come back and just put it all aside while I help Millie." She turns at the end of the office and walks the other direction, arms folded. "And I obviously can't give a man what he wants. Look how hard it was for Jake to deal with me. I wouldn't even *consider* a life away from Christmas Key. I knew it would make him happy, and I still couldn't do it."

"Well," Bonnie says, holding a blue pen up in the air for emphasis, "the two of you are both stubborn as mules, so maybe that was never going to work. But the babies would have been beautiful..."

Holly ignores Bonnie's comment about the babies she and Jake might have had together. "And River. All he wanted was to give me an adventure and show me the world, and all I could think about was getting back home." Bonnie tips her head from side-to-side, weighing this piece of information. She doesn't deny its validity. "Why do I get so lost inside my own head and my own dramas that I can't see what's happening right in front of my face?"

Bonnie is about to answer when there's a light knock on the open door of the office.

"Hi," Logan Pillory says. He clears his throat. "Sorry to interrupt."

"Hi, honey," Bonnie says cheerfully. "Come on in. You need something?" She stands up and straightens her emerald green shirt as she waves Logan in. As the mother of three boys, Bonnie has a soft spot for them in all shapes and sizes.

"I just wanted to talk to Holly," he says shyly, tapping the doorframe with his long fingers.

"What's up, Logan?" Holly waves him in and motions for him to sit in Bonnie's chair. "Have a seat."

"That's okay," he says, still standing by the door. "I just wanted to know if you had any work for me to do around here, or if you knew whether anyone was hiring."

Bonnie hoots. "I doubt anyone's hiring, doll. We don't have many people looking for work on Christmas Key. In fact, most of them are trying to avoid it!"

Something about Logan's crestfallen face makes Holly want to soften Bonnie's teasing tone with kind words. "The demand isn't super-high around here for new employees, but I wouldn't be surprised if we could come up with something for you to do. Are you just looking to make a few bucks?"

Logan lifts one shoulder and lets it fall again. "Yeah. My mom said my friend Owen could come down to visit, but that I had to help him pay for it. And I don't have any money."

"Gotcha." Holly picks up a pencil and a notepad. "Let's brainstorm a little. What are you good at?"

"Uhhhh, I'm not sure. I've never had a job."

"How about hobbies? Or things you did back home?"

"I like computers. And my mom used to make me mow the lawn every week."

"Okay, now we're getting somewhere." Holly scribbles on the notepad. "You could offer some unique services on the island, and I bet people would be willing to pay you."

"For what?" Logan steps out of the doorway and into the office, leaning his back against the wall where Holly usually hangs her purse on the coat hook. He puts both hands in the pockets of his shorts.

"How about lawn care services, for starters?" Holly looks up at him with the pencil poised over the pad of paper. "I know lots of older people who hate mowing their lawns anyway, but they especially hate it this time of year when the weather gets really hot and humid. It's not good for them to be out in the sun pushing a lawnmower when it's ninety-five degrees."

"I don't really mind the heat," Logan says. His eyes shift back and forth between Bonnie and Holly.

"So we could put together a flyer for that and see if the triplets will let you hang it at their store. And I bet Ellen and Carrie-Anne would be okay with you putting it up at the coffee shop. Those two stores alone would pretty much guarantee that everyone on the island sees your sign at least once a day."

"Okay." A smile spreads across Logan's face. "Yeah, I can do that."

"So why don't you go home and give it some more thought. Decide what you want to offer and how much you might charge, and then email it to me and we can print it out here if you want." Holly leans across the desk to grab a Christmas Key B&B business card from the holder on her desk and passes it to Logan.

He examines the card. "I took graphic design at school last semester."

"Perfect. Then I'm sure you can put together something great."

Logan stands in the doorway, still looking at the business card in his hand. He shifts from one foot to the other. "Thanks. I really appreciate it." A flush of red creeps up his young neck as he takes a step towards the hallway. "Oh," Logan says. He turns back to face Holly. "My mom said you two used to go kayaking when you were teenagers."

Holly smiles, remembering. "Yeah, we did. We used to hang out and do outdoorsy stuff together all the time."

"She's been pretty busy with my great-grandpa lately, and I was wondering if you'd go kayaking with me sometime."

Holly pulls one bare foot up under her thigh on the chair. "Me? Oh, I kind of..." Holly looks around at her neat work space, trying to find something pressing as an excuse to stay chained to her desk. "I've been gone for a while, and I have a few things I need to catch up on here."

"Right. Okay." Logan starts to walk out the door. "I'll send you the flyer as soon as I get it done."

Bonnie is smiling at Holly from the other side of the office. "You've gotten a lot accomplished here, sugar. Why don't you take Logan out on the water?"

Logan pauses hopefully.

"I guess I could..." Holly says, twisting her long hair into a knot at the nape of her neck and wrapping an elastic around the loose bun. "Maybe in an hour or two."

"Really?" Logan's eyebrows shoot up into his hairline. His eager expression reminds Holly of the look Pucci gives her when he gets wind of the fact that they might go on a walk.

"Yeah, we can do that." Holly nods. "Let me get a few things done around here, and then I'll text you. Here, give me your number." She picks up her phone and opens a new contact to add Logan's information, which he gives her eagerly.

There's a spring in Logan's step as he holds up a hand in farewell and disappears down the hallway. Bonnie is grinning at Holly with a knowing gleam in her eyes.

"There's no shortage of men for you, sugar. Even on a speck of sand in the ocean, you've got them clamoring for your attention."

Holly makes a disbelieving face and blows out a short puff of breath like she's dismissing the very idea. "Logan is sixteen," she says. "I'd hardly classify him as a 'man' who's clamoring for my attention."

Bonnie smirks. "Mmmhmm. A man is a man is a man, doll, and whether he's sixteen or sixty, if he turns pink under the collar while asking you for a date, then he's clamoring for your attention."

Holly is about to make a smart remark when her cell phone buzzes loudly on the desk. The name on the screen says JAKE in all caps.

Bonnie glances down at it. "Speaking of men who want your attention..." She cocks an eyebrow and turns back to the filing cabinets, sliding a drawer open slowly.

"It's just Jake," Holly says, hitting the button to send the call to voicemail.

"Mmmhmm," Bonnie says again, smiling to herself as she slips files into alphabetical order in the drawer. "Whatever you say, sugar."

28

Holly and Logan are dragging their kayak to shore after an hour on the water. It's actually been a fun escape from thinking about everything that's weighing on Holly's mind: Coco and the casino; River, who she still needs to respond to at some point; and—not least of all—Ray's memorial service that's coming up on Sunday afternoon.

"Thanks for taking me out," Logan says, pulling the boat by a handle and moving it onto the sand. "My mom's been pretty busy lately, and there isn't much to do around here."

"Trust me, I've been sixteen on this island," Holly says with a smile. "It's kind of a 'make your own fun' type of place."

"Oh, I didn't mean to say anything negative about the island—I'm actually starting to like it here," Logan adds quickly. He pulls the brim of his baseball cap down lower over his brows.

"No, it's fine. Don't worry about it for a second." Holly drops the side of the boat she's been dragging and puts both hands on her hips. "Hey, how's your great-grandpa doing?"

Logan shrugs. "He's okay. He doesn't really know who I am, but he only calls my mom by the wrong name sometimes. He mostly just watches television and takes naps."

Holly wipes her forehead with the back of her wrist. Hal Pillory's sudden decline has been a heavy weight on the shoulders of all the islanders, and the reminder that they live amongst so many people whose health and stability are tenuous—at best—is kind of a downer.

"I guess that's to be expected at his age. He held on pretty well after your great-grandma passed away," Holly says, remembering how lost Hal had been after Sadie's death.

Logan nods, dragging his bare toe through the sand. "Hey, sorry about that guy Ray," he says. "I didn't really know him, but it still sucks."

"Yeah." Holly narrows her eyes as she looks up into the tall palm trees that line the bluffs on the beach. "It does suck." It's a grand understatement, and a reminder of what life and love and loss mean to someone at Logan's young age. It's also a reminder to her of what life and love and loss mean at her own age, and Holly has a sudden urge to get some thoughts down in writing before they flee her mind.

"Listen, I need to get back to the office and work on something. Would you mind helping me move this kayak up to the HoHo Hideaway over there?" Holly points at Joe Sacamano's bar in the distance. "I'll come back later and strap it to my cart to take it home, but right now I just need to get back to the B&B before it gets too late."

"Sure," Logan says. They each pick up a side of the heavy plastic boat and lug it over to the HoHo.

"We can leave it here. Want me to drop you back at home?"

Logan glances up at the sky, squinting. "Nah," he says. "I don't mind the walk. Thanks again, Holly."

Before she can stop herself, the word is out of her mouth. "Anytime."

"Really?" Logan asks, his face hopeful. "Anytime?"

Holly is already walking to her golf cart. "Well, sometimes I have to work," she says, trying to make a joke of it. "But if I'm not working, sleeping, or being mayor, then we might be able to head out in the kayak."

"I'll check in with you tomorrow to see if you're busy. I've got your number in my phone!" Logan says, holding one hand up in farewell. "See ya!"

Holly waves at him, laughing to herself as she watches the teenage boy move down the sand on his stork-like legs, a red burn smeared across the back of his neck from the brief time he's spent in the tropical sun.

"See ya," she says quietly, letting her hand drop to her side.

THE THOUGHTS that she wants to get into writing are all over the place, and Holly's still at her desk long after Bonnie is gone for the evening.

Her first message is a draft of an email that she's planning to send to River, but she wants to make sure that it says everything she feels, and with the wisdom of someone who's given in to the itchy trigger finger and sent an email or two when she really should have just slept on it, she saves the rough draft and moves on.

The next message is a response to one that she got earlier in the spring. The nature of being mayor of Christmas Key means that she gets offers and ideas thrown at her pretty regularly, and she always vets each one carefully before accepting or refusing. This particular offer had come in as she was handling the aftermath of *Wild Tropics*, and Holly had responded vaguely and filed it away in her email folder labeled "Possibilities."

The idea had come to her as she'd paddled offshore with Logan that afternoon, looking back at her beloved island with the eyes of a visitor. It wasn't often that she got to just bob in the clear blue water and admire Christmas Key from a distance, and as she'd looked at the HoHo Hideaway with its grassy roof and rustic frame, she'd seen something in that view of the island that fit into a corner of her mind that had been waiting for a missing puzzle piece.

I'd love to talk to you more about this possibility, Holly writes, her fingers tapping at the keys as she sits in the semi-darkened office. *I think the time is right to consider what you've proposed, and I'm certainly open to having a discussion at some point in the near future.*

Holly reaches for the bottle of water on her desk and uncaps it. She takes a swig and goes back to typing, signing off and giving it a final read-through before hitting send.

"Okay," she says to herself, powering down the laptop and closing the lid. "We'll see what happens."

Holly slips out the side door of the B&B and climbs into her cart in the parking lot. The sun is almost gone for the evening, and the pink blush on the horizon means that she needs her headlamps on for the drive home.

"Hey," comes a voice from the sidewalk as Holly switches on her cart. "You never called me back today."

It's Jake.

"Oh. Hey." Holly turns the cart off and waits as he approaches, both hands in the pockets of his black shorts. He's still wearing his work shirt and black shoes, and even in the near darkness and with all that's happened between them, Holly has to admit to herself that he's devastatingly handsome. Her first instinct is to switch the cart on and put it in drive. To get away from him as quickly as possible. To save herself from the dangerous emotions that still come up in his presence.

"You don't have time for me, but I hear you had time for a date with another man this afternoon." There's an amused smile playing on Jake's lips.

"I didn't have a date," Holly protests. "Ohhh, right. Logan," she says, realizing what's causing Jake to hold in a laugh. "Yeah, real hot date." She rolls her eyes. "You caught me."

"Listen, I want to talk to you." Jake puts one foot on the passenger side of Holly's cart like he's about to step up and sit on the bench seat next to her. Instead, he puts one hand on the roof and gazes down at her. "It's been a crazy year, and I still think we have some unresolved stuff to work through."

Holly fights the urge to sigh loudly. There will always be "unresolved stuff" between her and Jake, but she's accepted that and is prepared to live without full resolution forever, if necessary.

"Jake," she says, reaching to switch on the cart again. "It's late—"

"It's not even nine," he says, turning his wrist so that he can look at the face of his watch. "And I know for a fact that Buckhunter would serve us something if we showed up at Jack Frosty's."

Holly sits there and thinks. Going with Jake to the bar would mean what—that she's ready to talk about their failed relationship? Or that she wants to hear about how things didn't work out with Bridget, or about their lost baby? Even thinking about that makes her stomach feel a little unsettled, and Holly is ready to beg off without another thought.

"How about if I talk and you listen?" Jake says. He hasn't let go of her cart, and she knows the look in his eyes: it's the one that's there when he's not ready to give in.

"Fine," Holly says, picking up her purse from the seat next to her and shutting off the headlights. "I guess I could eat something."

They sit at the bar counter at Jack Frosty's that looks out onto Main Street and order two beers and a pile of nachos. Holly's stomach is still twisting as she waits for Jake to come to the point, and when Buckhunter sets the plate between them, she picks one chip and nibbles at it nervously.

"Here's the thing about us, Hol," Jake says without preamble, scooping a helping of chips and toppings onto one of the small plates that Buckhunter's left for them. "When we're both single, chances are good that we're going to end up thinking we should give this another shot. It never fails with us."

Holly shoves the rest of the chip into her mouth and nods, chewing slowly so that she has an excuse not to speak.

"But we've been down this road way too many times, and it never works." Jake picks up his mug of beer and takes a long drink before setting it on the rough wood of the bar again. "So I'm going to propose right now that we end this thing for good."

Holly waits. This isn't what she was expecting from Jake—at all. "You mean..."

"Yeah, I mean we need to do anything and everything in our power to stop ourselves from climbing into bed together anytime we both find ourselves single."

"Oh." It's not that she's gotten back from Europe and is already thinking about taking a roll in the hay with Jake, but he does have a point. They'll most likely end up in a compromising position at some point, so long as they both stay single.

"I mean it," Jake says earnestly, grabbing a fork to spear a huge bite of seasoned meat and cheese off his plate. "Too much has happened since last year at this time, and at the very least, I don't think you're over River yet."

"I'm not," Holly agrees, picking another single tostada chip from the platter. "I've only been home from our trip for a few days, and I have no idea how we left things. There's no way I'd sleep with you right now, Jake."

It's Jake's turn to be surprised. "Oh." He pauses in the middle of devouring another loaded bite of nachos. "Okay. Then that's good."

This whole conversation has been a little awkward and totally unexpected. Holly laughs nervously. "Okay, then. I'm glad we got that settled. We're not hooking up under any circumstances." She picks up her mug of beer and holds it up in a toast. "I'll drink to that."

Jake picks up his beer with a slight hesitation. "I mean…I didn't expect you to be that happy about it, but sure, let's drink to celibacy."

They clink glasses and take sips of their beer. "Right. Celibacy." Holly lets her mind drift to the last night she spent with River, and a sudden sadness fills her as she realizes that her chances of waking up in the arms of a man in the near future have narrowed considerably in the past week. "So," she says, rolling the dice and hoping that she doesn't piss Jake off royally with this line of questioning. "Have you heard from Bridget lately?"

Jake takes another bite, chews the whole thing, and swallows before he answers. "We got closure," he says finally. "It's all good."

Holly nods. Brushing her hands together to get the salt from the chips off her palms, she stands up. "Be right back," she says. She puts a hand into the pocket of her shorts and digs out a quarter. At the jukebox, she chooses Springsteen's "I'm on Fire" and throws a look behind the bar at Buckhunter. In response, he holds up a thumb as he flips a burger on the grill. It's their little routine, and she missed it while she was gone as much as she's missed everything else about her life on the island. Rather than going directly back to Jake, Holly stands at the jukebox for a minute, one hand on each side of the machine as she scans the list of songs that are as familiar to her as the road she drives between her house and the B&B every day.

"Nice choice," Jake says when she returns to the stool next to his. "I thought you'd go with 'Glory Days,' but this is cool, too."

Outside on Main Street, one of the triplets walks by Jack Frosty's, arm-in-arm with her husband. Together, Holly still second guesses herself sometimes when it comes to identifying which triplet she's talking to, but when she sees them with their husbands, it's always a dead giveaway. "Hey, Glen!" Holly calls out, waving at her friend.

"Hi, sweetie," Glen says, blowing Holly a kiss. "Good to have you home." Glen and her husband keep strolling, and Holly and Jake go back to eating their nachos in companionable silence.

"Hey," Holly says when Springsteen is done wailing about being on fire. "I'm glad we got this all settled."

Jake takes the last few nachos off the platter and slides them onto his own plate. "What's that?"

"That you don't want to sleep with me ever again," she says coyly, reaching over to his plate to grab a chip. He slaps her hand lightly.

"I didn't say never again...did I?" Jake frowns.

"That's how I took it."

"Huh. Might need to rethink the way I phrase things." The corner of Jake's mouth pulls up into a smile. "But I do mean it for right now," he says. "It's way too complicated."

Holly's smile fades and she grows serious. "You're right. And neither one of us can afford to make our lives more complicated at this point."

They let a beat pass between them as they silently agree. "Anyhow," Jake says, breaking the silence. He pushes the empty platter between them out of the way and leans an elbow on the counter. "What's going on with the casino?"

Holly makes a pained face. "Uhhhhh," she moans, "the casino. Don't remind me."

"Is Coco still going full steam ahead on that?"

"I think so. But honestly, I've been more occupied with the B&B and with Ray's memorial this weekend."

"Speaking of Ray's memorial, is there anything I can do to help?" Jake offers.

"I think we've got it all set up. Ray and Millie's kids will be down here. The service will be at the chapel, of course, and we'll all meet back in the B&B's dining room for a potluck after. It's pretty straightforward."

"I still can't believe this happened." Jake stares at the wet ring that his beer mug leaves on the counter when he moves it.

"I don't want to be morbid," Holly says, reaching out a hand and resting it on his forearm. "But this island isn't getting any younger. You know how I feel about getting new people to move down here, and how important it is to look to the future if we're going to keep moving forward."

"I'm sorry it happened when you weren't here."

"Me, too." Holly's eyes mist over as she remembers all the times she'd laughed and talked with Ray, or the nights she'd spent at the HoHo, watching Ray lead his wife across the dance floor. The island won't be the same without him. "But we'll get through this, just like we get through everything else, right?" There's no use hiding the tears that have filled her eyes, and Holly swipes at them as they spill over and run down her cheeks.

"Yeah, we'll get through this. And we'll get through Coco's nonsense—I've got your back, Hol. You know that." Jake puts a hand on Holly's cheek and wipes away a tear with the pad of his thumb. It's a move that's at once intimate and tender, and it reminds Holly of all the good things they've shared.

"I know, Jake. You've got my back—just as long as I don't show up on your doorstep in the middle of the night looking to cuddle." Her joke breaks through the thick layer of sadness and they both laugh.

"Exactly. Don't show up at my place with those puppy dog eyes and a bottle of wine, or we're both doomed."

"It's a deal," Holly says, offering him a hand. She isn't totally sure, but Holly could swear that she sees the slightest flicker of heat in Jake's eyes as he hesitates for just a fraction of a second before taking her hand in his and giving it a hearty shake.

29

Cap Duncan starts Ray's memorial on Sunday afternoon by inviting everyone to take a seat.

"Please turn to the person next to you and take their hand," Cap says. He steps down from the small pulpit and stands between Maria Agnelli and Maggie Sutter, taking their hands in his as they all turn and face the rest of the islanders in the chapel. "Millie has asked that we do a non-traditional service for our wonderful friend Ray, and we'd like to honor her wishes by making this an afternoon of laughter mixed with tears, and of love intertwined with our loss."

Holly reaches out and takes Fiona's hand in her left one, then turns to Vance Guy next to her and holds out her right hand for him to clasp. He wraps his big hand around hers and gives it a squeeze. Next to Vance is his wife Calista, and on her right are the twins, who are holding hands and shoving each other lightly from side to side.

"Shhh," Calista whispers to her boys, trying to get them to settle down.

In the row ahead of them is Bonnie, and next to her is Wyatt Bender, who takes Bonnie's plump hand in his weathered one and pulls her closer to him. It's almost imperceptible, but Holly sees it and she smiles to herself. Across the row Jake holds hands with Kate-lynn Pillory, and on Katelynn's left is Logan. Logan leans forward slightly and looks around his mom so that he can make eye contact with Holly. He smiles shyly at her and she smiles back.

"I'd like to start by talking a little about what it means to move your whole life to Christmas Key," Cap says. "Ray and Millie are the proud parents of three grown children—Adam, Renee, and Courtney —and seven grandchildren." Cap nods in the direction of Millie and her loved ones in the front row. "When they decided to join this amazing community, they knew that in doing so, they were making a trade-off. The steep price we pay when we leave our families to move to Christmas Key is that we miss out on some of the big moments in their lives." Cap makes eye contact with the people in the chapel, knowing that they understand fully what this trade-off means. "And the bigger consequence is that sometimes they miss out on the big moments in our lives."

Millie lets go of her son's hand and puts a Kleenex to her eyes.

"None of us ever knows when the last good-bye we'll say to someone will actually be the *last* good-bye, but for those of us who choose to live so far away from our loved ones, we take a calculated risk. And even though Ray left us without getting the chance to hold his grandchildren one more time, and he never knew that the last phone call he made to his children would be the final time they heard his voice, I would wager that the years he and Millie have spent on Christmas Key have been amongst the best of their lives."

"That's true," Millie says, choking back a sob. "They have been." Her younger daughter puts an arm around Millie's shoulders and rests the side of her head against her mother's.

Cap pauses and lets his words sink in. "We'll all miss Ray and his big, boisterous personality. We'll miss him being first in line at Mistletoe Morning Brew—"

"And first into the bathroom at the coffee shop with the news-paper under one arm!" Jimmy Cafferkey pipes up from the back. Iris whacks his arm with one hand, but everyone laughs at this, knowing that it's true.

"But who else would have helped his wife open up a much-needed beauty salon on the island so that we don't have to look at each other's ugly, un-groomed mugs anymore? And which man amongst us would have offered up his toes to his wife so that she could try out the nail polish colors she'd ordered for the salon?" More laughter fills the chapel.

Joe Sacamano slips out of his pew and picks up his acoustic guitar from a chair in the corner of the chapel. He puts the strap over his shoulder and adjusts it so that the instrument is positioned correctly, then sits on the stool next to the pulpit and begins to strum gently.

"Anyhow," Cap says, winking at Joe. "All that Millie wanted today was for us to all be here together, and for Joe to play 'In My Life' by the Beatles while we all sing along."

A sigh runs through the crowd as Joe starts playing the familiar intro to the song, and within seconds, everyone is swaying slightly, the lyrics falling from their lips as tears run over their smiling cheeks. It's the perfect way to remember Ray, and Holly looks around at her neighbors as they sing together from their hearts, wrapping their arms around the shoulders of the person next to them rather than just merely holding hands.

The ceremony is brief and non-denominational, and Cap wraps things up by encouraging everyone to "love each other every day" after his reading of "Do Not Go Gentle Into That Good Night" by Dylan Thomas.

There are more tears and hugs outside in front of the chapel as Millie greets every person with open arms. Holly hasn't stopped crying since Cap's first words, and seeing Millie and her beautiful children and grandchildren standing together under the tall palm trees and scrub pine doesn't help to stanch the flow.

"Hey, honey," Millie says, tucking her curly auburn hair behind her ears. Her gold hoops glint in the sunlight as they dangle from her earlobes. "Come here." Millie pulls Holly in for a tight hug, and the women embrace in the humid afternoon. "Ray and I have sure loved watching you grow up," she whispers in Holly's ear. "And we both think that you're the best damn mayor this island could ever ask for."

It isn't lost on Holly that Millie uses the present tense, as if Ray is still around to offer an opinion. The sentiment is beautiful, but it also makes her a little sad.

"Thank you, Millie," she says, kissing her friend on the cheek as they part. "That means the world to me."

It's an emotional caravan of golf carts that makes its way over to Main Street where most people park along the curb. Holly leads the way into the lot so that Millie and her family can park there and head into the B&B through the back door. Inside, the women who've been caring for Millie and helping her get through her days without Ray have set up an impressive feast on the tables, and within minutes, people are mingling and serving up plates of cold fried chicken, potato salad, and cornbread muffins.

Buckhunter has invited people to wander down to Jack Frosty's if they'd like something harder than the Arnold Palmers that Millie has requested for the potluck—they were always Ray's favorite, and it's those little touches that people have suggested for the event (like fried chicken, another of Ray's favorites) that are keeping the weak smile on Millie's face.

"You holding up okay?" Jake walks up to Holly with two Arnold Palmers. He hands her one.

"Yeah, that was nice. Understated." She drinks the iced tea/lemonade combo and nods at Iris Cafferkey across the room.

"Where's your mom?" Jake looks around the room warily. His expression reminds Holly of a child who's been frightened by a jack-in-the-box one too many times.

"Oh, it can't be that bad, can it?" Holly smiles at him. "I'm the one who should be scared by the thought of Coco popping up out of nowhere." She sets her drink on the nearest table and picks up a cold chicken drumstick from her pile of food.

"I wouldn't be so sure," Jake says. He reaches over and plucks a cornbread muffin off of Holly's plate. "You owe me this for the nachos you stole the other night." He holds up the muffin and then takes a big bite.

"So what did my mother do now?"

"She got drunk and asked for a ride back to the B&B from the HoHo on Friday night."

Holly shrugs. "That seems like a responsible thing to do. I'm glad she didn't try to drive the B&B golf cart home after too many martinis." She takes a dainty bite of the drumstick, holding it between her fingers and leaning forward slightly.

"And then when I pulled up to the curb she asked if I'd cuff and frisk her."

Holly starts choking. "What?" she sputters, coughing as Jake whacks her on the back.

"You okay?" he laughs.

"No! No—I am definitely *not* okay." Holly reaches for her drink and downs a huge swig of her Arnold Palmer. "Jesus. You're kidding, right?"

"I would never kid about something like that. Trust me."

Holly spins around, searching the room for her mother. "I'll kill her."

"Hey, slow down there, sunshine," Jake says, grabbing Holly by the elbow. "She was drunk. And she told me all about how she and Alan were on different pages and how she needed to be down here so that she could clear her head—"

"Which does *not* include getting cuffed and frisked by my ex," Holly says hotly. The tips of her ears have gone red, and she's tugging her arm to free it from Jake's grip. "Between the casino and this, I'm seriously done with her. She's out of here."

Holly yanks her arm out of Jake's grasp and tosses the drumstick onto her plate, which she shoves into Jake's hand. "I'm going to find her," she fumes.

"Holly," Jake says, reaching out and catching her by the wrist. He tugs firmly, talking quietly through his clenched jaw. "This isn't the time or the place to duke it out with Coco." He tips his head in Millie's direction. "I only said that because I thought you would laugh. I wouldn't have told you if I thought you'd go ballistic in the middle of Ray's memorial."

Holly breathes in and out, her chest heaving with the exertion of keeping her cool. "You of all people should know how easy it is to send me into overdrive when it comes to my mother." She narrows her eyes at Jake. "And if you're refusing to sleep with me for the rest of our natural lives, then you're sure as hell not sleeping with my mother."

They stare each other down for several seconds before the levity of the situation breaks wide open with their laughter. First it's a surprised chuckle, but as Holly and Jake look into one another's eyes and weigh the ridiculousness of the the situation, the real laughter bubbles up and takes over. Before they know what's hit them, they're doubled over right there in the middle of the B&B dining room, leaning into each other for support as they howl.

"Sugar," Bonnie says, approaching them with a worried look. "Are you two hysterical? Do I need to slap someone?"

Holly shakes her head, putting her knuckles under her nose as she tries to mask the laughter that won't stop. "Not unless you're up for slapping Coco." Jake's shoulders start to shake all over again.

"Slap your mother?" Bonnie's eyebrows shoot up. "Do I finally have permission?"

"Let's wait until after everyone leaves," Holly says, wiping the tears that have sprung to her eyes again—only this time from laughing and not because of her sadness about Ray.

"That's a deal," Bonnie says, folding her arms across her chest and cocking one eyebrow.

EVERYONE LINGERS AT THE B&B until sunset. When Millie is finally ready to call it a night, people gather dishes and leftovers and head for their golf carts, lumbering across Main Street with full bellies and hearts.

Holly stays behind, as she often does after a function at the B&B. Once everyone is gone, she kicks off her sandals and walks around the dining room, straightening chairs and pulling tablecloths from the round tables. She'll start a load of linens before heading home, then come back first thing in the morning to keep the laundry moving through.

"I thought I might find you here."

Holly's head snaps around at the sound of her mother's voice. "Where else would I be?"

"I was upstairs and I thought if you were still here that we might have a chance to talk." Coco walks all the way into the room, her slinky figure clad only in a pair of satiny navy blue shorts and a thin, striped tank top. Her feet are bare, and her toes are painted fire-engine red.

Holly is leaning over a table, gathering the edges of the cloth that covers it so she can take the whole thing outside and shake off the crumbs before tossing it into the washing machine. She pauses and stares at her mother. "Oh, you want to talk?" She stands up straight and squares her shoulders. "Should we talk about how you tried to get Jake upstairs the other night? Or should we wait until Alan is around and share that little gem in front of him?"

"Holly..." Coco trails off. She at least has the decency to look chagrined, which she does—momentarily. "I had a few drinks too many that night. I didn't mean anything by it. And besides, he's only about fifteen years younger than me. It wouldn't be that big of a deal if it'd actually happened."

"It wouldn't be a big deal? Are you kidding me? Jake and I almost got married, Mom!"

Coco sits on the edge of one of the dining room chairs and crosses her tanned, toned legs. The muscles of her thighs are taut and defined. "Let's not get carried away here," Coco says, holding up one finger. "He asked, and you said no. In my mind, that means he's on the market and that you've relinquished all right to have a say in who he spends his time with."

Holly is almost speechless. *Almost.* "But, but—how...I mean—" she stutters. "What were you even *thinking*? Number one, that's disgusting. I dated him! And number two—possibly even more important than number one—you're married. To Alan. Who is patiently waiting for you to get it together and come back to New Jersey."

"Oh, he is not," Coco says, waving a hand at her daughter. "He's as bored of me as I am of him. Let's be honest."

"I talked to him the other day, and he didn't sound bored at all. He sounded worried. He sounded like he wanted you to find what you were looking for."

"Wait—you talked to Alan?" Coco frowns at Holly. "Did he call here?"

"No, I called him."

Coco stands up. "Who told you to do that, Holly? You have no right to get in my business."

The irony of this statement is like a punch in the gut to Holly. "Are you out of your mind?" She pulls the tablecloth off the table and drops it onto the pile she's already gathered, forgetting altogether about the crumbs that need to be shaken off outside. "All you *ever* do is come down here and get in my business! You go after my business like it's your full-time job. You're so far *up* in my business that I feel like you know more about me than my gynecologist does."

"Don't be vulgar, Holly."

"That's not vulgar, Coco—that's honest. But you wanna know what *is* vulgar? My mom trying to cheat on her husband with my ex-boyfriend. My own mother trying to sell the island that her parents built from scratch. You coming down here and bringing investors and trying to turn us into a floating casino while I'm away on vacation. All of that is vulgar."

"Let's be fair, while we're at it," Coco interrupts. "I didn't come down with Gator and the Killjoys because I knew you were on vacation. I was coming here to pitch this idea long before I knew about your European adventure."

"Ooooh," Holly says sarcastically, holding up both hands and wiggling her fingers. "That makes it so much better." She shakes her head and lets her hands fall to her sides. "I want you to stop coming here and trying to change everything, do you hear me? I want you to take your bored self back to your husband and forget all about moving showgirls and card dealers to Christmas Key. I'm not letting you wreck this place."

"You know what, Holly?" Coco says, stepping behind the chair to put something physical between her and the daughter who has suddenly turned into an angry, ranting businesswoman. She rests her hands on the back of the chair and leans one hip against it. "The truth is, you're incredibly small minded, and I blame your grandparents for that. They taught you to say no to everything that didn't suit your every whim, and because of it, you're stuck. You can't see what this place could be because you'll never say yes to anything."

"Is that what you think?" Holly rears back, looking at her mother with disbelief. "I'd honestly love it if you'd leave now, but I'd actually like you to stick around until Wednesday for the village council meeting I'm calling. There are some interesting things that I'm about to say yes to."

Coco laughs. "Is that right?" She folds her arms the same way that Bonnie had done just a few hours before. "Then I'll definitely stick around for *that.*"

30

Plans to open the bookstore are in full swing. Vance and his mother have met with Holly twice by Tuesday afternoon, and they've covered most of the particulars when it comes to rent, utilities, supplies, and the basic ins and outs of running a business on Christmas Key. Holly is satisfied that they have a decent business plan in place, and while she's certainly questioned how much of the current push to get the doors to the bookstore open is coming from Vance and how much is coming from his mother, Vance's enthusiasm has tipped the scales in his favor in terms of Holly believing that this project is still his baby.

"So do we have a new business on the books?" Bonnie looks up from her computer when Holly returns from her most recent meeting with Vance and Idora.

Holly sets her purse on the hook by the door and kicks off her Birkenstocks. "I think we do." The humidity is inching up drastically with each passing day, and Holly holds her arms out to the sides as she lets the cool air-conditioning inside the B&B dry out the perspiration that's left damp rings on either side of her ribcage.

"Any idea what they're going to call it?"

"I think they're leaning towards—" The ringing of the phone cuts Holly off.

Bonnie picks it up. "Christmas Key B&B. This is Bonnie."

Holly waves her arms around as she watches Bonnie's face to see if she can gather who might be on the phone.

"Yes, of course. Right! No, we have the dates all blocked out. Right —I completely understand, honey," Bonnie says, using her sweetest, most placating tones. "I wouldn't want a single thing to go wrong, you hear? Okay. You got it. Yes, that's our email address. Mmmhmm. Very good. Bye now." She hangs up and takes a deep breath.

"The October bride?" Holly guesses. She slides into her chair across from Bonnie's and looks at her watch. It's nearly four o'clock, and they still need to get the agenda typed up and printed out for the village council meeting that she's called for the next day.

"How did you guess?" Bonnie asks sweetly. "Am I starting to make a face whenever I hear her assistant's voice on the other end of the line?"

"Kind of." Holly types in her password and her computer screen comes to life. "What does she want now?"

"She said they're going to need to get their marriage license in Florida and that she'd prefer it if whoever we secure to do the ceremony doesn't know the real names of the bride and groom until that weekend. I'm supposed to use placeholder names."

"Huh?" Holly's mouth drops open and her brows pull together in an exaggerated frown. "I don't get it."

"Sugar, I don't either. But we've got too many irons in the fire as it is, so let's put John and Jane Doe on the back burner for now and get everything ready for tomorrow."

Holly closes her mouth and shakes her head slowly. "I mean...it's weird, but whatever. 'Placeholder names,'" she says, reaching for a pencil and a notepad. "Now I'm really curious who these people are."

"All will be revealed in time," Bonnie says, trying to sound profound and wise. "But until then, we need to worry about Coco and her friends. I heard her at the coffee shop this afternoon talking about the Killjoys coming back for the meeting tomorrow."

"You're kidding me," Holly groans. "We're not taking commentary from the peanut gallery on this one."

"Honey." Bonnie reaches across the desk and puts her hand on top of Holly's. "We *have* to take commentary from the peanut gallery on this one. That's essentially what a village council meeting *is*."

"Oh. Right." Holly puts the yellow pencil between her teeth and bites down gently as she thinks. She takes the pencil out of her mouth and tosses it onto the desk. "Damn. But I don't want to hear from my mother again, and I don't want to listen to these Killjoys talk about how many slot machines they can have installed by the end of June. I'm not interested, and neither is Buckhunter."

"But you've got another proposition to offer, so that should appease everyone and draw the attention away from Coco."

"I'm not so sure that it will appease everyone," Holly says, taking the pencil out of her mouth and dropping it on the desk. She leans back in her chair and laces her hands behind her head. "We still have some holdouts who aren't fans of the larger scale ideas I have for progress, and I think all of this coming on the heels of Ray's memorial service might be a lot for them to handle. Too much change at once is kind of panic-inducing, you know?"

"Yes, sugar," Bonnie says, smiling at her sadly. "I do know a little something about how terrifying change can be."

"Okay," Holly sighs. "Let's get to work on this agenda for tomorrow. Oh, and we need to introduce the bookstore and let Vance say a few words if he wants to—we can't forget that."

"Do you have all the information for your pitch? I printed off the details for you so that we can make a Powerpoint if you want to."

"That's not a bad idea. It wouldn't hurt to compare and contrast my idea against Coco's in a subtle way. Maybe show everyone what the impact of this development would be as compared to her casino."

"Oooh, nice, sugar! I like that idea. Let's get this put together, and then how about we hit the HoHo for a margarita?"

Holly picks up the discarded pencil and a notepad in one rapid movement and holds them in front of her like an ace reporter about to get the scoop. "How fast can we get this done?" She starts to scribble on the notepad.

Bonnie laughs. "Lightning fast. A frozen margarita awaits us, milady. Let's get crackin'!"

~

"You've got a lot going on these days," Joe Sacamano says, setting the margaritas in front of Bonnie and Holly on the bar at the HoHo Hideaway. "And it looks like Coco has her sights set on the mass destruction of paradise."

"As always." Holly lifts her glass and rolls her eyes simultaneously. "When has Coco ever set foot on this island and *not* turned everything upside down?"

"Good point," Bonnie agrees, clinking her glass against Holly's. "But I think we've got a solid plan in place to block her this time."

Joe sets a bottle down on the bar and leans his weight against one strong, tanned arm. "Do I get a preview of this plan?" He winks at Holly. "You know, since I'm bringing the margaritas to the relationship *and* babysitting your secret admirer?"

Holly's smile fades. "What secret adm—..." Before she even finishes the question, her eyes scan the bar and land on the tall, narrow figure sitting on the top step that leads out to the beach. It's Logan. "Are you kidding me?"

Bonnie reaches out a hand and rests it on Holly's arm as she stands up from her stool. "Sugar," she warns gently. "Be kind."

But Holly has no intention of being unkind. She leaves her margarita on the bar and strides over the unfinished floorboards of the beach bar.

"Logan," she says, picking a spot next to him on the step. They're sitting side-by-side, facing the ocean. "What's up?"

Logan's surprise is almost tangible as he sits up straighter and clears his throat. "Holly. Hi. Nothing—I'm just here to make some money."

"Does Joe know that? I'm not sure he's prepared to put you on the payroll just yet. Or even let you inside the bar."

"Oh, I'm not working at the HoHo. And that's why I'm sitting out here: Joe won't let me in." Logan shakes his head and leans forward, pointing at the sandy parking lot next to the bar. "I've got a new service. It's called Guber."

"Guber?" Holly's amusement is written all over her face. "Sounds interesting."

"Yeah, it's like Uber, but I drive a golf cart instead of a car, obviously."

"Ohhhh, Guber—like a golf cart uber. Clever." In spite of herself, Holly's mild annoyance at seeing Logan lingering on the steps of the bar starts to melt.

"And also my mom has always called me Goober, so it kind of worked." Logan shrugs. "Do you want one of my business cards?"

"Sure." Holly reaches for the small rectangular card that Logan pulls from the back pocket of his shorts. He passes it to her and watches her face intently as she reads it. *"Glaucoma and cataracts make night driving hard? Too many gin & tonics at the HoHo? Need a lift anywhere on Christmas Key? Call Guber—I'll come to you!"*

"So? What do you think?" Logan rubs his hands down the front of his cargo shorts like he's drying off sweaty palms. "It's okay, isn't it?"

Holly reads the card again, one side of her mouth turned up at the corner. She's impressed. And entertained. "Yeah, I think so. You only have to be fourteen to drive a golf cart in Florida, so as long as your mom is okay with it, and if you've run it by Jake, then I think it's great."

Logan's face breaks into a relieved smile. "I've got other ideas. I'm trying to be creative."

"I admire that."

"I heard that women were into that sort of thing," Logan says knowledgeably. "They like industrious men."

Holly can't help herself; she laughs out loud. "Yeah, I guess we do like industrious men. Nice work, dude." She stands up and, without hesitation, reaches down and ruffles Logan's hair. He watches her as she walks back to the bar.

"He's not bothering me," Joe says to Holly. "I was just teasing you, kid."

Holly slides back onto her stool and picks up her drink. "He's got a pretty good head for business."

"He gave Iris and Jimmy a lift the other night after they'd both had too many. I know they appreciated it." Joe turns on the faucet behind the bar and fills a small pitcher with water. "And if he makes a few bucks while he's at it, then I think that's great. I was up to much worse when I was his age."

"I'm shocked," Bonnie says sarcastically, lowering her chin as she gazes at Joe.

"Hard to believe that a mild-mannered guy like me was ever a wild teen, huh?"

"About as hard to believe as the fact that a sassy redhead of a certain age was ever a chaste Southern belle," Bonnie says, smiling at him over the rim of her margarita.

"So then we have no chance in hell of ever convincing anyone that we were young once, huh?" Joe pulls out a pitcher of blended frozen margaritas and tops off Bonnie's glass.

"Probably not. And if you keep filling me up, I'm going to have to take up Holly's little friend on the offer of a ride home." Bonnie taps the side of her glass with one long fingernail.

"We're in cahoots," Joe says confidentially. "I get kickbacks every time I over-serve someone and they pay him for a lift."

"Logan's learning all the tricks of the trade right here on Christmas Key," Holly says, glancing at the boy again. He's still sitting on the top step, looking out at the ocean with his bony elbows propped on his equally bony knees. "Who needs the bright lights and the big city when he can learn about business and backdoor dealings from all of us?"

"Nothing wrong with the boy figuring out early that greasing a few palms will get him everywhere. It's part of the cost of doing business." Joe holds up a clean glass in the waning evening light and inspects it for spots. He pulls out a rag and polishes the glass.

"And whose palm are you greasing, Sacamano?" Holly asks, nudging Bonnie with her elbow. "Because I haven't seen any kick-backs from you yet!"

"Here's your kickback for this month, Mayor: I'll keep your young gentleman friend busy in the evenings so that he doesn't wind up on your doorstep asking to earn a few bucks by washing your cart or walking your dog. How's that?"

Holly takes another sidelong glance at Logan and turns back to her margarita. "It's a deal."

31

The village council meeting convenes at noon the next day. Fiona walks in wearing her white lab coat and a stethoscope around her neck, her thick, wavy strawberry blonde hair held in place with a few pins on top of her head. She waves at Holly and slides into a chair next to Buckhunter.

Frankly, it's too soon for Millie to be out and about, but Iris Cafferkey and Maggie Sutter have been unable to convince her of that, so she walks in between her two friends, each holding her by the arm as if she's an invalid and not a recent widow. It's obvious as she walks down the center aisle that being in the same setting where she last saw her husband alive is going to take a toll on her, but Millie is tough and she's tired of being cooped up in her house, so she forges ahead, taking a seat in the front row next to Maria Agnelli.

As Holly shuffles through the stack of papers on the podium, Cap and Heddie walk in together. Heddie leaves him in a seat near in the middle of the room and walks up to where Holly is standing.

"Ready for this?" Heddie asks, setting her purse on the floor next to the chair she always sits in to take the meeting minutes.

"To go head-to-head with my mother in front of the whole

island?" Holly whispers, raising an eyebrow at Heddie as she turns one of the pages she's been looking at. "I can't wait."

Almost as if on cue, Coco walks into the dining room wearing a knee-length yellow chiffon dress with spaghetti straps. She's pulled her dark, glossy hair back on one side and pinned it with a small comb, and her tanned legs are enhanced by a combination of Pilates and wedge sandals. She waves at the triplets and then turns back to the door. Holly's eyes follow her mother's gaze.

Two people stand silhouetted in the doorway, the midday sun filling in the space behind them. They're about twenty years older than Coco and the second they step into the room, Holly smells money.

"The Killjoys," Heddie says simply, turning her head so that she's looking up at Holly from her seat by the podium. "They are the money behind Coco's casino."

Holly nods. She chews her lower lip and pretends not to watch as her mother squires the couple to a spot at the front of the dining room. Within seconds, Coco approaches the podium.

"When are we up?"

"Mommmmm," Holly says sweetly. "How are you? And who are your guests?"

"Cut the crap, Holly," Coco says, flicking a loose strand of hair out of her eyes. "I called Bonnie yesterday and told her exactly what I wanted to have happen at this meeting."

"I don't remember any mention of you bringing guests," Holly says, picking up the agenda and scanning it unnecessarily. "Nope. It's not on the agenda."

"The Killjoys were a last minute addition." Coco leans on the podium and lowers her voice so that the couple in question can't hear the conversation. Netta Killjoy is only feet from Coco, and she's watching intently as Holly's face remains impassive. "They were able to come in from Key West this morning, so I'd like to give them a chance to speak during my time slot."

"About what?" Holly picks up a pen and taps it against the

wooden podium. "About how to throw an obscene amount of money at an island and turn it into a Vegas outpost?"

Coco shifts her weight on her feet impatiently. "No," she says with a clenched jaw. "I'd like them to talk about their vision for what the casino will actually look like. They've been through this before with a place they opened up in Biloxi, so I think of them not just as investors, but also as potential resources for how to do this the right way." As she talks, the volume of Coco's voice climbs. "I think if you'd just listen for once, Holly, you'll see that this is actually a very good plan."

Heads in the front rows have started to turn, and several people are following the conversation between Holly and Coco intently.

Cap Duncan stands at his seat and holds up a hand. "I know this meeting hasn't officially begun yet, Mayor," he says to Holly. "But I'd like to weigh in on this if I may."

Holly looks around the room and realizes that they've got almost everyone in attendance at this point. "I think we can call this meeting to order now if we're all ready," she says, lifting her gavel and tapping the block lightly. "Welcome to the village council meeting for May thirtieth. I know this isn't one of our regularly scheduled meetings, so I do appreciate you all being here and putting up with another round of discussions about the potential changes that have been proposed."

Heddie starts scribbling furiously on her notepad.

"Can we just launch in here?" Cap asks, still standing. "Or is there something that comes before this issue?"

"I think this is our first and main order of business today," Holly says, glancing at her agenda like she isn't aware of what's on the menu for the meeting. "We were also going to discuss new business opportunities on Christmas Key, but we can start with this discussion. Cap, what would you like to say?"

Cap takes a deep breath and tugs lightly at the gold hoop earring in his ear. "I'd like to know why in the hell these people keep showing up here wanting to buy up our island and turn it into some sort of gambler's paradise." He jabs a finger in the direction of the Killjoys.

"I'd really like to know the same thing," Jimmy Cafferkey says, standing up next to Iris and folding his meaty arms across his chest. "No one here has shown any interest in sharing Christmas Key with a bunch of people who want to throw their money into slot machines and order endless rounds of drinks from cocktail waitresses in bunny suits."

Coco spins around in front of the podium to face the crowd. "No one said anything about bunny suits, Jimmy," she spits. "This isn't going to be *that* kind of establishment."

"But if we wanted bunny suits, could we make that happen?" Wyatt Bender raises a hand. From the smirk on his face, Holly can tell that he's trying to stir the pot.

"Let's bring this back to the issue at hand." Holly shoots Wyatt a look. "Coco has a proposition that she thinks will be beneficial to the island, and she'd like to bring it to the table." This attempt at being diplomatic nearly kills Holly. "So I'll give her the floor here, and if she'd like to have her guests add anything..."

"Thank you." Coco steps behind the podium and nearly shoulders Holly out of the way in the process. "I've been looking into ways to better use this island and to bring in a profit that will make Christmas Key more sustainable. At the rate we're going, this will be an empty island with shuttered businesses in the next decade."

An audible gasp runs through the crowd and eyes flicker towards Millie's stunned face. It's only been a week and a half since Ray's heart attack in this very dining room, and Coco's insensitivity stuns everyone.

"To that end, I'd like to propose a casino to be constructed on the north side of the island, along with a hotel and a larger dock to support it." Coco nods at the Killjoys. "Brice and Netta Killjoy have come back to the island for another visit—I know many of you met them the first time they were here—and they'd like to give us some of the highlights of running a world class casino and resort." With one delicately boned hand, Coco waves them up to the front of the room. Heads are still shaking in disbelief and displeasure as they wait for the Killjoys to speak.

"Hi, everyone," Netta says into the small microphone that Holly never uses. "Is this thing on?" She taps the padded head of the microphone.

"You probably don't need it," Holly says, leaning in to switch it on. "But here you go." Might as well let everyone in the back of the room hear the Killjoys as they drive the final nail into Coco's coffin. Even without hearing what these people have to say, Holly knows her neighbors well enough to know that they aren't going to be in favor of the casino, so she takes a seat at the end of the front row and waits her turn, running through the Powerpoint in her head that she and Bonnie have created for the occasion.

"We've worked closely with our architects to draw up some specs on the kind of resort we're envisioning," Netta says, gripping the sides of the podium with her liver-spotted hands. Her fingers are laden with gold rings and giant diamonds, and each slightly pudgy wrist is wrapped in snaky gold chains and bangles. "To begin with, Coco agrees with us that we need to go big or go home, so we're looking at a three-hundred room resort attached to a twenty-thousand square foot casino." Netta Killjoy's voice is high-pitched and scratchy, and a few of the men in the crowd reach up to adjust their hearing aids. "In our experience, casinos are year-round money makers, and you can count on a steady stream of income and a strong influx of visitors to the island that will keep you on your toes and making money at all the local establishments."

"I have a question," Joe Sacamano says, putting a hand in the air. All eyes turn to look at Joe, his blue eyes flashing beneath a cap of snowy curls. "What kind of staff would we need to run an operation like the one you're describing?"

Brice Killjoy steps up to the podium next to his wife. He speaks loudly, ignoring the microphone altogether. "In order to fully staff a casino and resort like the one we're describing, we'd have to look at a rotating staff in the hundreds," he says. "It would invigorate and repopulate a dying island."

Another gasp tears through the crowd. Millie's hand flies to her mouth. Coco steps up to the podium to cover Brice Killjoy's unintentional gaffe.

"Rather than think of it as a dying island," Coco says, holding up a hand to shush the whispers in the crowd, "I'd like to think of it as an island with untapped possibilities."

"But with an investment this large, we're going to need total buy-in," Brice Killjoy continues, scanning the crowd with his eyes. "The money you could all make would change your lives, but in order to keep the tourists coming your way, they have to feel that you're welcoming them and catering to them." Brice's balding head gleams under the overhead lights of the dining room. "But what I see when I look at this crowd is a group of unconvinced old-timers."

"And if you took a good long look in the mirror, you'd see the face of an *uninformed* old-timer." Jimmy Cafferkey's sense of loyalty kicks in, and he throws Brice Killjoy a murderous look. For once, Iris refrains from swatting his arm. In fact, she nods her head in vigorous agreement, putting one protective hand on the thigh of her daughter, Emily.

"Now, Jimmy," Coco says, crowding the podium so that Netta Killjoy has to take a step back. "We don't need to be defensive here. Brice is simply talking about the reticence you all obviously feel about moving forward. But at this point, we really don't have any other plan. I'm simply trying to offer all the possibilities—"

Without warning, Idora Blaine-Guy stands up and clasps her hands in front of her midsection. She looks around the room, silently willing anyone to interrupt what she's about to say.

"Now, young lady," she says, addressing Coco. "I'm well aware of my newcomer status on this island, and I haven't even decided yet whether I'll stay on permanently or just see my grandsons out of their mischievous stage before I head back to my real life in Toronto." Idora squints knowingly at her son next to her; Calista has stayed at home with the twins to occupy them during the meeting. "But what I see here is a woman who wants to capitalize on something valuable to her family." Her eyes bore into Coco like two hot coals, and the thick enamel bangles on her wrists click together as she gestures. "And while family isn't perfect, cashing in on them to line your own pockets is a shameful way to go about things."

"I don't think you've been around long enough to talk to me like that," Coco says. She blinks several times, her face going red under the scrutiny from a near-stranger. "And what my *family* does with *our* island is really none of your business." In a sudden move that reminds Holly of someone opening the door to a birdcage and letting its inhabitant fly free, Coco lets go of her composure. "In fact, it's none of *anyone's* business. We simply play along with this formality of kowtowing to you all to keep the peace."

"Mom," Holly says, standing up and striding towards the podium. Even she can't bear to watch Coco spin out of control in front of the entire island, though a tiny part of her has known all along that this was coming. Ever since her phone call with Alan on the beach, Holly's sensed that her mother was on the verge of some sort of intangible meltdown.

"Hear me out, Holly," Coco says, pounding a fist on the stand. "I'm only trying to make everyone see what kind of a grim future this island has if we don't make a bold move, and it's my turn to present something that you and Leo will actually consider." She waves a hand at Buckhunter.

"But I don't think this is the way to do it," Holly says quietly, taking another step closer to her mom. "Telling us that we're dying off and that we won't survive without a casino that no one wants isn't going to convince us to make any 'bold moves'—it's just going to alienate everyone who lives here."

Brice and Netta wisely step away, letting Holly and Coco speak quietly. But they've forgotten that the microphone was switched on for Netta, so as Coco leans closer to Holly, it picks up her every word.

"The people on this island *are* dying off, Holly. Ray Bradford dropped dead on your carpet here not even two weeks ago. We could probably start a pool to guess who's going to be next."

Holly's mouth falls open in horror; she can't believe her mother would be this callous. Even for Coco, this is unbearably offensive.

"My money is on Maria Agnelli," Coco goes on. "But Bonnie puts away the pastries and iced coffees like there's no tomorrow, so there might be a heart attack in her future," she says meanly.

"You're completely out of line." Holly makes a face, holding up one hand like it will shield her from her mother's cruel words. "Just stop talking."

"I'll stop when I'm done." Coco taps the podium with an acrylic fingernail.

"I think you're done." Buckhunter is up from his seat and approaching his half-sister before she can get another word out. "We don't need to hear any more."

The sound of Buckhunter's firm voice when he normally holds his tongue startles Coco out of her tirade. She pauses and looks around. All eyes are on her—and most of them don't look happy.

"I've put a lot of work into this idea," Coco argues, her voice faltering. "And Brice and Netta have come all the way back here to talk about the casino."

"Mom," Holly puts a hand on Coco's shoulder. "There isn't going to be a casino," she says quietly. "We were never going to green light this."

With the look of a woman who's been publicly and embarrassingly defeated, Coco steps back from the podium. She smooths one hand over the bodice of her yellow sundress and stands up straighter.

"This was a good idea," she says in a voice barely above a whisper. "This was a really good idea, and I had it all set up." It comes as a shock to Holly to see her mother's eyes fill with tears. "I don't know what you're going to do with this place, but I want you to mark my words: you *will* regret not getting on board with an idea that would have made us millionaires." She looks at Buckhunter and makes a face that's meant to hold back her angry tears. "And for the record, I really don't think your vote should count."

With that, Coco steps away from the podium and walks down the center aisle of the dining room, her head held high.

Holly looks at the Killjoys helplessly. "I'm not sure we're going to need your input anymore."

Netta Killjoy moves back to her seat and picks up her straw purse, but Brice stays put, looking more than a little perturbed.

"Now, we came a long way out here—not once, but twice—to talk seriously about working together on this project," Brice says, putting two meaty hands on his hips as he addresses the front row. He looks back and forth between Holly and Buckhunter. "You kids are making a big mistake here. This place is a gold mine and Coco sees it. You really oughtta listen to what she has to say rather than being so damn stubborn."

Netta reaches out a short arm and takes her husband's hand. "Let's go, hon." She gives him a gentle tug and they follow Coco's path down the aisle and out the door, Brice shaking his head the whole way. Near silence engulfs the room in their wake.

"This has been some month, sugar," Bonnie says to Holly from her seat. There are a chorus of "amens" and "hallelujahs" from around the room. Some of the islanders wrap supportive arms around one another's shoulders to soften the blow of Coco's harsh words about their dying island and dwindling numbers.

"It's been some kind of month for all of us," Holly agrees, addressing the crowd and thinking about everything that's gone on in her absence as well as her trip to Europe with River. Her eyes unintentionally seek out Jake's. When she finds him, he's sitting towards the back of the room in a seat next to Katelynn Pillory with Logan perched in a chair on the other side of his mother. An inexplicable pang of discomfort rips through Holly before she can find the words to speak again.

"And while I appreciate my mother's continued attempts to drag us forward towards what she sees as our inevitable salvation, I do have an idea of my own that I'd like to share."

Heddie signals Holly from the chair next to the podium. "Did you want to address the new businesses on the island first?" she whispers.

"Oh! Right!" In the aftermath of Coco and the Killjoys' sudden mass exodus, Holly's forgotten completely about this item on the agenda. "I'd like to share the exciting news that we have some new business activity on Christmas Key. Vance, would you like to give us the scoop?" She seeks out Vance Guy in the crowd and nods in his direction.

Vance stands and his mother gets to her feet again at his side. "Hi, everyone," Vance says, clearing his throat. "Many of you know that I've been flailing around a bit here since Calista and I arrived on the island with the boys, but I'm happy to announce that we're opening a new business on Main Street next month."

Those in the crowd who haven't yet heard about the bookstore start buzzing with the news.

"The empty spot next door to Mistletoe Morning Brew is about to become the new location for the island's first bookstore." Vance smiles down at the faces around him. "We're clearing off the land right behind the store and adding a covered reading area where you'll be welcome to sit and read the paper, or bring your coffee over from next door to hang out and see what's new on our shelves."

"I think a bookstore is a wonderful idea," Ellen says, turning to Carrie-Anne for confirmation. As always, they've closed the coffee shop for an hour to be at the meeting, and they're both thrilled with the idea of a business going in next to theirs.

"What will you stock?" Fiona asks, leaning forward in her seat so that she can see Vance's face.

"New releases, classics, any special requests that people have, weekly papers, monthly magazines, and of course we'll do special orders," Vance rattles off.

"So what's this place called?" Maria Agnelli pipes up. She turns around in her seat in the front row to find Vance. "It'd better have a Christmas theme or Holly'll tan your hide," she adds.

Holly holds her breath and watches Idora's face. She's not the kind of woman who seems like she'd take too kindly towards anything vaguely threatening being thrown at her son, but she smiles at Mrs. Agnelli beatifically. It's clear that she's already picked up the lay of the land and knows what to take seriously and what to ignore, and most of what comes out of Maria Agnelli's colorful mouth falls into the latter category.

"It'll be called *A Sleigh Full of Books*," Idora says, looking pleased with herself. "My grandsons and I brainstormed all of the Christmas terms we could come up with, and we settled on that one."

Heads around the room nod in approval. The idea of a bookstore seems to be going over well, and though it's a tiny step in comparison to what Coco's just proposed, it excites Holly to see her neighbors appreciating these little changes as they come. It gives her hope for her own mid-sized proposition that she's about to make.

"Thank you," Holly says to Idora and Vance. "I think it's going to be a popular place on the island, and we're all really excited for you." There's a smattering of applause in the crowd and the general feeling of agreement.

"Now," Holly says, "our next business is actually an umbrella of one proprietor who has several ventures up his sleeve." She gestures for Logan to stand at the back of the room, and he gets up nervously, glancing at his mother for encouragement. Katelynn looks at him proudly and reaches out to give his hand a squeeze.

"Logan Pillory, our resident teenager," Holly smiles at him, "has some great ideas for ways he can contribute to the island and also—hopefully—make himself a few bucks in the process. Logan, do you want to give us a rundown of your ideas?"

Logan's face goes up in flames almost immediately and he begins to stammer. "I, uh, I—I have a few things I, um, want to offer you guys," he says, pausing to swallow. "Like my driving services. I started a little operation called Guber, and I'm available to drive you around the island any time you need a lift. I have business cards over there by the door," he says, pointing awkwardly at the table near the dining room's French doors. "And I also offer specialized lawn care services, pet care, and I'm happy to be a personal shopper or errand-runner for you. I can meet the boat at the dock and bring anything to you that you've ordered, and I can also run over to Tinsel & Tidings and grab groceries or other items that you might need."

Maria Agnelli turns around in her seat again and puts one knotted hand in the air. "You're a good boy, Logan Pillory. You'd make your great-grandmother proud," she says. Everyone in the room nods in agreement. Sadie Pillory would have indeed been proud of her industrious great-grandson, and all of the gray heads in the room bob politely in unison.

"Thank you, ma'am," Logan says, blushing even more furiously.

"So that's it." He starts to sit but then stands up again. "Oh, and my rates are reasonable and we can negotiate for any special services that you might like that I don't offer yet. Thank you." And with that, he sits down quickly, looking relieved to be out of the spotlight.

"Excellent," Holly says. "That concludes our overview of new island businesses." Bonnie raises an eyebrow in question, and with Holly's slight nod, she gets up and turns on the laptop that they've set up to project the Powerpoint onto the screen at the front of the room. "Now our last item is one that I'm hoping you'll all see the value in." Nervous butterflies flutter around behind Holly's navel as she tries to gauge the crowd's potential reaction to her pitch.

"While I was in Europe, I had the chance to give some real thought to my approach to island development," Holly starts, veering off of her pre-charted course to give some insight into her idea. "It was brought to my attention that, while I aim to move us ahead and work towards real progress in both island business and in my personal life, I occasionally dig in my heels and refuse to see opportunity and possibility." It's almost unnoticeable and it's definitely subconscious, but Holly's eyes land on Jake's face for the briefest of moments.

Bonnie clicks the Powerpoint on and the first slide comes to life on the screen behind Holly.

"To that end," she says, blinking a few times to refocus her thoughts, "I'm entertaining an offer from a company that would like to help expand tourism to Christmas Key." The slide behind Holly shows a large boat and the logo for a company called Island Paradise Excursions.

"This company came to me a couple of months ago with the idea of bringing in bigger groups for day tours and smaller groups for multi-day stays. At this point," she says, nodding at Bonnie so that she'll move the slides ahead, "the B&B only has 20 rooms, and we have no plans to build any other hotels on the island. Which isn't to say that we never will," she adds hastily, "but right now we're not equipped or prepared to start adding the potential for hundreds of guests to stay on the island at once."

The next slide shows some figures that Island Paradise Excursions have given her with regards to the number of guests she can expect to visit Christmas Key during any given month, based on their historical figures. It's a modest number compared to the huge waves of humanity that Coco has been hoping to see at the proposed casino, but it's certainly enough to cause an uptick in patronage at all the local businesses and to bring some new faces to the island.

"The only concession we'd have to make in order to bring this plan together would be the construction of a newer, bigger dock. I'm not talking anything cruise ship-worthy," Holly promises, sweeping a hand across the crowd to let them know that she has the building under control. "But we would need to be able to accommodate something larger than our ferries and delivery boats."

"Permission to add my two cents, Mayor?" Cap stands up slowly, patting the pockets of his khaki shorts. "Not that I've ever waited for permission before."

"You read my mind, Cap," Holly says, leaning an elbow on the podium. "Go for it."

"I think this sounds like a damn fine plan. You've got some good projections here for visitors, but no plans for them to stay. You get a gold star on this one." Cap reaches for the chair behind him and sits back down, giving Holly a wink and a thumbs-up as he does.

"Controlled growth," Fiona says from her spot next to Buckhunter. She's nodding slowly as she thinks about Holly's presentation. "I think that's important for an island our size. We've tried a couple of wacky things—and I mean no offense, because they were both really fun and different—like the reality show and the pirate weekend, but those are one-offs. They might bring us residual visitors and visibility, but this is a long-term plan for continued tourism, and I think that's an important factor here."

Holly can feel the pleasure of her neighbors' approval swelling in her chest as the nerves give way to excitement. "That's why I wanted to give this proposal a second look," she says, smiling at Bonnie. "We get several things that come across our desks and I normally just see the cons, but this one really seems to have potential."

"So the next step is...?" Wyatt Bender, whose business has always been in oil and property, tosses out this open-ended question. It's a practical one, and it gives Holly the opening she needs.

"The next step is to make it happen. Buckhunter and I are on the same page with this, and, well, frankly we don't need Coco's vote to make it happen, so I think we're ready to move ahead with the construction of a new dock at the end of Main Street."

The room buzzes as the meeting breaks up, and several people stop by the podium to talk to Holly and to express their relief about the fact that there won't be a casino on Christmas Key, its gaudy beacon lighting the way for travelers like a Las Vegas lighthouse winking on their shoreline.

Holly is relieved, too—not just about the fact that Coco is done dragging investors around the island (at least for the time being), but also because the general consensus seems to be that they're ready to move ahead on a project that she sees as productive and worthwhile. Her preparations with Bonnie have paid off, and the people at Island Paradise Excursions appear to totally understand her vision.

There are still a couple of things weighing on her mind as she leads Pucci down Pinecone Path later that evening, but for the most part, she feels lighter and happier than she has since the day she left Paris.

Paris. River. The strange way they left things. It all comes back to her now like a bad feeling that's been pushed aside and temporarily forgotten. She still hasn't spoken to him, hasn't sent the email she'd started to write, hasn't dealt with the fact that they traveled half a world away together and came up empty-handed. It's been far too easy for her to come back and fall headfirst into island business and life, and she's pushed him out of her mind as much as possible. But the time to deal with River is coming.

Pucci sees a marsh rabbit ahead in the underbrush and goes bounding off after it, his ears flattened as he tears through the grass in search of a playmate.

"Pucci!" Holly whistles, trying to call him back. "I've got your ball!" At the mention of his favorite toy, Pucci stops short, forgetting about the rabbit. He looks back at Holly questioningly. "Let's hit the sand, and then I'll throw it," she says, breaking into a slow jog in spite of the syrupy-thick summer air.

On the beach, the sky is changing with the oncoming sunset, and Holly rears back and wings the red ball as far as she can, watching it sail through the air and land in the waves near the shoreline. It bobs there like an apple as Pucci gives chase.

"Holly!" A female voice calls her name. Holly turns to see Katelynn Pillory walking across the sand, her feet bare, her toned legs jutting out through the slit of a sarong that's tied at her waist as she takes long strides. "Mind if I walk with you?" she asks as she draws near. "I was just out for a stroll myself."

"No! Join me," Holly says, waving her over. "Pucci was cooped up all day while we had the village council meeting and I got work done, so I thought I'd bring him down to the beach for a run."

"Nice night for it," Katelynn says, falling into step beside Holly. "Christmas Key is as beautiful as I remember it."

"It never changes much." Holly reaches down and takes the wet ball that Pucci offers her. "Watch out, this thing holds water," she warns, nodding at Katelynn's skirt. She pulls her arm back and throws the ball, and sure enough, the red ball sprays them both with sandy ocean water as it sails away again.

"I like your plans for the new dock, though. Sounds promising," Katelynn says, watching as Pucci runs into the water again.

"This has been an ongoing thing for a while," Holly explains, walking again as the waves crash and break just feet from them. "I've been trying to look ahead and see what our long-term vision for the island should be, but it's a delicate balance of progress and sustainability."

"I hear you." Katelynn nods in agreement. They walk in silence for a minute. "Hey," Katelynn says, "I wanted to thank you for taking Logan under your wing."

"Oh, it's nothing," Holly assures her. "He's a great kid."

"Yeah," Katelynn smiles, "he really is. And he seems to have taken a shine to you. I think Jake is calling it a crush, but of course no mother wants to imagine her sixteen-year-old falling head over heels for a woman twice his age. Though I can see why he would," she adds, giving Holly a mock appraisal followed by a wink.

"Oh, jeez," Holly says. "Stop. He's just looking for a friend. It's either me or the twins in terms of people he could hang with, and I'm the one who can kayak and approve his money-making schemes. I think I won by default."

"Don't shortchange yourself, Hol." Katelynn says. "I can see why any man would be smitten by a fun-loving island girl with a pair of stems like that." She nods at Holly's tanned legs. "Hey, remember that summer when my parents let me bring my boyfriend down here for a week and he ended up falling for you?"

Holly squints as she thinks back to that summer: it feels like a million years ago and the image of a young Katelynn and the boy she'd been smitten with at seventeen comes rushing back to her.

"Justin, right?" Holly smiles, remembering the tall, skinny boy with the floppy, bleached-out bangs and the charming scar across his right cheek. He'd come down to Christmas Key with eyes only for his lanky, volleyball playing girlfriend, but had left with a huge crush on Holly, who wasn't the kind of girl to steal a friend's man.

"Yeah," Katelynn laughed. "Justin Cromford. I saw him at our ten year high school reunion, and he had a receding hairline, a drinking problem, and a pregnant wife. I think you and I both dodged a bullet there."

"Whew!" Holly jokes, wiping a hand across her forehead jokingly. "I've been wondering all these years whether I missed my golden opportunity at true love that summer."

"Well, you can stop wondering now," Katelynn assures her, tucking her hair behind both ears. "Justin was definitely not the love of *either* of our lives."

"What about Logan's dad?" Holly asks boldly. "Where did you two meet?"

"History class. Right after I dumped Justin. I needed a prom date and I ended up with a corsage, burgers for dinner...and Logan." Katelynn elbows Holly to let her know she's teasing. "I guess Coco and I have that whole teen mom thing in common."

"I think the similarities end there," Holly says. "I take it you've been here long enough to see her in action?"

"I've had the whole Coco experience, yes." Katelynn laughs. "When we first got here and I bumped into her on Main Street, she looked me up and down and asked how I'd managed to avoid inheriting the 'Pillory tree trunk legs.'"

"Oh, she did not!" Holly's mouth falls open.

"Believe it. And then she congratulated me on managing to keep my legs closed after Logan, because 'having one kid as a teenager was enough punishment for a lifetime.'"

"You know, that does sound like her," Holly says, wagging a finger at Katelynn. "And that voice you just used," she shivers, "it felt too real to me."

"She's an original," Katelynn says with a smirk. "But I have to say I'm kind of glad that her plan for the casino fell through. That sounded like a nightmare."

"To you and me both." Holly walks along next to Katelynn, her eyes focused ahead on the long stretch of sand and ocean. "But I think we've found a happy medium here with the boat tours—it'll kick things up a notch in terms of tourism, but it won't upset the delicate balance of the island too badly."

The women stroll in easy silence for a while. Finally, Katelynn clears her throat and speaks.

"So, word on the street is that you and Jake were an item a while back—true? False?"

Holly mentally shifts gears. "True," she says honestly. "We were definitely an item."

"And now..."

"Now we're just friends. Cop and mayor. Neighbors," Holly says, feeling the words catch in her throat as she forces them out. She can sense from Katelynn's stiff nod that she's asked for a reason.

"Ah, I see. He's a good guy, isn't he? Jake?"

Holly takes a deep breath. "He is. One of the best." She smiles and meets Katelynn's eye. "We're lucky to have him on Christmas Key."

The turn in conversation leaves Holly with mixed emotions. She and Katelynn part ways at the end of the path that leads up to Holly's house, and while she waves her off with the invitation to drop by for a drink on her lanai anytime, there's a part of Holly that wonders—childishly—whether Katelynn's interest in Jake has anything to do with getting back at her for Justin Cromford's fickle heart all those years ago.

Inside her house, she flips on lights and turns on the stove. She hates making dinner (or any other meal for that matter), but it's just late enough that a couple of scrambled eggs and a piece of toast will satisfy the hungry ache in her stomach. The canned light over the kitchen sink casts a glow over the countertop as Holly cracks three eggs into a bowl to whisk together with a splash of milk and a dash of salt and pepper.

"You ready for dinner?" she asks Pucci, looking down at his eager face as she tosses the eggshells into the trash can under the sink. "Let me get this on the stove and then I'll feed you."

The eggs sizzle as they hit the pan. Holly turns down the heat and uses a spatula to move the mixture of whites and yolks around on the hot surface. Across the lawn, the light in Buckhunter's kitchen goes on, and she glances at his window as she rinses the egg bowl in the sink and sets it down under the faucet.

Her cell phone rings on the counter; Holly runs her hands under the water and grabs a dishtowel to dry them before picking it up.

On the screen is River's name. She hesitates with her finger over the button, unsure about whether she should pick up or not. It's May thirtieth. She hasn't seen him or talked to him in nine days, but it feels more like nine months. The email she'd begun drafting to him the week before had gone unsent. Wiping her hand on the back of her denim shorts, she swipes the button and answers the call.

"River." Holly holds the phone between her cheek and shoulder while she stirs her eggs in the pan.

"Hi. How are you?"

Holly sets the spatula down and takes the phone in her hand again. She stands in front of the sink and watches Buckhunter's window absentmindedly. It's still early enough in the evening that he should be at Jack Frosty's, so the fact that his light's come on is slightly puzzling.

"I'm okay. A lot happened around here while I was gone. Where are you?"

There's a slight hiss on the line and Holly thinks she might have lost him when his voice finally comes through again. "Dublin," River says.

"Ah. Sarah. Of course. I could see that one coming."

"Hol—"

"No, it's fine," she says, turning back to the stove in a panic as the smell of rubbery, burned eggs starts to fill her kitchen. With a fast hand, she yanks the pan off the stove and sets it on a cool burner. "I could tell you were interested in her—"

"I wasn't interested in her!" River interrupts defensively.

"If you would let me finish," Holly says slowly. "I was going to say that I could tell you were interested in her *offer*."

There's silence on the line. She knows that River knows what she really meant: she saw the mutual interest between him and Sarah, and could sense an adventurous streak in the girl that mirrored his own. Would River have cheated on her? Dumped her for another girl and run off to Dublin? Certainly not. But the unpleasant rift that had grown between them throughout their time together had started to feel more like a chasm as she'd watched the way he gravitated towards the kind of adventures that put Holly off...the kind of adventures that a girl like Sarah would probably welcome with open arms.

"Yeah," River continues. "Well, after you left I did some real soul-searching and some thinking, and I decided that it was time for me to keep moving."

"To Dublin?"

"To wherever. We've had a good time, Hol. I loved visiting you on the island, and I think this trip to Europe was a good idea, but it was a real make-or-break kind of deal for us."

"And I broke it."

"Well, I wouldn't put all the blame on you. We're just different. I'm a wanderer and you're tied to that island like a prisoner who'll never escape."

Holly's face falls as she listens to his words. They sound so much like Jake's. "But I don't want to escape," she says softly. "This island is all I've ever wanted."

"You said it, kid." River blows out a breath from across the ocean. "No man will ever hold a candle to Christmas Key, and no adventure out in the big, wide world can compare to what you have right there. So I'm choosing to accept that—finally. It's not me you're objecting to, it's loving anything as much as you love the island."

Holly has nothing to say to this, so she takes the spatula and pushes the slightly-burned eggs around in the pan. They've already gone cold.

"Anyway, I just wanted to put a period at the end of our sentence," River goes on. "I couldn't leave anything hanging, or I'd never be able to move on."

Tears spring to Holly's eyes as she realizes what he's saying. He's moving on—nine days after she left, and he's already moving on.

"So basically you need to close this chapter so that you can open up a new one with Sarah from Seattle?"

"That's not what I said." River's voice is firm. "That's not what I said at all."

"You didn't have to." Holly walks across the kitchen with the pan in one hand and turns it over, dumping the eggs into Pucci's bowl. She's not hungry anymore.

"Listen, Holly...you're amazing. And I'm really going to miss you."

"But?" She tosses the pan into the sink with a loud *clank*.

"But this is for the best. For both of us. You see that, right?"

She stares out the window and sees Fiona walking through Buckhunter's kitchen, totally unaware of Holly's gaze on her.

"I see that," she agrees. "And I wish you all the best. Really, I do. Have fun in Dublin, okay?"

River is quiet for a moment. "I'll talk to you sometime?"

Holly smiles to herself. The tears she'd felt just a few minutes earlier have dried up. She knows he's right and that this is for the best. "Yeah, we'll talk sometime."

They say their goodbyes and Holly sets her phone on the counter again. Without even slipping on her flip-flops, she wanders out the front door, leaving it wide open. Fiona throws open the door to Buckhunter's house at Holly's first knock.

"Hey, what are you doing?" Fiona searches her friend's face. "Are you okay?"

"He's in Dublin. With Sarah," Holly says, walking up the steps and through the front door without invitation. Fiona opens her arms and wraps them around Holly, holding her close as she exhales deeply.

Fiona pulls back and looks up at Holly. "No tears?" She puts her hands on Holly's cheeks and looks deeply into her eyes. "You saw this coming?"

"I did leave him in Paris," she says. "So I guess it was kind of inevitable."

"Still...it sucks." Fiona shuts the door. "Come in. I'm about to make dinner for Buckhunter. Want to join us?"

Holly follows her into the kitchen where three bags of groceries from Tinsel & Tidings are resting on the counter. "I just burned my eggs," she says, as if this answers the question. And for Fiona, it kind of does.

"Perfect. Then you'll eat with us. Here, start chopping." She passes Holly a white onion and points to the block on the counter with a variety of knife handles protruding from it.

For the next thirty minutes, the women cook side-by-side in Buckhunter's small bungalow kitchen, sipping at the white wine that Fiona's poured into tumblers, for lack of any real wineglasses.

"Why is Buckhunter coming home this early for dinner?" Holly asks, looking at the watch on her wrist. It's only nine o'clock, and he normally stays at Jack Frosty's until closer to midnight, even on a Wednesday.

Fiona takes a swig of her wine and tops off the glass. "I wanted to ask him to marry me."

"What?" The glass in Holly's hand nearly falls on the floor, but she catches it and sets it on the table heavily instead. "You're asking him?"

Fiona shrugs. "Yeah. I thought I might. It's time. I decided while you were gone that I was ready to make a move."

"No thoughts of waiting for him to ask you?"

Fiona shrugs again. "Sure. I considered it. But the clock is ticking. I'm ready. And we're unconventional, so...it kind of works."

Holly thinks about this. Fiona's right. She watches as her best friend takes the pot of noodles off the stove and dumps them into a strainer in the sink. They are a pretty unconventional couple, but somehow it works. Fiona and Buckhunter have been happy together for the better part of a year, and Holly feels an inexplicable sense of joy flood her heart at the thought of her uncle and her best friend sharing a happily ever after.

"Come here," she says to Fiona, pulling her into an embrace in the middle of the kitchen. "Congrats, girl." She lets Fiona go and grabs her glass off the table to drain the last of the wine. "I'm going to leave you to it."

"No! Stay!" Fiona insists. "I want you here."

"I shouldn't be here. This is a special night for you two. Call me tomorrow." Holly leans in close and plants a kiss on Fiona's cheek.

It takes her less than five minutes to find a pair of shoes, load Pucci into her golf cart, and drive across the island in the dark. The night sounds surround her as she bumps down Cinnamon Lane with her dog next to her, a hot summer wind rustling the leaves of the trees overhead and all around her. Holly reaches out a hand and rests it on Pucci's side, feeling the comforting rise and fall of his steady breathing. This is all she needs right now: familiarity, reassurance, things she knows and understands as well as she knows and understands herself.

There's really no point in giving her destination any thought. Overthinking it will only lead to her turning around, and she can't afford to do that tonight. She drives down the quiet streets in silent contemplation, passing the B&B with its soft front desk lamp shining through the front window.

When she gets to where she's going, she puts the cart in park and switches off the headlights, leaving Pucci on the seat with the instruction to stay put until she calls for him.

Her hand feels detached from her own body as she stands in front of the door, fist raised and ready to knock. But before she can rap her knuckles against the wood, the door swings open.

"I saw you pull up. Is everything okay?" Jake is standing in his doorway, shirtless and concerned. His black basketball shorts hang low over his toned hips, and his hair is disheveled and slightly damp as if he's just come out of the shower.

Holly's heart skips a beat as the words fall from her mouth, unbidden and unconsidered. "Is it still too complicated?"

Jake frowns, moving his mouth to speak. Before he does, understanding dawns over his dark features. "Holly…"

They stand there—Holly on the porch in her jean shorts and untied Converse, Jake inside the house, one hand on the doorjamb as he looks into her wild and pleading eyes. The summer night sky winks above them. An entire unspoken conversation passes between them, but it yields no real conclusions, only more questions that will need answering.

"Is Pucci going to come in, or are you making him stand guard out here?" Jake says, nodding at the golden retriever sitting obediently on the seat of her cart.

Holly's head whips around, her loose hair flying around her shoulders. She gives a whistle that her dog recognizes instantly, and they both watch as Pucci hops out of the cart and trots up to Jake's front door. Without invitation, the dog slides past them both and disappears into Jake's house. Holly laughs.

"Well, I guess you'd better come in then, too, huh?" Jake says, looking down at her with a flash of understanding in his eyes.

Holly slips in, turning her shoulders so that she won't brush up against Jake as she does. She kicks off her shoes in the entryway and pads across the cool tile in her bare feet, disappearing into the kitchen to pour a bowl of water for Pucci. The way she does this feels so familiar to both of them—so right—that there's really no question about whether she should or shouldn't have come to him on a night like this.

Jake stands in the doorway for another moment, looking out into the night. Satisfied that the street is quiet and that no one has seen Holly come in, he closes the door and follows her.

ABOUT THE AUTHOR

Stephanie Taylor is a high-school teacher who loves sushi, "The Golden Girls," Depeche Mode, orchids, and coffee. Together with her teenage daughter she writes the *American Dream* series—books for young girls about other young girls who move to America. On her own, Stephanie is the author of the *Christmas Key* books, a romantic comedy series about a fictional island off the coast of Florida.

https://redbirdsandrabbits.com
redbirdsandrabbits@gmail.com

ALSO BY STEPHANIE TAYLOR

There's Always a Catch: Christmas Key Book One

Wild Tropics: Christmas Key Book Two

The Edge of Paradise: Christmas Key Book Three

Coco's Story: A Christmas Key Novella

Jake's Story: A Christmas Key Novella

Made in United States
Troutdale, OR
08/20/2024

22195086R00136